SECOND LIFE OF MR. HUNT

Book 2 – Sacrifices

GERRIT S. OVEREEM

ISBN: 0-692-12457-8
ISBN-13: 978-0-692-12457-4
Library of Congress Control Number: 2018944549
OTKE INC. Independent Publishing Platform
Indian Land, South Carolina
Cover Design by Yvonne Less, Art-4-Artists

This book is dedicated to my wife Jennifer.
Her support is what makes my writing possible.

CHAPTER 1

TRIALS AND TRIBULATIONS

Another shovel of dirt poured into the artifact scanning system. Professor David Winslow watched the exit ramp of the sorting machine to see if any new relics were discovered. Unfortunately, this shovelful, like all the others this morning, was just plain dirt. He shook his head and wiped the sweat from his brow as he looked at the terraforming town not too far from him down the hill. It had been about six months since he and his family settled on this distant world. Then again, it was his wife who had talked him into coming. His wife, Dr. Anna Winslow, was hired by a terraforming company to be the lead medical technician for this farming colony in a newly found planetary system on the edge of explored space. This would be the furthest any human had settled. He was against going until a scouting expedition found the remains of a prior civilization that had once called this place home. Since he was a Professor of Archeology, it didn't take much for Anna and his daughter Katalina to talk him into this adventure.

"Dad, taking a break again?"

"Shoveling dirt and staring at a scanner is hard work. Shouldn't you be at the learning center, Kat?"

"It's more fun to learn with you," said Kat with a big smile.

David smiled back at Kat and shook his head. "Yeah. It's more fun searching for antiquities. Grab a shovel and don't let your mother know. We'll say you got dirty roughhousing with the boys again."

"Yay," cheered Kat as she grabbed a shovel and started digging in the dirt. "Someday I'm going to be an archeologist like you."

"Kat, you can be whatever you want," said David. "Hey, look, a transport is taking off."

Both David and Kat stopped what they were doing as a transport full of farm goods blasted off. Its loud engines roared as it started to head upward in the sky. David loved how Kat was always in awe of the great transport ships. Something that big shouldn't be able to fly but somehow it did.

Her smile vanished as soon as the loud explosion echoed across the terra-forming town. The transport started smoking and listing to one side as the front of the ship violently plunged back into the planet. From the smoke of the explosion, two Woland fighters pulled upward as they fired their las-guns into random town buildings. A Woland troop transport followed them in and started making its landing in one of the fields.

"Kat, run!" David shouted, bending over and pulling a las-pistol from his bag.

Kat stood in shock.

"Run! Run now!" David shoved Kat toward the town.

Kat ran toward her house, which was close to the edge of town. Explosions shook the ground and small pieces of debris rained down on her as she headed for home. She could hear sounds of fighting and screams of injured people. As she neared her house, the building erupted in a ball of flames, knocking her to the ground. Kat looked around, her ears whistling from the explosion—everything seemed to be moving in slow motion. She wanted to run but her body wouldn't listen as she sat there in shock.

"Kat...Kat!" screamed her mother, shaking her.

Kat looked up to see her mother covered in blood and talking, but every word was incoherent. Looking past her through the smoke and people scrambling for safety, she could see the Woland systematically killing everyone in their path. She looked back to make eye contact with her mother but couldn't say anything.

"I will always love you, Kat." Her mother injected her with something. Kat's vision started to fade as she felt her mother wipe her own blood onto her face, and then all went black.

Kat opened her eyes, but she couldn't make out where she was. Her body felt wet, confined, and she was disoriented…until the stench hit her, bringing her back to reality and to the horror before her. It was unlike anything she had ever seen. Her vision adjusted to the darkness to focus on her mother's head— with the side exploded out. Kat screamed and…

She shot upright in her bed, sweating and hyperventilating. It was only a nightmare. She looked around her darkened room as the rain hit the glass doors of the bedroom balcony. Kat grabbed the bedding with her left black-gloved hand and wiped the sweat from her face, taking slow deep breaths.

It had been nine months since her plans to secure a Gravel artifact from Earth to kill the Woland had failed. Ever since then, the memories she had long buried started coming back. Sleep was something that rarely came, but horrifying when it did.

The stress was starting to get to her and interfering with everything in her life. Whatever Ryan and she had, or were trying to move on to, was not going well. They barely spoke to each other, Nora still wanted to kill her, and her coworkers didn't trust her. On top of all that, today was the day she and her uncle, Commander Seymour, were to go on trial for what happened on Earth. There was no longer any happiness or bright colors. All her thoughts in the present were dark, and shadows of the past echoed from the darkness. There was no sight of a future.

Thunder echoed outside, shaking Kat out of her thoughts as she looked at her reflection in the balcony window.

"Damn, they should have let me die."

Ryan skidded around the turn and accelerated. This modern remake of his 2007 Grabber Orange Mustang GT gripped the wet ground as if it was dry. It was early in the morning, just before sunrise. Rain was pouring down as lightning bolts lit up the sky, followed by crashes of thunder. It was mesmerizing seeing the futuristic buildings in the distance outlined by the lightning bolts. He still had to thank CEO Klein for getting him permission to drive through the emergency ship docking and repair area. Currently it wasn't being used, but in times of crises they could land big ships here for repairs, rearming, or whatever else they needed to do to them. Along with this area, he had found some old hidden roads outside of the facility he liked to use. There was even a road he could take to Brian's Antiquities shop to show off the antique car, but this morning he figured he would stick to the emergency ship area.

Any other morning he'd be out jogging in the botanical gardens, trying to keep himself in shape. Compared to modern humans with their DNA, genetic and bio-cybernetic modifications, Ryan was decaying at a rapid rate for someone twenty-nine years old. However, today was one of those mornings where he needed to get out and clear his head, and driving the Mustang fast did that. For the most part, things were going pretty well. It seemed he was financially better off in this second life. He consulted on old Earth antiquities for Brian at the Ye Olde Earth Antiquities shop, and the Artesian Bakery Corporation had bought the license for his waffle and syrup recipe. But he was kept awake by his thoughts on the trial of Commander Seymour and Kat. He may be called down to testify against one or both of them.

Things hadn't been going well between him and Kat. It wasn't as if they hadn't tried to work things out, but they just seemed distant. On top of that, he had been focused on studying for the test that would allow him to remain in the scientific division of OTKE Corporation.

In the grand scheme of things, the studies weren't too bad. Yesterday's class focused on the origins of humanoid species with partial DNA matches to Earth humans. Even thousands of centuries since his twenty-first century life ended, science is still open for debate on the nature of the universe. OTKE Corporation and Earth Consortium scientist did have two theories they were heavily focusing on. One being that asteroids or comets containing the same bacteria slammed into multiple planets, giving those worlds the seeds for life. The second theory is a long extinct alien race seeded the various planets in their own image or for some unknown purpose. Then there was still the possibility of divine intervention, a theory still being debated by various religious and scientific groups, or even wilder theories about how our universe is a remnant of a prior universe, or a branch off a universe tree.

Besides the various theories of evolution, there was a ton of other information he needed to remember for the test:

- There are many worlds still to map out and explore.
- Some colonies on the edges of explored space have not been heard from in a long time.
- Many colonies are based on the country of origin from Earth. They were settled to keep the culture of each race alive—and some are thriving historical vacation spots. Other colonies have picked times throughout human history and live as if it was that era, some with just a flare of technology to enhance it.
- Space is not as safe as it appears. Ships go missing all the time from wormhole accidents, pirates, mechanical failures and other unknown reasons.
- Some humanoids can do more than other humanoids with the technology they have implanted in them, but it's up to the individual whether to get such implants.
- C-Tec stands for: Cybernetic - Technology Enhanced Corporeal.
- All diseases from Ryan's era have been cured, but many new ones have evolved over time and from other worlds.
- The time system is based on a numerical calculation of the universe, which is based on various expansion of galaxies into the expanding universe, rotation of the planet a person is on, and then a bunch of other calculations to take into account wormhole travel and blah, blah, blah…

Ryan accelerated faster as he went through the list of items he had to remember for the test, but stopped when it gave him a headache. The thunder crashed louder, and the sight of lightning made him smile. He always loved watching storms as a kid.

He drove around for about another hour until an incoming call from Nora flashed on the Mustang's heads-up display. Driving with a virtual heads-up display had taken him a while to get the hang of, but the fact that he had a clear viewing screen in a rainstorm without windshield wipers was pretty cool. Plus, the green tint of the viewing screen matched the ambient green light in the car's gauge cluster.

"Answer incoming call from Nora."

Nora's face appeared on the lower right-hand-side of the heads-up display.

"Mr. Hunt, excuse me for interrupting you. Even though you should be jogging instead of out for a pointless drive."

Nora was Ryan's personal assistant, watchdog, or whatever else people whispered behind her back. Nora the AI was finally set free once she was able to download herself into the top-secret Female Assassin AI. Since then, her role was to make sure Ryan was safe, sometimes taking it to the extreme.

"No need for the lecture, Nora. I'm allowed to take a mental break now and then."

"If you say so, sir. It is your significantly short lifespan, not mine. Squander it how you see fit."

Ryan rolled his eyes. "What is it you need, Nora?"

"The trial starts in two hours. You should begin heading back so we can be there on time."

"Already? You know I'm not looking forward to this."

"Understood, sir, but I am looking forward to Dr. Katalina finally getting what's coming to her for what she did to you."

"Nora, technically Commander Seymour is on trial and if things go well they may not bring up any charges on Dr. Kat."

"Yes, but what she did will have to be brought up once they start questioning her accomplice, Commander Seymour. Then she will be incriminated and then off to a prison planet where she will rot away the remainder of her days."

"Well, glad to see you have this thought out. Don't wait for me. I'll meet you there."

"Very well, sir. Out."

The communication closed and, unlike Nora, who was grinning ear to ear as she talked about Kat rotting away on a prison planet, Ryan was hoping everything would go smoothly for her. Ryan slammed on the brakes, spun the car around and headed back to the main hangar bay.

⋏

It was the day everyone had been dreading. The trial of Commander Seymour and his niece Dr. Katalina Winslow. The room was large, with five virtual screens in front and an area in the center for the defendants and their counsel. A half circle at the back overlooked the room. Ryan and Nora joined OTKE Corporation CEO Klein and his personal assistant Jack as the only onlookers and possible witnesses that could be called down to testify. Due to the sensitivity of the crimes, the Earth Consortium wanted to keep the trial isolated to only those involved.

Commander Seymour and Kat entered the courtroom with their counsel, took their places in the center of the room, and sat down. Kat was dressed in a gray business dress and knee-high boots. As always, she wore a glove on her left arm that went just past the elbow. This time it was black in color, and the normal matching streak of color in her hair was missing. It was the first time Ryan had ever seen her without color in her hair and a matching colored glove. He knew she was having a tough time getting along with coworkers, and he and Kat were still finding it difficult to work together. Kat had lost the peppy side of herself and now sat there absent of any emotion.

Commander Seymour was dressed in his OTKE military officer's uniform and, as always, had a stern look on his face. His signature sideburns ended in a carved skull. Neither Kat nor Commander Seymour made eye contact with each other or any hint they noticed one another at opposite ends of the table.

"CEO Klein, from past experiences, how tough are the judges in trials like this?" asked Ryan.

"The five judges make up the main Earth human settlement systems that form the Earth Consortium. It is hard to gauge, but they are usually tough with matters relating to the Earth home world."

"This isn't going to be good," said Ryan, shaking his head.

Ryan leaned back in his chair and placed his elbows on the armrests, pyramiding his fingertips to his mouth. He recalled giving a detailed statement of what happened, and it was difficult not to give too much evidence to convict both of them, but there was not much he could do, especially since discussing it flooded him with a variety of emotions and the investigators had technology that could tell if he was lying.

Everyone in the courtroom stood up as the virtual screens came to life and the five judges, three men and two women, looked down on the courtroom. The male judge in the center banged a gavel, and everyone in the room gave him their undivided attention.

"Court is now in session. Please be seated. Will the prosecutor please step forward and present the charges against Commander Seymour of OTKE Corporation?"

A man in a blue robe virtually stepped into the room, looked around and began to speak.

"Your honors, we are here today to pass judgment on Commander Lance Seymour Winslow. The charges are kidnapping, dereliction of duty, attempted murder, and breaking the Earth Consortium charter of quarantine. We are also planning on presenting evidence to further convict his niece, Dr. Katalina Winslow, who is also an employee of OTKE Corporation."

"Yes," cheered Nora in a whispering voice.

Ryan turned and gave Nora a dirty look and then went back to focusing on the trial. His stomach was now in knots. He noted that neither Kat nor Commander Seymour showed any reaction to the charges against them.

"Those are serious charges," stated the head judge, and all the other judges nodded in agreement.

"They are, your honor, but the Earth Consortium has agreed to a plea bargain if the council of judges would allow it to be entered into the court record for consideration," said the prosecutor.

Kat looked around, confused, as did Ryan. CEO Klein continued watching the proceedings, while Nora and Jack leaned in, sparked by the trial's turn of events.

The five virtual screens went black for the judges to deliberate about the plea bargain. About five minutes later the virtual images of the judges reappeared.

"Prosecutor, we agree to have the plea bargain entered into record for our consideration. Please continue."

"Thank you, your honors. I shall now read the plea bargain put forth by Commander Seymour and agreed to by me, the Earth Consortium Head Officer of Prosecution, and Commander Seymour's defense team."

"Commander Seymour, please rise," said the head judge.

Commander Seymour stood up and straightened his uniform as his defense lawyer stood up as well. Kat looked at him, befuddled. She glanced at Ryan and quickly turned away.

The prosecution began: "I, Commander Lance Seymour Winslow, being of sound mind, admit to the kidnapping of my niece Dr. Katalina Winslow and OTKE employee Ryan Hunt. I further admit to conspiring with outside individuals to hack Earth defense platforms for my own personal gain on the home world of Earth."

Tears started to fall down Kat's face as the shock of what he was doing hit her.

"I further admit to dereliction of duty by falsely leading my troops into harm's way and getting them killed when some of the defense platform splices failed and they opened fire, destroying the tactical transport vessels. There is no excuse for my actions. I acted alone and take full responsibility for everything that happened. May the judges have mercy on me."

"That's not right! That's not what happened!" Kat exclaimed, jumping up. She struggled as her defense attorney forced her to sit back down as the head judge banged his gavel and asked for order.

The virtual screens of the five judges went black to deliberate and discuss the plea bargain, and it didn't take long. The virtual screens came back to life in about thirty seconds, and everyone stared at them intently.

"We, the Earth Consortium panel of judges, agree to the plea agreement and find Commander Lance Seymour Winslow guilty of all charges. He will be stripped of his OTKE and Earth Consortium ranks. The normal verdict would be execution, but considering his past military record, that penalty will be waived. Instead, he will serve life of hard labor on the prison planet in the remote Carcerem system and will never be allowed visitation rights. This court is now adjourned."

The gavel banged down and the virtual screens faded away, as did the prosecutor.

"Congratulations, Dr. Winslow, you are a free woman," stated Kat's counsel as he rushed out of the room.

Kat stood there, dumbfounded. She made eye contact with her uncle and ran over to him with tears streaming down her face and banged on his chest.

"What the hell have you done? This was all my doing! I should be punished! I should be punished!"

"Katalina, I promised you I would always protect you like the daughter I never had. Please be safe," replied Seymour. He kissed her on the head before being escorted away by armed guards.

Kat turned, looked up at CEO Klein with a fire in her eyes, and then stormed out of the courtroom.

⟑

"What the hell just happened?" asked Ryan, just as dumbfounded.

"Politics, Mr. Hunt. Pure politics. Centuries may have gone by for you, but protecting one's interests have never changed. If the Earth Consortium tried to convict both of them, they would have to admit the Woland were involved and there were alien artifacts hidden on Earth for thousands of centuries. It would seem someone made Commander Seymour an offer that protected everyone's interests," replied CEO Klein.

"Unbelievable. After all these centuries, governments are still playing the same political games."

CEO Klein stood up, as did Jack, and looked at Ryan.

"By the way, Mr. Hunt, I have promoted you to senior level in the scientific division. With your bravery on Earth, the OTKE board of directors felt it was well earned. You will be equal to the rank Dr. Kat once was and the Earth Consortium military will recognize the rank as well. I apologize for the informality."

"Thank you. No need to apologize. There is a lot going on."

"Again, congratulations and good luck on your medical procedure. I must head back to my office before Dr. Kat starts yelling at me in the halls."

Ryan watched CEO Klein and Jack leave.

"Nora, what just happened was frigging unbelievable."

"Yes, sir, unbelievable. Once again, the treacherous Dr. Kat got away without being punished. I was hoping for the death penalty for her and would have eagerly volunteered and recommended numerous painful ways to carry it out on your behalf. We did not even get a chance to see her rot on a prison planet. Again, sir, just unbelievable."

Ryan slowly turned to stare at Nora. He then put his head down and shook it.

⚔

CEO Klein sat at his desk, patiently waiting. His cybernetic eye rapidly followed the lines of corporate data being transmitted across his monocle that was wired to a port in the side of his neck. As he had predicted, his office door slid open as Kat stormed in, red-faced and ready for a fight.

"Good evening, Dr. Kat. I have been expecting you."

"Don't you 'good evening' me! What the hell was that? You had something to do with this! I know you did!" yelled Kat, pointing her finger at him.

"Sorry to disappoint you, but I had no prior knowledge or involvement in what just occurred between your uncle and the court. It was a surprise to me as well, but in hindsight expected."

"Oh, I'm supposed to believe that. You have your hand in everything and are always manipulating things from behind the scenes."

"If I was able to know that many outcomes and change things from 'behind the scenes' as you state, Dr. Kat, Ryan would still be dead, there would have been no plague, and you would never had made it to Earth to find lost artifacts."

Kat wanted to yell at him some more, but he made it impossible to do with his damn logic. She started pacing back and forth, clenching her fists and then releasing them.

"First Ver'Lin leaves, I can tell Ryan is still angry with me, and now my uncle takes the fall for my mistakes. My mistakes! I'm not sure how much more of this I can take!" Kat grabbed the sides of her vein-bulging head.

"Katalina, first you need to calm down and regroup. Clear your mind and focus on the now. With bad, there is good. With dark, there is light. You are going to need to rebuild yourself from the foundation, learn from your mistakes and move forward. Do not live in the past. Learn from it and move on."

"Yeah, right. Easy for you to say. You're always calm and in control. You never get angry and nothing goes wrong for you." Kat slumped down in one of the hovering office chairs.

"I wish it were that easy, Dr. Kat. I will let you in on a little secret. My mystical cybernetic eye and all-powerful monocle I see people envy…I would give it up in a heartbeat if I could forget the memory of my eye being carved out of my head while I was being tortured, or if I could just forget the screams of the innocent people around me from the mistake I made."

Kat looked at CEO Klein with her mouth open. She could not figure out what to say about his personal revelation. He had never told anyone about his past.

"As you can see, Dr. Kat, we all do not have perfect lives. We all wish we had things we could forget or redo, but in life that is not possible. You need to move forward. It will not be easy but there is always hope."

Kat lowered her head and calmly said, "I understand."

"Good. Now if I am not mistaken, you need to prep the lab for Ryan's medical procedure that Ver'Lin developed. Please keep me updated with his condition."

"Yes, sir," replied Kat in a quieter voice. She got up and left the room, not as angry but more confused than when she entered.

CHAPTER 2

UPGRADE AND JESTERS

It was the morning of Ryan's Gene and DNA manipulation, or just "plain body upgrade" as he called it. Nora had gone over the numerous procedures with him again last night, but it still didn't make any sense to him. The more she explained it, the more worried he became. Especially when she mentioned the three-month coma he would need to be in—that bothered him the most. The thought of not waking up from it made his stomach churn.

Ryan was sitting in the same chamber that had brought him back from the dead. He could see AIs running about as they took orders from Kat. The setup was taking longer than it should—Nora insisted on double-checking everything to make sure Kat was not trying to kill him. As much as he appreciated the concern, the long delay was making his anxiety grow.

"Are we sure I have to be out three months? Maybe Ver'Lin's notes were read wrong," said Ryan.

"Yes, Mr. Hunt, three months is the correct incubation time for this procedure. Especially since Gene and DNA manipulation is never done on someone your age. The procedure was the last thing to be developed by professor Ver'Lin before he left, and he specifically documented that it needs to be applied slowly over a three-month period," replied Nora.

"Are you sure they're able to modify and fix everything in this one procedure and I won't have to do it again?"

"Yes, sir, they will be modifying your genes and DNA for issues you currently have and for diseases your genetics carry such as acid reflux, ten different types of cancer, diabetes, eye degeneration, heart disease, rheumatoid arthritis, tendon and muscle irregularities, and a host of other issues and possible ailments. On top of that, they will be adding technology for interior bodily waste disintegration, intergalactic language translation, integration with complex combat clothing for personal energy shields, and integration with specialized combat firearms."

"Fine. When you put it that way. I will assume Ver'Lin was correct. Although it seems odd he just up and left like he did without saying goodbye. He gave me some information and just vanished. I never got the chance to thank him."

"I inquired about his disappearance as you requested, but was unable to find any trace of him. You should feel honored he kept you in mind as his last OTKE scientific work."

"You're probably right. Still odd though."

"Sir, I wish you would reconsider getting a communication device embedded into your brain along with other neural interfaces. It would make life a lot easier for you in the long run."

"No. I'm not going to have that much stuff implanted into my head. There is already too much going on up there without me hearing random voices calling me, or odd devices connecting to my brain. The language translator and the shielding and firearm connections are as far as I will go."

"Very well, sir."

Ryan closed his eyes, took a deep breath, and exhaled slowly to calm himself.

"Nora, do me a favor. On the table behind you, I left a storage crystal. Please keep it safe for me."

Nora walked over, picked up the crystal, and walked back to Ryan.

"Sir, is there something top-secret on here?"

"It's my daily journal, my last will, and I have been transcribing the rules for my favorite tabletop role-playing game as I remember them. Eventually I will remember enough of the rules to be able to play it again."

Nora was about to say something, but stopped when she saw Kat approaching. She placed the storage crystal in her pocket and whispered, "I will take good care of it, sir." She eyeballed Kat with suspicion.

"It's that time. Is the patient ready?" asked Kat.

Ryan went to answer but Nora interrupted him.

"Mr. Hunt is perfectly ready for this procedure, and I am ready to make sure you are not up to any foul deeds."

Kat looked blankly at Nora and back at Ryan.

"Yes, Kat. I'm ready as I ever will be. And Nora, let's keep it civil please."

Nora's eyes narrowed. "If you say so, sir." She then glared at Kat, spun around, and walked away.

"She's a piece of work, Ryan. I cannot guarantee one of us will be around when you wake up."

"If you two want to blow each other up while I'm out, go for it. Just make sure my Mustang stays in one piece."

"Figures a man would care more about his toy," joked Kat, trying to crack a smile.

Ryan laughed a little with her, and Kat could tell he was nervous. She placed her gloved hand on his arm.

"It will be OK. I promise I will not let anything happen to you."

"I know. You would be bored without me."

Kat wanted to jest with him like they used to do, but she could only muster a business-like reply. "Lay down, close your eyes and just breathe normally as the chamber door closes."

Ryan laid back and closed his eyes. He could hear the chamber door seal.

"Now, start counting back from a hundred," said Kat over the communication system.

Ryan began to count from a hundred, and somewhere around ninety-seven all went dark.

The master bedroom of the house was filled with a king-sized bed and various pieces of furniture. A large open area on the floor at the end of the bed was the perfect spot for the slot car track. Ryan gripped the yellow lever on the controller to make his car go faster as it went into the turn and took out his little sister's car in the process. She laughed as their father reminded him about slowing down in the turns, but it was fun when he and his sister could make the cars go flying off the tracks.

The happy vision floated away in a mist.

⋏

The crying of his mother and the appearance of his grandmother alerted Ryan that something was wrong. He was playing a game with his sister in the living room when it all began. He listened to the conversation the adults were having, and the sadness hit him. His papa, his grandfather, had passed the night before his ninth birthday. The military funeral stuck in his mind as he recalled Taps, the twenty-one-gun salute, and the folded flag being given to his grandmother. The only birthday gift he could recall receiving that year was Monopoly.

The sad vision seemed to move on.

⋏

The butterflies in his stomach told Ryan he was nervous looking out at all the people in the pews while he stood at the altar of the church. It would seem everyone showed up for the wedding. The butterflies vanished once the music was playing and he saw his lovely wife coming down the aisle in her white dress. "Until death do us part" was what he recalled, as the rain hit his old face. Leaning on his cane as he looked down on the grave of his wife, his tears mixed with the droplets of water and were lost.

The happy and sad vision floated away in a mist.

⋏

Being brought back from the dead, dancing at a ball, flying around in space-ships and seeing distant worlds. It all sounded cool, except for Kat turning on him, being kidnapped, and having to be put in a life-or-death struggle with an alien twice his size.

His mind continued to race with various scenes and thoughts. Almost like a movie in front of him.

Dr. Katalina Winslow stood out in his mind. That twist he did not see coming. He trusted her and she betrayed him. It worked out in the end, of course, after being beaten half to death by the Woland Ambassador and dragged out afterward by his friend Nora. Ah, Nora. What to make of her? An AI that found her own body to move around in and his best friend, personal assistant—but sometimes he felt like her pet.

Ryan was brought out of his trance of thoughts when he heard a swoosh of a door sliding open. Looking around he realized he was in a small movie theater and his memories were being shown on a big screen in front of him. A woman in a white robe and veil entered and took a seat in the row across from his.

"OK. This is very odd."

"It's your head we are in, Mr. Hunt," stated the calming female voice.

"Your voice sounds familiar. Have we met?"

"We have, but I was fashioned a little differently, with armored wings, sword—"

"And an electrified shield," interrupted Ryan.

"You are correct."

"Who are you? I never got to thank you."

"My name is Anatia, an angel."

"Never met an angel before, but that answers a boatload of questions I had."

Anatia giggled at the comment.

"So why is an angel in my...I guess...dream?"

"I have been watching you and I see you are recalling both good and bad in each of your lives. I wanted to let you know that unfortunately, no matter what time period you live in, there will be both good and bad. It is the nature of the universe and it's up to the living at that time to tip the balance to one or the other. You are having to go through this twice and I am truly sorry."

"Why are you sorry?"

"I'm the one that put your soul back in your body when it was at peace. I owed Ver'Lin a debt and he called it in."

"I see. I should be angry at you, but I feel blessed to have a second chance at things."

"You don't know how much that means to me. Thank you. I should warn you though, your path ahead will be rough, but life is what you make of it."

Anatia got up and walked out of the theater. Ryan turned to watch some more of his memories on the big screen and smiled.

⅄

The large unidentified battle cruiser exited the wormhole in the Nilor system, where all that remained of the great Nilorian race was several asteroid belts. The Nilorians were a highly advanced race, but their lust to control other galaxies was their undoing. At the height of their power, they were pushed back to their home world by a multi-race fleet of ships that banded together to put an end to the Nilorian conquest. The Nilorians had the last laugh. Instead of surrendering, they blew up their own planets, taking out the unified fleet of ships. The war was over, but the Nilorian race was wiped out due to their own arrogance.

The battle cruiser moved to the edge of the asteroid belt and a small torpedo-shaped ship shot out of its hangar bay into the spiraling mess of tumbling rocks. The small ship made pinpoint turns and rolls to avoid colliding with the random movements of the asteroids. The ship danced its way through the mess for about an hour until it found the huge asteroid it was seeking. This one floated along its trajectory, and no other asteroids seemed to get close to it. As the ship moved closer, multiple ship-docking bays and defense platforms were revealed. This was no asteroid, but a base of some kind.

The defense platforms immediately opened fire, but were unable to neutralize the small nimble ship as its quick random movements kept the base defenses from gaining a lock on it.

The energy shield around the small ship turned red and the ship accelerated as it breached the asteroid base defense shield and embedded itself into the interior wall of one of the docking bays. Smoke emanated from the small ship as a bottom hatch opened and a scraggly man covered in a tattered robe made from rags slid out from the small cargo hold to the floor. The man slowly stood up, wobbly from the rough trip and stood amongst the debris, blaring base defense alarms and flashing lights, waiting for the guards that would be rushing in shortly.

Four guards with dog-like snouts and protruding brow lines, dressed in tight brown combat suits with red and yellow stripes and matching lower face masks, came running in and strategically surrounded the ragged individual.

"Please. Don't shoot. I bring a message for your master from mine," said the ragged man, holding up his hands in front of him.

A guard with four red stripes on his shoulder armor stepped away as he communicated through his embedded comm link to find out his orders. It took only a few seconds and then he approached the ragged man. "You are to come with us."

Three guards fell into formation behind the ragged man and shoved him forward as the lead guard started to move.

The group moved deeper into the base and passed by a variety of training areas and simulated buildings where various humanoids practiced infiltrating them. The final lift brought them to the main floor and to a large audience hall. A variety of humanoids from different worlds and crosses—human-animal hybrids—practiced martial combat, knife throwing, juggling, and other odd things while people who were in charge overlooked and corrected any errors they noticed.

"Wait here," ordered the lead guard, who then walked through an open doorway and out of site.

The ragged man continued to look around. To his right was an ornate throne-like chair. Behind it was a large old banner hanging across the wall with the word "Carnival" written across it. A pair of flags hung on each side. The flag pictured a skeleton jester from the waist up with its skeletal hands holding a pair of daggers crossed in front of its body. To the right of the throne was a small table with an old ceramic jester puppet dressed in flamboyant dirty yellow and red clown clothes. The puppet wore a matching three-pointed jester hat that at one time must have had a bell on each point. Now only one bell remained.

The ragged humanoid froze in horror as he realized where he was. This was the Jesters Freak Show mercenary guild. The mercenary guild took in anyone considered an outcast from their society. It was your loyalty and skill they were after. Some of the guild members were descendants from the gene wars of the past. Many humanoids were crossed with various animals and were shunned from society after those wars. Here they found a home along with others of odd skills like knife throwers, mime assassins, and magicians that can kill with a simple card trick. The Jesters Freak Show was known in the underworld as the best assassins and mercenaries that credits could buy, and no outsider had ever entered their base of operations, until today.

The place went quiet as people snapped to attention when a middle-aged man of about five hundred and fifty years old entered the room. He had short, gray and black speckled spiky hair that stood out against his exotic tan skin color. His face was cleanly shaved, and he wore a tight-fitting leather looking body armor as a jacket and bright orange pants.

The man made his way to the throne and sat as the lead guard finally caught up and took a position on the left side of the throne, the opposite side of the jester puppet.

The man looked around with a grin on his face. "Please everyone, line up and pay attention. It appears we have an intruder, visitor, or a possible new recruit—depending on how you perceive things."

Some of the mercenary guild chuckled at the new recruit comment.

The man in the chair brought his hand up and the chuckling stopped. He began to wave his hand toward himself as he looked at the ragged man. "Please now. Don't be shy. Come over and present yourself."

One of the guards nudged the man forward with his las-rifle and the ragged man hesitantly moved forward as the two guards followed closely behind.

Once the ragged man reached about ten feet from the man on the throne, he cleared his voice. "I, I seek the one called Fredrick LaRue."

The man in the chair smiled and charismatically replied, "Well you're in luck today. You have found him. I'm Fredrick LaRue, leader of this fine organization. Now, Mr. Rags, if you don't mind me calling you that, which I doubt you will, what brings you to my humble place?"

"Please. I want no trouble. I only need to deliver a message from my master and then leave," said the ragged man. He held up a box with his head bowed.

Fredrick crooked two fingers at one of the mime assassins in line and pointed at the box. The mime walked over, observed the box, and made a gesture as if opening a lid and pulling the box out of a much larger one. Once he had the box in his hand, a light shined up in the air as a black circular cloud appeared above it.

A deep voice spoke: "Fredrick LaRue, your organization is known for accomplishing the impossible. I'm in need of your services."

"I like compliments," said Fredrick, sitting up taller in his chair. "Please continue."

"I need you to retrieve an item from the OTKE Corporation Headquarters in the Gliese star system and kill a human named Ryan Hunt. Your payment will be substantial, but failure will not be tolerated."

"Hmm…we do like high-paying jobs, but I'm afraid we do not take kindly to threats. It's with much regret, I must decline this business proposition."

The black circle was silent for a second. Then without warning, a black tentacle reached out and sliced the head off the mime holding the box. The head thudded onto the floor, followed by the body and the box, which continued emanating the black circular cloud.

"Let me be a little clearer. You don't have a choice."

Fredrick pursed his lips as he gazed at the dead mime. "There is a joke in this somewhere about a waste of a mime," he said with a laugh, and the tension in the room subsided. "Well then. It appears we accept the job."

"You are a wise leader. A data crystal located in the box will provide additional information. Please dispose of the messenger as you see fit. I will be in touch at the completion of the job."

Everything went silent and the black circular cloud vanished.

The ragged humanoid looked at the dead body and box in horror. Then looked up at Fredrick.

"Wait. Please. I beg of you. Don't kill me." He fell to his knees—begging.

"What to do? What to do?" said Fredrick, rocking his head back and forth.

He then smiled, leaned over and picked up the jester puppet. Fredrick carefully slipped his right hand into a cloth section on its back while seating the puppet on the right arm of his chair so that its legs dangled down. "So, Mr. Jingles, what do you think we should do with this messenger?"

Fredrick leaned in, put his ear to the puppet's mouth and nodded as if listening to the puppet talk.

"My life is in the hands of that? It's a doll. You people are insane," said the ragged man.

"No. It's a puppet. A doll is much different. Please do not interrupt Fredrick when he is in audience with Mr. Jingles," said the lead guard near the throne.

The ragged man looked at him with utter confusion.

"Mr. Jingles, that's it. Really? That's it?" said Fredrick aloud.

Fredrick moved his hand to make the puppet nod.

"You realize I would only have one more of those left and the one on the other side makes a bigger impact?"

Fredrick moved Mr. Jingles closer to his ear and nodded.

"Yeah, you make sense. I am holding you with my right arm. One last time, are you sure?"

Fredrick moved his hand to make the puppet nod again.

"Well, if you say so."

Fredrick pointed his left arm toward the ragged man, and a small missile shot from a hidden launcher. It hit the ragged man with blinding speed, and before the man could scream out, an electrical burst fried his internal organs.

"Kind of undramatic if you ask me. The one on the other arm is much better," said Fredrick as the ragged man's body slumped to the floor. "Oh well."

Fredrick put the puppet back on his stand and looked at the members of his guild.

"Everyone, listen up. We have a job to do. Let's reach out to our comrades already embedded in various worlds. Get me all the data on the OTKE Corporation, and I want to know who this Ryan Hunt fellow is. I would like to get to know my prey before I kill him."

CHAPTER 3

AWAKENING

Kat entered the dimly lit lab to check on Ryan's progress. Ryan was into his sixth month of the induced coma and she was concerned. The DNA re-sequencing process should have only taken three months and was going smoothly until the nanobots making the changes slowed down the process. They went from upgrading DNA to rebuilding them along with muscle tissues, bones and internal organs. Only recently did the lab find an unknown compound with the markings of Florarien DNA mixed into the serum Ver'Lin had created. How it got there was a mystery. Nothing like this was listed in Ver'Lin's notes and many people were now worried about how it was affecting Ryan. It was already risky to try to upgrade DNA at his current maturity, but rebuilding DNA and other bodily areas was taking him into the danger zone.

Kat reviewed Ryan's vitals on the virtual screen beside the chamber. She was intently reading a new scan that revealed his brain was also modified when she got the feeling she was being watched. Kat turned slowly to her left and peered into the darkness of the lab to see a pair of red eyes appear. Kat put her head down and sighed. She knew it was Nora once again stalking her and it was starting to get on her last nerve.

"Dr. Katalina Winslow returns to the scene of the crime. Come to add more unknown compounds into Mr. Hunt's procedure. Finally here to finish him off. Make it look like a lab accident so no one can point the finger at you," said Nora, stepping out of the shadows holding some metal computer part.

"Nora, please. I'm not in the mood for this nonsense again. Don't you have something better to do than stalk me? Like build a cyborg army or something?"

"Not in the mood. Just trivial nonsense you say. Please explain to me how that compound got into the re-sequencing processes? You have tried to kill him once already. Admit your guilt and give me a reason to enact swift justice on you."

Kat violently turned and got right into Nora's face.

"Enough! I've had enough of you and your ridiculous over-dramatic comments! Yes. Yes, I admit to a lot of things. I admit to having feelings for him. I admit to betraying him and those feelings. I admit to hating myself every living second for what I did. Ryan accepted my apology and we're trying to find a way to work things out!"

Nora's eyes went back to blue as Kat's face turned bright red with anger and she shook from the adrenaline rush.

"Are you yelling at me?" Nora crossed her arms and raised her eyebrows in shock.

"Yes. Yes, I am! Enough with you already! You know what your problem is?"

"I have no problems."

Kat smirked. "Oh, yes you do. It's called jealousy. That's your problem. You're jealous."

"Me? Jealous of you?" Nora laughed, shaking her head and putting her arms down.

"Yes, you are. The mighty and superior Nora. By far much smarter than me. You can process information in yoctoseconds and can kill a man in a blink of an eye, but the one thing that bothers you is that Ryan will never have the same feelings for you as he can for me."

"That...that is absurd."

"Is it? Think about it. At the end of the day, Ryan thinks of you as Nora the AI, or Nora the robot from his era. Not flesh and blood like me. Not a real woman, to be touched and to be loved!"

The two locked glares of anger. Nora went to say something, but for the first time she could not process anything to say. An anomaly was getting in the way of her logical thought cortex. Kat could see tears begin to form in Nora's eyes and she heard an odd sound: Nora's hand crushed the metal computer part she was holding.

"If you will excuse me, Dr. Kat, I need to get things in order for Mr. Hunt when he revives." Nora handed Kat the crushed computer part and stormed out of the lab, slightly hitting Kat with her shoulder as she went by.

Kat watched her leave and finally felt relief from standing up to her, but she also felt guilty for the mean things she had said. It was the first time she had seen an AI tear up naturally. Maybe Nora was becoming more?

The chamber alarm brought Kat out of her thoughts. She put down the crushed metal thing and turned toward the chamber controls.

"Procedure for Ryan Hunt has completed. Initiating wake up," stated the lab AI.

Kat turned to the virtual screen to monitor the vital signs. All looked normal as the chamber made a swoosh sound as it opened. It took a few seconds and then Ryan's eyes started to open slowly as they got used to the light. He moved his mouth from the bad taste and started stretching his head side to side.

"Ryan, how do you feel?"

"I feel like I need a waffle," he said with a grin.

⅄

It took a few hours for Ryan to get the clean bill of health and clearance to leave the lab. Kat hadn't told him the length of time he had been out, just that the procedure went great, and then she took him back to his apartment.

Ryan's apartment door slid open and the smell of waffles emanated into the hallway. Upon entering, he stopped in shock when confronted with Nora in an apron preparing waffles, looking like a 1950's housewife. The sight baffled him.

"Mr. Hunt, it is satisfying to have you back," said Nora, awkwardly hugging him.

"Nice to…ah…see you too, Nora," replied Ryan.

Kat rolled her eyes and shook her head.

"I have waffles, warm maple syrup, and fresh-squeezed orange juice with no pulp waiting for you on the table. Just how you like it."

"Thanks!" replied Ryan, quickly sitting down and pouring maple syrup on the waffles. "It feels like I haven't eaten in a year." A look of satisfaction appeared on his face as he ate the first bite, savoring it.

Kat leaned against a couch close by. She and Nora were silent as they stared down each other while Ryan was eating, which made him uncomfortable.

Ryan stopped eating, his eyes shifted between Kat and Nora.

"OK. You two are acting very odd. I'm happy that you didn't kill each other while I was out, but I'm sensing you're not telling me something. Did my medical procedure go as planned?"

"Yes, kind of…sort of," said Kat.

Ryan put his fork down, leaned back in his chair, and crossed his arms. "Sort of, like almost good, bad, somewhere in between?"

"Sir, she is beating around the bush and being cryptic as always. You have been out for six months due to an unknown compound found in the procedure. Your DNA was not just upgraded, but some of it was rebuilt in an undocumented fashion."

"Six months! What the hell is she talking about?" exclaimed Ryan, staring at Kat.

"So much for being subtle. Fine, if you must know the details. There was a Florarien compound found in the procedure that integrated with the nanobots and rebuilt your DNA almost from the ground up. I have my guesses, but I think the compound may just turn out to be pure Florarien DNA. We are unsure what purpose it had in Ver'Lin's mixture, how it got there or what ramifications it may have, but other than that, all your scans show everything to be normal."

"Great. Just great. We're going to have issues if I start sprouting leaves or turning into a tree."

"Dr. Katalina, you forgot to mention the brain modifications," said Nora with a little grin.

"Wait. What about my brain? What is she talking about?" Ryan touched his head.

Kat gave Nora a dirty look, while Ryan looked back and forth at each of them with sudden concern.

"We noticed you have additional neuron pathways and some parts of your brain also got rewired, which gave you access to other parts of the brain you weren't using. Could mean something and then again it may be nothing," said Kat, lifting her hands and shrugging her shoulders.

"Huh, I don't feel any smarter."

"Mr. Hunt, what is the geometric shape of a neutron under pressure of a time distortion in a collapsing wormhole?" asked Nora.

"Ah, three...blue...twenty-two...square."

"You are correct in your assumption, you are not smarter," said Nora.

"Now that we have proved I'm still an idiot, any other big news I may have missed that someone would like to share?"

"To summarize, the Earth Consortium voted in favor of repopulating Earth and the neighboring planets and system outposts, while the Florariens and Woland are on the brink of war," said Kat.

"War...What? Why?"

"The Florariens are holding the Woland responsible for the kidnapped children you rescued last year, and other missing Florarien citizens. In response to the accusations, the Woland recalled their diplomats. Recently the Woland entered Florarien space as they normally do with every race as a show of strength. However, this time, the Florariens opened fire and took out the Woland scout ships. That didn't go over well with the Woland and their allies. Other smaller skirmishes have been taking place ever since, and, even though it is not being reported, the death toll is starting to rise."

"What about the other races? Anyone trying to intervene to end it?"

"The other races are trying to stay out of it the best they can. OTKE is trying to broker peace accords, but no one is backing them. The Earth Consortium is focused on resettling the home world and, to be blunt, doesn't care."

"Lovely. Another wonderful day in my second life. Year 2001 or 50,001 and nothing has changed. People are still killing each other over foolish reasons or ideologies."

Ryan rubbed his face as the horrifying memories of watching planes crash into buildings on the TV flooded his mind.

"You OK?" asked Kat.

"Yeah, just some memories. I'm fine."

"Alright. I would love to stay and chat, but I have to attend another review of the alien artifacts you recovered from Earth. We can talk later if you want. Maybe dinner?" asked Kat, heading for the door.

Ryan pursed his lips and looked at her. "I think it's best I take a raincheck. This was a lot for me to take in and I would like to rest."

"Sure, I…understand. I'll see you around then," said Kat. She put her head down and left the apartment without looking back.

"Sir, eventually she will get the hint you no longer want her in your life. There are better, superior women out there for you anyway," said Nora. "Here, have another waffle."

Ryan looked down at his food and poked at it. "Yeah. Well…maybe."

Nora woke up Ryan at the crack of dawn, and he was not happy about it. A morning person he was not. Her new idea of training him to handle himself better was to get him up earlier than usual every other day to train hard physically and tactically. So far, the DNA and gene sequencing was paying off. They had jogged five miles and performed some functional training, and when they were done he was barely winded.

"Not bad. This is the best I've ever felt."

"I am glad to hear that, Mr. Hunt. We will continue pushing the pace to see what will get you out of breath. Eventually we will hit marathon levels of running."

"Oh joy. Yay me. Go Team Hunt."

"Mr. Hunt, your attempt at sarcasm will not deter me. What I am doing is in the best interest for us…I mean you."

"Nora, did you just confuse your wording?"

"Let us not dwell on words, sir. Take a break and meet me over there by the mats. Today we will focus on hand-to-hand combat since we did firearms and room breaching training the other day."

Ryan watched her walk away, not sure what to make of her odd behavior.

Something had changed, and he was not able to put his finger on it yet.

After a short rest, they continued with martial combat training. Ryan could tell she was taking it easy on him. Even with his enhanced modern body, Nora was still quicker and stronger. But after another hour of training, he was still able to get back up and keep going.

"Mr. Hunt, I have a simple question for you," said Nora, working her way out of his grip.

"OK, shoot."

"Do you prefer training with me or the field work you did with Dr. Katalina before she betrayed you?"

"Nora, we really don't need to go there. I think there have been advantages to training with both of you."

Ryan fainted his attack and went the other way to get behind Nora. He attempted to grab her around her neck. Without hesitation, Nora threw Ryan over her shoulder to the mat with great force. He slapped the mat with his left hand as he yelled a *kiai* in an attempt to control the fall and his breathing—something he learned to do in his Nihon Goshin Aikido training days a long time ago. Even with all that, he still had the wind knocked out of him.

"I am glad to hear both have advantages, sir. Perhaps you should take a quick break to catch your breath and think about your answer. When you are ready to continue, meet me in the hangar bay where we will start with your flight training."

Ryan lay there and watched Nora walk away.

"I may have to become a hermit. These women are going to be the death of me."

"No, sir! Not that interface," yelled Nora. The ship crashed down hard on the hangar bay floor, bounced up and then slammed down again. Only this time it magnetically clamped to the floor, due to Nora reaching over Ryan to activate the magnetic seal on the heads-up display.

Ryan was trying to get used to moving his hands around the virtual screen instead of using a steering wheel, but it had been a few hours, and so far, the hangar bay crew had to run for their lives, clean up a cargo spill, and chase after training missiles that had fallen off the training ship and rolled across the hangar bay.

"Why can't we just put a damn steering wheel in this thing? Can't I just let the ship's AI manage everything?"

"The AI may encounter an issue that requires you to manually operate the ship. You need to be prepared for all situations in case of emergencies," said Nora.

"Yeah, well…I'm just not understanding this virtual nonsense of swiping fingers and glowing circles in the air."

Nora stared at him. "Sir, if you would stop being so hesitant to learning something new, you would get it. We are only practicing lifting the ship up and then putting it down. I am not sure why you are finding it difficult to land in the lines. We are not even up to the actual flying yet. I told you that getting the technical implants to interact with ships during your procedure would have helped, but you declined. Perhaps if you listened to me, things would go better for you."

"Yeah. Easy for you to say. You're a superior AI that can do anything in a blink of an eye."

"Yes, sir. Just an AI. If you will excuse me, I am going outside to check how much damage the ship has taken from your carelessness."

Ryan watched Nora leave and he was even more confused than he was earlier. He must have missed a lot in six months. Everyone seemed to get all pissy when he said anything. Shaking his head, he leaned back into the ship's command seat, and rubbed his face, when he noticed Kat loading crates onto her ship, the *Retribution,* on the opposite side of the hangar bay. He didn't recall Kat saying she was going on a trip.

Ryan immediately left the training ship and headed over. He knew something was wrong.

Kat was about to board her ship. "Kat," he yelled with a wave. He jogged over as Kat came back down the rear ramp. "Looks like you're going somewhere. I don't remember you mentioning anything."

Kat looked at the ramp and then back at Ryan. "Yeah. I've decided to leave for a little bit."

"Oh. Where're you going? How long will you be away?"

Kat looked straight into his eyes. "I'm not sure. I wish I knew."

Ryan broke eye contact and looked past her, not knowing what to say. Before he could reply, Kat interjected.

"Ryan, let's not kid ourselves. We're still having trust issues, I said a final goodbye to my uncle who is going to jail for life for something I did, and people are doing everything they can to avoid working with or talking to me. On top of all that, I don't know who I am anymore."

"Kat, I…we—"

"Please, Ryan, don't. I need to go somewhere far away and clear my head, or I'll just…"

"Just what, Kat?" asked Ryan.

Kat tried to pick her words. "I'm not sure. All I know is I need to get away from you, this place…everything."

Ryan looked at the ground and then back at Kat. "OK. I understand. Do what you think is best. I'll…see you around then."

He wanted to hug her, but there was too much tension and negativity. Kat gave a quick grin and walked up the ship's ramp. Ryan took a few steps back and watched the ramp close. He walked away so Kat could blast off to wherever.

Ryan watched the ship leave. "Please be safe, Kat."

CHAPTER 4

LITTLE LAMB

Ryan's comm pad on his hand lit up red to alert him of an incoming communication. It had been a long time since he had used it and had almost forgot about it.

The incoming message crackled, "This is Victoria Van Buuren, trying to reach Ryan Hunt. Under attack…" Ryan pulled his hand away as Vicki's message was interrupted with the sounds of loud las-fire and explosions "…need assistance at Little Lamb…come alone. Please—"

The message ended as fast as it started. "Hello, Vicki, can you hear me? Are you there?" he replied, but all he received was static.

Ryan raced back to the training ship to find Nora inspecting some hull damage.

"Nora!"

"Yes, sir," replied Nora.

"I just got an odd communication from Vicki at the Little Lamb. We need to get there fast. She's in trouble."

"And?"

"It sounded like someone was trying to kill her and we may be the only ones who can save her."

"Why? She is nothing to us."

"We don't have time to get into this discussion. Someone I know is in trouble. Look at it this way: you get to fight something."

Nora perked up at the chance to get into a fight.

"OK, sir. If you put it that way. We need a fast ship, a stealthy one. Follow me."

Nora headed to hangar bay eighty-five and pointed at the ship in the back corner. It was a charcoal-colored four-seater craft. A smoke-colored canopy covered the seats, and it was streamlined like a SR-71 Blackbird spy plane Ryan had admired when he was a kid.

They boarded the ship, at the displeasure of the hangar master, and Nora instantly connected to the ship's systems. The canopy closed, and the ship blasted off for space. Once they broke the planet's gravity, the ship sped up to wormhole speed and entered the wormhole. The ship AI estimated it would take two hours to get there.

Ryan hoped he was not too late.

λ

The two hours went fast for Nora, but Ryan was ready to eject after getting a non-stop lecture from her on how the ship worked and combat strategies for the rescue mission.

"Wormhole disengaging," stated the ship's AI.

Nora brought the ship to a stop as they evaluated the Little Lamb club that Victoria Van Buuren ran out of the old Woland battle station. Remains of destroyed ships floated eerily around the space station and two larger transports were docked in the customer area. A few humanoid bodies floated by the OTKE stealth ship, which made Ryan jump when he looked out the window to see another face peering back at him.

"No need to be jumpy, sir. They are already dead."

"It's not being jumpy, it's called reacting. It may save my life someday. Aren't you afraid of dying?"

"If you say so, sir. And if you must know, the answer is no. I am quite superior. The thought of ceasing to exist has not even occurred to me."

"Let's hope you're never in a position to think about it. Anyhow, it looks like there was an intense space battle. Are the sensors picking up anything?"

"No other active space craft are in the area, only the docked ones. Some of the station's anti-scanning systems are operational. From what I can detect, there are multiple power outages on the low levels and the station's weapon systems are down," said Nora.

"Weapons down is a good thing for us. If I recall from my last visit, Vicki's office was toward the top of the station."

"Sir, if that is the case, I recommend we enter the top side of the station and work our way down. There is a chance I can splice into the station's system to get better schematics once we are inside."

"OK. That sounds like a good idea. How do we get in?"

"This ship's bottom is flat for a reason. We can connect to the side of the station and use the ship's cutting device to make a hole for us to enter. The panel on the floor behind us slides free leading into a small lower deck of this ship. From there, a hatch lines up with the hole cut into the station. We get in from there."

"You could have left out the dictation about the engines for the last hour and just mentioned that important detail."

"I could have, sir, but that would have been in section five and I was only up to four."

"Fine. Never mind. Let's just do this."

Nora manually navigated the ship as Ryan took the chance to grab a las-pistol and two small black anodized-colored golf-sized balls, which he guessed were some type of explosive device, from the side compartment.

The ship glided in as small thrusters controlled the speed and stabilized the ship, bringing it to rest against the hull of the space station. Ryan could hear the cutter begin its work, and a sucking sound told them the job was done and the cut piece was pulled into the ship, leaving a perfect hole for them to infiltrate the Little Lamb.

Nora went first, and then Ryan entered the lower deck of the stealth ship. Ryan stuck his head out of the newly cut hole and scanned the darkened hallways. Anything still working blinked on and off. The faint sound of music starting and stopping from damaged equipment could be heard in the distance. Two men in everyday clothing walked by. Ryan turned to Nora, held up a fist to tell her to hold, then two fingers and pointed down the hall. Nora gave him a nod that she understood.

Ryan watched the men disappear down the darkened hallway and then waved to Nora. He held onto the side of the opening, lowered himself down and then dropped the remaining four feet to the floor. He drew his las-pistol and knelt to provide cover for Nora. She held onto the opening with one hand as she dropped down, holding a case with the other hand.

Once she hit the floor she immediately knelt, opened the case, pulled out a combat belt with small pouches, and hooked it around her waist. She then pulled out pieces of some type of gun and assembled them into a high-powered las-rifle.

"Hey, where did you get the bigger gun?" asked Ryan in a whisper.

"It is in the back of the ship. If you were paying attention when I was discussing this on the way, you would know that."

"Yeah, yeah."

Nora gave him a look. "In any case, let us go down the opposite way that the targets you spotted went. We should be able to find a system console along the way."

Ryan nodded and started nervously down the hallway with Nora behind him. He noticed his vision in low light was better than what he could remember, which he figured was either from being young again, or an effect of the DNA and gene upgrade procedure.

Las-blast marks scarred the walls and pieces of the ceiling hung down from explosions on the level above. The lights continued to flicker and every now and then sparks would shoot from fried circuitry in the walls. As they headed further down, they came upon a site with bodies strewn about. Some of them were torn to shreds, and pools of red and green blood mixed together formed an icky yellow color. The smell of the bodies made Ryan crinkle his nose.

"It's OK, sir, not everyone is prepared to see the dead," whispered Nora. "Just remember your training. I am sure we will find a console a little further up."

Nora was just starting to train him in the ways of tactical combat. He was far from being a soldier and he doubted he could ever fill the shoes of those brave men and women he remembered seeing on the evening news in his first life, or like his father who had served in Vietnam, or his grandfather who served in World War II.

Ryan nodded, covered his nose to try to mask the smell, and continued past the remains. Up ahead, the corridor ended at a t-intersection and the stuttering music was much louder in this area. Ryan moved to the edge of the t-intersection and leaned against the left-side wall. This allowed him to see down the right corridor, which was difficult due to lack of lighting. Nora followed him, and she went against the right-side wall, knelt and peered down the left corridor. She pointed to her eyes and held up one finger.

Ryan gave her a quick thumbs up that he understood.

Nora moved to the other side of the hallway next to Ryan and picked up a shard of metal from where part of the ceiling had been blown out. She placed the las-rifle against the wall and tossed the shard of metal down the opposite hallway from the target, who turned around and headed over to the sound to investigate. As the target walked by, Nora flicked her wrist to pop a knife into her hand and moved behind the individual. She cupped her hand over the targets mouth, jabbed the knife into its jugular and pushed the knife forward, slicing open its neck. Green blood shot everywhere, and the target struggled. Nora stabbed it a few more times as its las-rifle fired a few shots into the ceiling.

Everything happened so fast, Ryan didn't have time to jump in to help Nora. Another person came running from the darkness of the hallway. The bio-neuro weapons technology implanted in Ryan during his upgrade procedure interfaced with the las-gun he was carrying. Just as he thought about shooting, a green dot appeared in his eyesight, which allowed him to aim and fire the weapon with precision. The weapon also adjusted to his breathing and the unsteadiness from his nerves.

Ryan fired off a three-round burst and two las-blasts hit the person in the chest, spinning him around while the other one hit the wall. It seemed like a lot happened, but it was over in milliseconds and Ryan was glad he had practiced this similar scenario repeatedly at the range with Nora.

Nora wiped her blade on the targets back, walked back over and noticed Ryan was breathing heavily and sweating.

"Mr. Hunt, please relax. You are showing signs of nervousness."

"Of course I'm nervous," whispered Ryan. "We just killed two people. Are we sure they were the right people?"

"Considering they are both oozing green blood, I would say yes. There is a terminal over there, so please watch my back. Again, remember our training sessions."

Nora grabbed the las-rifle and headed down the hallway. Ryan moved halfway down and knelt in the corridor to cover her.

Nora's fingertips opened, and tendrils extended into the terminal.

"Mr. Hunt, if we continue down the right hallway there is an emergency tunnel. We can climb down forty feet to the floor below us where the main office is. There is a strong energy reading down there. Perhaps this is where Vicki is hiding, or the enemy, or maybe both. Are you sure you wish to continue on this rescue mission?"

"Yes, but we need a plan. What other options are there to get to that floor?"

"There is a non-functioning transport tube near the emergency tunnel."

"OK, Nora, here's an idea. You think you can climb down the transport tube?"

"Yes, that would not be a problem."

"Great. I will go down the emergency tunnel and I will relay to you what I see. Then I will cause a distraction so you can blast out of the transport tube. We then get in quick, find Vicki and get out."

"It may work, sir. If not, I will let Dr. Katalina know you died heroically before I terminate her."

"Really. I'm stressed enough. So not necessary, Nora. Let's just get this over with."

⚔

Nora crept along the wall to the transport tube. She made sure Ryan was guarding her rear before she put her weapon down and forced open the doors. The transport pod was nowhere to be found. She leaned her head in and found empty darkness in all directions. Nora assessed the situation for a few seconds, then reached into one of the small pouches on her combat belt and pulled out two small round disks with straps on them. She slid a strap over each hand, so the metal disks were centered in her palms and the straps auto-tightened around her hands. Nora slung her las-rifle over her back and placed her right palm against the inside wall of the transport tube. The climbing disk clung to the wall like a magnet. She proceeded to do the same with the other hand and swung herself into the transport tube. Now hanging from the wall, Nora moved hand over hand as she cautiously climbed down until she reached the door to the next floor. She paused as she realized the door was bent inward and severely damaged from some sort of blast. Trying with all her might to push the door open with one hand, it did not budge. This was not good.

⋏

Ryan watched Nora enter the transport tube. Once she was out of sight, he scanned the area for any other guards, holstered his las-pistol and carefully opened the wall. He started his climb down the ladder in the center of a round vertical tunnel, at one point cringing when his foot slipped off one of the rungs causing a loud sound, forcing him to stop and listen to make sure no one heard him. Ryan continued his descent and paused at a small circular room about a floor down, looked in every direction, took a deep breath, and continued climbing down. He stopped at the next floor, which should be the floor Nora was talking about, and straddled the opening of the ladder's tunnel below him. It was the only way to stand in the tiny space.

Looking over his shoulder at the wall behind him, he saw a well-placed door that must appear like part of the room on the other side. A small lever was positioned next to two eye slits. Ryan carefully turned around to face the door and moved the lever downward. The eye slits opened to reveal a familiar room. It was the room he and Kat had first met Vicki to discuss the alien book. He always figured it was a movie thing, but he must have been looking through the eyes of one of the paintings on the wall he recalled seeing when he was talking to Vicki.

The last time he had seen the room, it was perfectly white and showed off unique antiques. Now it was dark with scorched walls from explosions and weapon fire. A large number of bodies were strewn about the room. Piles of dust mounds smoldered, the antiques were shattered, and there was debris everywhere from the blown out walls and parts of the ceiling.

On the opposite side of the room, he saw Vicki. She was sitting on the ground behind some sort of energy shield, bloody and with a las-pistol in one hand and something else in the other. Two men with masks stood in front of Vicki's small electrified prison, while another fiddled with something on the wall to their right. The shield flickered, and he could see a nervous look form on Vicki's face. If he had to guess, the men were about to bring down Vicki's emergency defense shield.

Leaning into the eye slits, Ryan tried to get more of the room in view. One of the large wooden doors in the entranceway was lying on the ground, and he couldn't see the transport tube door Nora was going to come out of from this position. Carefully kneeling along the edge of the tunnel's opening, Ryan tapped the comm pad on his hand.

"Nora, are you there?" he whispered. "Nora, come in."

Ryan waited a few seconds and tried again, but no reply. He went back to peering through the eye slits. The shield flickered again.

"Almost have it. Get ready," said the person fiddling with the wall control. The other two attackers backed up and raised their las-rifles in preparation to shoot.

Vicki, exhausted from battle, shook as she ejected the empty 5,000-shot mag-cell from the las-pistol, slammed in the fresh mag-cell she had in her other hand, and brought her weapon up for a last fight.

Ryan blasted through the secret door, interrupting the attackers' plan, and dived to the ground behind some debris as he tossed his two small black anodized-colored golf ball-sized devices at the attackers.

The shield dropped as the two attackers ran in opposite directions, trying to find cover, but nothing happened. The round devices rolled around and eventually stopped when they hit some debris. Everyone slowly peered out of their covered positions and paused for a moment, waiting for something big to occur, then Vicki opened fire at the person by the control console, killing him with shots to the chest and neck. Ryan provided cover fire as Vicki made her way to some cover nearby, while the other attackers joined in the firefight, lighting up the areas where Vicki and Ryan were hiding.

"Vicki, try to get to the door behind me!"

"I'm working on that!" screamed Vicki over the las-blasts.

More attackers entered through the blown-open main doors and took up positions.

"What the hell?" said Ryan.

"I guess you didn't know about the other secret entrances," said Vicki. "It seems they have been compromised."

Ryan spun around as additional las-blasts came from behind him. Nora was now firing from the secret door he had come through.

"Sorry, Mr. Hunt, the transport tube was not accessible, and the communications are not working for some reason."

"I thought I said come alone! Maybe next time we'll just invite everyone!" yelled Vicki. "I need you and your friend there to cover me on my signal."

"Why?"

"Just do it."

Ryan turned to Nora and nodded. Nora switched her weapon to full auto as her eyes changed to red.

"Now!"

Ryan and Nora provided cover fire as Vicki dived out, grabbed one of the balls Ryan threw earlier and crawled back to cover.

"Get ready!" shouted Vicki.

Vicki quickly and firmly squeezed the metal ball twice. The black anodized shielding changed to a bronze color before she threw it. The small ball exploded into a blue shimmering electrical field, covering her limping dive over the debris Ryan and Nora were kneeling behind.

"Huh, so that's how you use those things."

"I'll show you later, now let's get the hell out of here. It doesn't last long," said Vicki.

The three of them entered the secret room, climbed back up the emergency tunnel ladder and headed to the stealth ship. Ryan assisted Vicki, who was having difficulty walking, while Nora made sure their path was clear.

Ryan kept looking back as they finally reached the entrance to the stealth ship.

"Don't worry, they're not following us. They sustained too many casualties and they have what they wanted…my precious home."

"Who were they?" asked Ryan as the stealth ship detached from the Little Lamb and headed back to OTKE base.

Vicki smirked. "Old friends."

CHAPTER 5

DELEGATE

The OTKE stealth ship exited the wormhole in the Gliese star system. Vicki was still sleeping off her ordeal, while Ryan and Nora let the ship's AI navigate them to Gliese Major.

"Nora, I know the planet is always a hub of activity, but there seems to be a large number of big ships in orbit around the planet and what appear to be fighter spacecraft flying in formation."

"Sir, that is an Earth Consortium attack fleet. It is rare they would be here. They are usually on deep space patrols for years at a time," said Nora.

"Do they detect us?"

"Since I am getting a communication, it appears they do. I will output it to the virtual screen for you."

"OTKE ship. Please continue your current heading to the OTKE headquarters hangar. Any deviation in your flight path will result in us intercepting and disabling your ship."

"This is OTKE vessel, we acknowledge and comply," replied Nora.

"Well that seems to be a bit on the harsh side. Can we contact the OTKE headquarters?" asked Ryan.

"No, sir, they are jamming all planetary and interstellar communications. We have no choice but to land. We would never make it back into a wormhole in time."

"Never a dull moment with you, Ryan, is there?" said Vicki, stretching her arms out from her nap, looking refreshed.

"Oh, how I wish for dull. This should be interesting."

⋏

The stealth ship made its way to the OTKE hangar bay, followed by five of the attack fleet's fighters. Earth Consortium heavy defense platforms and mechanized AIs equipped with heavy weaponry guarded all the hangar bay entrances. The three of them exited the stealth ship and headed out of the hangar bay. Earth Consortium soldiers patrolled while heavily armed OTKE troops watched them. The situation looked like a time bomb waiting to go off at any second.

Nora moved close to Ryan and whispered out the side of her mouth, "Sir, CEO Klein has sent me a secure request to meet him in his office."

"Go. I will take Vicki back to my apartment so she can clean up and then I will meet you at the CEO's office."

The team parted ways at the first intersection. Ryan grabbed a hover AI transport to get him and Vicki to his apartment faster.

Vicki sauntered in after Ryan. "Not a bad little place, Mr. Hunt. Luxury apartment in the diplomatic wing. You're moving up in the world."

"You could say that, and I apologize for the dollar tour of the place, but I'm in a hurry. Shower is over there. The food processor works, but you have to use it manually since there is no AI to run the apartment yet. And the clothing replicator has a wide selection to choose from."

Vicki smiled as she watched Ryan rush to change his shirt. "Very kind of you to let me use your place to clean up. I will make myself at home."

"Do whatever you need to do. I'm running over to the CEO's office, and while I'm there I will get you credentials so you can move around. Again, there is no room AI, so you need to activate everything manually," said Ryan, bolting out the door.

Vicki watched him leave and looked around the room. "Anything I want. This could be fun."

⋏

Navigating his way to CEO Klein's office, Ryan counted many heavily armed Earth Consortium forces. Two Earth Consortium soldiers stood guard outside the office door. As he approached, one of the guards stepped forward and put out a hand to block his path.

"Sorry, sir, no one is permitted into the office at this time."

"Can you let your superior know Ryan Hunt is here to see CEO Klein?"

The guard raised his index finger to indicate Ryan to wait.

Ryan could tell the guard was contacting someone via an implanted comm chip based on how he was moving his head.

"You may enter. Sorry for the inconvenience, Mr. Hunt," said the guard.

Ryan entered the room to see CEO Klein talking to Nora. Jack and two OTKE guards stood about ten feet behind them.

"Mr. Hunt, glad you could join us," said CEO Klein.

"I got down here as soon as I could. What the hell is with all the ships and the Earth troops?"

"I am as in the dark as you are. It would seem the Earth Consortium wanted to make a point about something with their grand entrance and show of power."

"Yeah. Seems more like a takeover than a friendly chat."

"Yes. Indeed it does, Mr. Hunt. On another note, were you successful in your unauthorized rescue attempt?"

"Oh, you found out about that?"

"I reported it as soon as I arrived here, sir," said Nora. "As per OTKE guidelines, all armed missions must be reported to the CEO if not authorized, in case of any political fallout. Also, all guests must be reported to security, in this case Jack, when brought into the main building."

Jack rubbed his fist with his other hand, causing the servos in his cybernetic arm to whine. "I think someone will be attending my next security review meeting."

"Mr. Hunt, I think there is something I should mention about your friend Vicki. She is—"

The door to the office slid open. A man wearing a black sleeveless long coat buttoned diagonally across his body, a red shirt that emphasized his arms, and a pointed goat patch beard, entered the room with two well-armed guards and an AI assistant holding a data pad. The guards took up a strategic position to keep an eye on Jack and his troops.

The man stopped and whispered something to the assistant, waited for a whispered reply, nodded his agreement, and then turned with a big smile to the attendees in the room.

"Greetings. Greetings everyone," said the man with a suave wave of his hands. He continued into the room and approached CEO Klein, who was now moving in between Ryan and Nora.

"You must be CEO Klein. It's a pleasure and honor to finally meet you. I have heard so many grand things about you and your company," said the man with a slight bow. "I am High Executive Glumet, delegate from the Earth Consortium of Planets."

CEO Klein nodded back. "Glad to make your acquaintance under these odd circumstances. Let me introduce—"

"No, no. Let me guess. I love seeing if my research of people and places pays off," interrupted Glumet with a wave of his index finger.

Glumet faced Ryan, crossed his right hand over to his left bicep and brought his left hand up to his mouth as he thought.

"You must be Ryan Hunt. The man making a second appearance on the stage of life."

"Yeah, that would be me," replied Ryan.

"We have heard a great many things about you. If you're interested, there may be some distinguished positions for you in the Earth Consortium once Earth is resettled. We should talk again sometime."

"Perhaps we shall," said Ryan cautiously.

Glumet then walked over to face Nora, who made no facial expression. He stared at her stunning blue eyes and with a quick flick of his right hand, a beautiful pink flower appeared.

"The flower is called 'Nora Barlow'. A unique flower for a unique and beautiful woman."

Nora tilted her head slightly as she stared at the flower. "No one has ever given me a flower before."

"That is sad to hear," said Glumet.

Nora hesitantly reached out and took the flower from Glumet. As she grabbed the flower and touched his hand, she twitched.

"Nora, you OK?" asked Ryan, clenching his fists.

"Yes, sir, I am fine," replied Nora, twirling the flower in her fingers before placing it in her hair and smiling at Glumet.

"I hate to break up the pleasantries, but why are Earth ships surrounding the planet and appear to be taking over my headquarters?" asked CEO Klein. "I am getting worldwide reports of upset and nervous citizens."

"No, no, no. You misunderstand. We are here to assist in the defense of your headquarters. You are holding some extremely valuable artifacts retrieved from the Earth Consortium home world."

"Oh, I see where this is going now," interjected Ryan. "I bet the next thing you're going to say is that you're also here to retrieve them, and who better to guard them than you and your fleet."

"Very perceptive of you, Mr. Hunt. I'm assuming diplomacy was not something you did in your previous life."

"No, it wasn't. I could never act that fake to be a diplomat. I'm too honest."

Ryan and the delegate grinned at each other.

"I think it best we have a seat and discuss the matter," said CEO Klein, "before a war of words escalates. Nora and Ryan, you should clean up and check in on the injured guest you brought back with you."

"Shall we, Mr. Hunt?" said Nora with a wave of her hand.

Ryan was getting better at figuring out Nora's expressions, and he could tell she wanted him to leave and not cause a fuss.

"That's probably a good idea," said Ryan, keeping eye contact with Glumet, and then left the office with Nora.

Nora stuck her hand out to stop Ryan as soon as they cleared the office and were out of range of any Earth Consortium troops. She scanned the area to make sure no one was watching and whispered: "Mr. Hunt, CEO Klein gave me direct orders to get those artifacts out of here before the Earth Consortium troops took up positions around the facility, but their actions were quicker than anticipated. The artifacts are too powerful to hand over, and he thinks something else is going on. I would also like to point out that this conversation would have been more secure and easier if you had received the neural comm implant like I told you."

"Well, it's too late for that and I'm still not getting it done. Now back to the task at hand. This isn't going to be easy. They have all the hangar bays and airspace heavily guarded. So, if you have any ideas, I'm all ears."

"CEO Klein mentioned the *Tempus* would be our way off the planet if we can get out of the headquarters."

"Did he mention where we should go?"

"No. He just said to get the artifacts off the planet and away from here. He also said he had faith we would figure out what to do with them."

"I trust him to know what he is doing. With that said, the *Tempus* must be well hidden, or we would have seen it grounded and guarded." Ryan looked at his feet in thought. "I have an idea. Can you get the artifacts without attracting too much attention?"

"Yes, I can get them."

"Good. I will go get Vicki, you get the artifacts, and then meet me in the back storage area of the hangar bay."

"I think I know what you are up to, sir, and I agree," said Nora. "I will meet you there."

Nora fixed the flower in her hair, while watching Ryan walk away. She was calculating various tactics when odd thoughts flooded her mind. *"I can give you all you desire...Give him to us...Kill him..."*

Nora's eyes flared red and went back to blue. Her head twitched, and she looked around with a blank stare. Unable to recall the last few seconds of processes, she ran a quick diagnostic on her system and recalled she was calculating tactics and heading to one of the labs.

She adjusted the flower in her hair one more time and headed off toward the main scientific research labs.

A

The artifacts were hidden behind the wall in one of the microbiology labs that contained everyday average microscopic organisms. Since the Earth Consortium troops had no idea where the items were, they were guarding every lab and storage area. On the way, Nora grabbed a yellow lab coat, two virtual protective field devices, and a data pad. It was time to use some of her non-lethal infiltration programming.

She eased up to the corner of the hall near the lab and heard two guards talking. Nora fixed her lab coat and walked around the corner, staring intently at the data pad, and ran right into the first guard.

"Oh, my god. I'm so sorry. I was reading and…again, sorry. I have a bad habit of doing things like this when I'm concentrating," said Nora with an innocent smile.

"Totally understandable, ma'am. It happens, no worries. But this area is off limits to all personnel."

"Oh, I saw all the troops, but I wasn't aware of any lockdown. This is bad."

"Ah, what is bad, ma'am?"

"This lab holds some of the deadliest viruses in a cryogenic state. There was an issue with one of the pathogen storage devices earlier this morning and it was unfortunately my turn to verify the stability of the system."

"Sorry, we can't let you in there without approval from our commander."

Nora looked at the ground, getting ready to pull her hidden knife and change her tactic to lethal, but the other guard interrupted.

"Hold on a second. What isn't stable?"

Nora looked up and gave a shy smile. "Well, it's known as the 'Dealer of Death' or in some cultures the 'Melter of Eyes'. I wouldn't want to be anywhere near it if the storage system failed, but we'll have to take that chance now."

Nora gave them a few seconds to contemplate what she said, then turned around and started walking back the way she came as she heard the two guards in a whispered argument.

"Wait one second, ma'am."

Nora gave a devilish smile that she erased from her face as she turned around.

"We'd hate to have something happen. We'll let you in, but I'll accompany you," said the second guard.

"That would be great. It won't take me long, but I need you to put on a virtual protective field device," said Nora. She reached into her lab coat pocket and pulled out two small disks.

The guard going in with her now looked concerned.

"Don't look at me. It was your idea," said the first guard, grinning.

"Whatever." The guard handed his las-rifle over to his companion.

Nora placed the small disk on his uniform and a slight orange shield formed around him. She then did the same thing for herself.

"OK, we're now safe to go in," said Nora. She turned and placed her hand on an access panel while the system initiated a facial scan.

"Access granted," replied the lab AI. The door slid open and closed once they entered the lab.

Nora led the guard into the main lab area and then into the storage room. A small gaseous fog lingered as the cryogenic AI kept the specimens in the hover fields cool. Of course, none of them were lethal in any manner, but Nora could see the concern on the guard's face.

"Now this is the part where we need to be extremely careful. Since you're taller, I need you to hold this data pad up really high to get a reading off the specimens at the top," said Nora, handing the pad to him.

"Sure thing, ma'am." The guard smiled at Nora, stood on the tips of his toes and reached his arm up high. "Maybe when I'm off duty later, you and I could meet up for a bite to eat?"

Nora hesitated for a second. The thought of someone asking her out on a dinner date threw her off. She eagerly wanted to say yes, but knew she could not and for the first time she felt awkward.

"How long do I need to hold this up here to get a reading? Um…If you are not free later, maybe tomorr—"

Nora reached her arm around the guard's throat and placed him in a rear naked chokehold. The guard pushed backward, slamming Nora through some of the hovering specimens and into the wall, but her grip was too tight. The guard fell to his knee, then the other, and passed out on the floor. Nora looked at him sadly, wondering what a dinner date might be like. Those silent voices entered her head again. *"Ryan holds you back... This man could have loved you..."*

"No, no...odd thoughts. Must be a malfunction," mumbled Nora, shaking her head.

Nora tapped a few areas of the wall to reveal a hidden compartment. She verified the guard was till unconscious, grabbed the energy Orb that was sealed in a small metal container with clear protective walls and placed the vial of Gravel Goo into her lab coat pocket.

Looking around, she saw a cooling hose had become dislodged from the ceiling. She pointed the cooling hose toward the main part of the lab so the chemical mist would start flowing in that direction. Once it started to spread and fill the lab, Nora ran out toward the entrance, acting in a panicked state.

The storage room door slid open. "Oh god! There was a system malfunction! Lab AI initiated emergency containment protocol!" yelled Nora.

Red lights twirled around the lab and outside hallway, while alarms blared warnings in a variety of alien languages.

Gas started to filter into the hallway where the other guard was. He put his arm across his face and moved into the lab to meet Nora.

"There was a malfunction. Some of the specimens started to fall and he shoved me out. Oh my god, I think he's infected. He saved my life."

The guard looked around nervously, distracted by all the commotion and the fear of dying by some horrible pathogen. "What do we do?"

"Make sure no one enters this area. Take my protective shield. I will go and meet up with the emergency crews and inform them of the situation." Nora removed the disk from her clothes and slapped it on the guard's chest.

"Will do, ma'am."

Nora nodded and hurried back down the hallway. She fixed the flower in her hair, smiled and headed to the hangar bay.

⅄

Ryan took off to his apartment as fast as he could. He assumed Earth Consortium troops were monitoring all communication and video feeds but, then again, Jack probably would have done something to disrupt things. Not taking any chances, he made sure not to contact Vicki, run or do anything that looked out of the ordinary.

He finally reached his apartment and rushed inside to find Vicki leaning against his kitchen counter reading a data pad. Her shoulder-length red hair was damp, and she was only wearing one of his tee shirts, which ended just low enough to cover her private area. He stopped with his mouth open, not sure what to say and trying not to stare at her legs.

"Close your mouth, Mr. Hunt, you're going to catch flies."

"What? Ah, I mean…why are…why are you dressed like that?" stuttered Ryan.

"By your response I'm assuming you like. I thought I would personally repay you for my rescue."

"As much as that sounds appealing, I need you to get dressed quickly. Things have gotten complicated and we need to get the hell out of here. The Earth Consortium ships and troops are not here for a casual greeting."

"Oh pooh. Always interruptions. Are you sure? I can make it quick and satisfying."

Ryan's face flushed, he took a deep breath and let it out slowly. "I'm sure you could, but we need to meet Nora in the hangar bay fast."

"Fine," said Vicki. She put the data pad down, took off the shirt and headed off to the bedroom to change.

Ryan's mouth fell open and he found it hard to blink.

She turned with a smile and said, "Your loss," and disappeared into the bedroom.

"Wow," thought Ryan, shaking his head and wishing for a cold shower. Once he regained his composure, he put on his holster and las-pistol, and grabbed his adventurers backpack and hat.

"Well, I'm ready, Mr. Hunt," said Vicki, entering the room dressed very steampunkish with leather pants, baggy medieval style shirt and leather corset.

"Awesome. What a fashion statement. Let's go." Ryan grabbed her hand and rushed her out of the apartment.

CHAPTER 6

ESCAPE

Ryan and Vicki made their way to the hangar bay, trying not to draw too much attention to themselves, but some OTKE guards noticed their odd behavior. Instead of saying anything, they casually moved in front of the Earth Consortium troops at just the right time to block their line of sight.

Ryan was starting to think everything was going smoothly, until alarms started blaring and Earth Consortium troops rushed about. He and Vicki were able to get into the hangar bay and sneak around using ships and cargo as cover. Ryan noted that Vicki seemed well versed at sneaking around. He would have to interrogate her about her history later.

Once they made it into the storage bay, Ryan whispered into the comm on the back of his hand, "Nora? Nora are you there?"

Two familiar red eyes lit up in the darkness and vanished. He headed toward them and found Nora hiding behind some cargo pods.

"Did you get the items?" asked Ryan.

"Yes, Mr. Hunt. I have them wrapped up right here."

"Excellent. Here, place them in my bag," said Ryan, opening his backpack.

"So, what is our grand escape plan?" asked Vicki.

"Duck," said Ryan. He dropped down as a light came by.

Nora grabbed Vicki by the arm and pulled her down. Vicki pulled her arm away when she saw Nora's eyes turn red.

"Not here. Not the time," said Vicki, shaking her head and giving Nora a devilish grin.

"Did someone say something?" whispered Ryan.

Nora's eyes went back to blue. "Nothing, Mr. Hunt. We better keep moving."

"Agreed. That room just over there is where we want to get to," said Ryan, pointing to a dark opening about fifteen feet ahead of them. "I think we can make it without being seen if—"

Louder alarms started blaring before Ryan could finish his sentence.

"Screw it, run," yelled Ryan, and the three of them made a break for the room.

"Hey! Where do you think you're going?" yelled one of the Earth Consortium soldiers.

"That's them. Stop them!" screamed another soldier who started firing warning shots from his las-rifle.

Nora ordered the hangar AI to shut the door as they entered the room and the lights came on. Ryan ran over to a covered item and removed the sheet to reveal his recreated 2007 Grabber Orange Mustang GT.

Vicki started laughing. "That is your great escape plan? A car that has been outdated for thousands of centuries."

"Well, do you have any better ideas at this point? Their guns are all pointed up. They'll never expect it."

"You're a crazy one, Mr. Hunt. As I said earlier, never a dull moment," said Vicki.

"Crazy, strange, whatever... Just get in and hold tight."

Vicki jumped into the back, Ryan slid into the driver's seat and handed Nora the backpack with the artifacts once she was in the passenger seat.

"Start," said Ryan.

The Mustang started up with a rumble. Seat restraints automatically wrapped around the occupants and the heads-up display in the windshield lit up.

"Nora, get the doors open."

A few of the soldiers stood outside the hangar storage door. One was communicating with his command staff over his embedded comm chip on how to get the doors open. They all paused as they heard the roar of some type of machine. It seemed to rev up and then return to a low rumble. It was unlike anything they had ever heard. One soldier moved closer to the door to try to hear better and, without warning, the door shot open. The squealing of tires made the soldier dive aside as the unknown vehicle shot by him.

Ryan shifted through the gears as the Mustang accelerated through the hangar bay. Earth Consortium soldiers and AIs took cover as the recreation of an ancient machine took them by surprise. By the time Ryan had shifted into sixth gear he was already going over two hundred miles per hour. The Mustang shot out of the hangar door and onto the hangar bay runway. Earth Consortium las-gun platforms currently pointing up tried to swivel to point downward, but all the soldiers could do was watch the orange blur disappear into the distance.

Ryan made a hard right and headed toward the emergency ship landing area. Normally this area was empty, but some large Earth Consortium transport ships were now using it as a staging area. Ryan didn't slow down and drove under the ships. He blew past the Earth Consortium soldiers, leaving them confused in his wake. If they fired, they risked hitting their own ships.

Watching through the rear window, Vicki smiled, they were leaving the men and ship's in their dust. It had been a long time since she had been in a car at high speed, and she found it exhilarating. Her smile faded when she saw two silver blurs fast approaching.

"Better speed up. I think we have company," said Vicki.

Ryan looked in the rear-view mirror out of habit even though Nora was pointing at the pursuers being tracked on the virtual heads-up display.

"Sir, if you look to your right you can see two AI attack platforms coming at us and you are heading right toward the bases force wall it uses for shielding."

"I see them, but I have a trick up my sleeve."

As the Mustang neared the wavering energy wall, a section of the wall vanished, allowing the Mustang to exit the base onto the old roads. Just as the AI attack platforms reached the opening, the wall reappeared, and two explosions flashed on the car's virtual heads-up display.

"You have a security beacon installed in the car. You are not authorized to have one," stated Nora.

"Yup. I was able to get one in trade from some of the ship engineers. They wanted to drive the car and I told them about my issue of getting to the old roads. So, they installed the security beacon in the car if I let them drive it."

"They will probably send more after us," said Vicki.

"Let's hope not."

"Why is that, Mr. Hunt?" asked Nora.

"Because I'm out of tricks."

"So, CEO Klein. I come here under the flag of friendship and mutual cooperation and this is how you repay me."

"I am not sure what you mean. If I am not mistaken, your troops are the ones shooting. Not very friendly if you ask me."

"Games, you like to play games. You forced my hand to sound the alarm once I found out a pretty blonde female took out one of my guards and fled with something. Sounds a lot like a familiar AI we know, and I assume those are the artifacts she fled with."

"I know plenty of pretty blonde females. Was in the company of one in my younger years. What great times we had," said CEO Klein.

"Smile all you like. We will get her and her companions," said Glumet. "Assistant, status."

The Assistant AI moved closer. It had no covering so all its mechanical workings were visible.

"High Executive, it would seem that three individuals have escaped OTKE headquarters in an orange land machine."

"An orange what?"

"The description is an orange machine on four wheels with no flying capabilities."

Glumet's face went red, but he took a deep breath and tugged on his uniform.

"Mr. Hunt," said Glumet. "There is no one else who would own such an archaic contraption."

CEO Klein only shrugged.

"Assistant, dispatch two fighters and order them to disable the orange machine with any force necessary."

"Yes, sir. Two fighters are en route to intercept."

"Now we will end this game."

⚔

"Where are we headed, Mr. Hunt?" asked Nora.

"Not sure. I never got that far into the planning. We might be able to lose them in the main part of the city. Maybe sneak into the storage bay of Brian's shop."

The heads-up display started alarming and tracking two red circles coming in fast.

"Ah, Nora, why is it doing that?"

"Two Earth Consortium fighters are locking on to us."

"Crap."

"Orange vehicle, you are ordered to stop, or we will open fire."

"Can't this thing go faster?" yelled Vicki.

"I'm doing over three hundred miles per hour—it's all it can do. We're not going to stop now."

"Orange vehicle, this is your last warning."

When the fighters received no reply, they opened fire on the Mustang. Ryan swerved as las-blasts hit the ground around them. If it wasn't for the onboard AI assisting him, he would have probably wrecked at this speed. Finally some shots hit the Mustang, but bounced off as an energy shield activated around the car.

"What the hell?" said Ryan

"I was not aware the vehicle had shields," said Nora.

"Neither did I. Kat said she made an upgrade. I'm happy she did."

"Mr. Hunt, we have an incoming secure communication," said Nora.

"From who?"

"The *Tempus*."

Commander Gordon of the OTKE ship *Tempus* appeared on the virtual screen.

"Mr. Hunt, I have prepared an escape for you. I need you to continue on your present course and take the turn to the old city bridge in about two miles."

"Part of that bridge collapsed many centuries ago," said Nora.

"Nora is correct. I need you to drive off the end of the bridge. Trust me. Out," said Commander Gordon.

"Great! My parents would always say 'If all your friends jumped off a bridge, would you do it too?' I guess the answer this time is yes," said Ryan. He blasted through a barricade and headed to the bridge looming in the clouds ahead.

"Mr. Hunt, it is a two-mile fall from that bridge into a large deep river. Vicki and I have a chance at surviving the fall, but you will perish in a horrible death."

Ryan took a deep breath as he drove onto the bridge. Las-blasts hit the ground all around him and the heads-up display was alerting him that the shields were beginning to fail.

"Thanks for putting such a great image in my head. I really…hey, wait a minute, why does Vicki have a chance and not me?"

Nora turned and looked at Vicki, who shook her head and mouthed back, "No."

Nora shrugged and said it anyway: "Vicki is a vampire, Mr. Hunt."

With all the stress of the current situation, it took Ryan a moment to process that statement. "A freaking what? I see her in the mirror."

Vicki smiled as two fangs grew out.

"Jesus Christ!" exclaimed Ryan as he lost control of the car, causing it to swerve and almost crash into the sidewall of the bridge.

"Actually, I'm too old for the mirror thing to work anymore."

"Screw the mirror. Were you seducing me to feast on me?"

"Perhaps I might have had you for dinner in the beginning, but I'm not sure now. You've rather grown on me. Either way you would have enjoyed the foreplay," said Vicki, licking her fangs.

"If I live through this, we're having a long talk."

"Sir, we have more pressing issues at hand than you being eaten by a vampire. The end of the bridge is coming up. You have to decide to slow down or drive off it."

Ryan looked at Nora, gave her a nod, and kept the accelerator pedal planted to the floor as the end of the bridge came up fast. The Mustang shot off the end and seemed to float for a while before gravity took over. Then it started to fall, and Ryan closed his eyes and screamed.

Like the breaching of a large whale, a wall of water rose up as the *Tempus* shot out of the river. Its tractor beam grabbed hold of the Mustang, slowing its descent and forward motion and then pulled it toward the open hangar bay.

The two Earth Consortium fighters banked in opposite directions as the *Tempus* fired its Gatling las-cannons and headed directly at them.

Ryan opened one eye, then the other, and breathed a sigh of relief as he felt the Mustang being pulled to the open hangar bay of the *Tempus*. Once the Mustang was inside, the *Tempus* accelerated into orbit.

⋏

"What do you mean they escaped in a ship? What ship? I gave orders to secure all vessels from leaving!" yelled Glumet at his assistant.

"An OTKE ship called the *Tempus* docked the orange vehicle after it drove off a bridge, and then took off into orbit," replied the assistant.

Glumet peered at CEO Klein with distaste.

"Very unlike him, but it appears Commander Gordon must have gone rogue. Funny how things like that happen," said CEO Klein. He leaned forward with both hands on his cane. "Jack, remind me to have a conversation with Commander Gordon when he returns, and to tell Mr. Hunt that it is not safe to drive off the end of a bridge."

"You think you're clever, CEO Klein. I will show you I'm not one to be trifled with," said Glumet. "Assistant, order the fleet to intercept and disable the craft with all means necessary."

"As you wish, sir, but I am getting new information. There is an issue."

"Just order them to do it!"

"I…well…There is—"

"Stupid, AI! Transfer the fleet commander to Klein's virtual office screen," Glumet ordered. "Commander, why are you disobeying my orders to intercept?"

"Sir, there is another fleet entering the system from a wormhole. You need to see this."

The virtual screen flashed to a scan of orbit. A giant battle cruiser with an energy reading higher than several of his cruisers combined was now moving into position with an escort of ten other medium-sized cruisers and a star fighter carrier.

"Commander, whose fleet is this?"

"They have the magnetic signatures of an OTKE fleet, but we have never seen anything like it. They're targeting us, and we're being hailed."

"Put it on the virtual screen now!" yelled Glumet.

The virtual screen flashed to show a woman in a military uniform with a metal plate of blinking lights covering a small section of her head behind her right ear.

"This is Commander Indigo Williams of the OTKE Heavy Destroyer *Tolerance*. It appears you are conducting an illegal blockade of Gliese Major and are targeting the OTKE ship *Tempus*. You have ten seconds to disarm your weapons and lower shields or you will be destroyed."

"This is High Executive Glumet of the Earth Consortium. We will not be threatened!"

"Greetings, High Executive. I was not threatening, I was giving your fleet the option to survive. You are currently outmatched, and I would recommend you comply. Your ten seconds starts now. Out."

"Sir, the OTKE fleet weapons are powering up to fire and OTKE star fighter squadrons are deploying."

Glumet banged both of his fists on a nearby table, making the hovering table drop a few inches and then rise back up.

"Assistant, order our fleet to stand down. Order our troops back to their ships and we will take our leave."

"I have relayed your orders. Fleet is standing down and the *Tempus* has opened a wormhole out of the system."

Glumet pulled down his jacket to fix himself and smiled at CEO Klein. "Well played. Well played."

"It was nice to have a visit from an Earth Consortium delegate. Please make sure you come by again and we will do tea," said CEO Klein.

"Oh, I shall. Assistant, let us depart this world and notify command there was an issue gaining the items."

Jack, who was standing in the back with his guards, moved up as the office doors closed behind Glumet.

"You should have let me engage his troops. My men could have taken them," said Jack, his cybernetic arm whirring as his fingers tapped his holstered las-pistol.

"Jack, sometimes it is better to let things play out. We got lucky Commander Williams arrived when she did. Something is not right. The odds of an Earth delegate arriving on our doorstep in such a hostile way on the same day the Earth Consortium leaders are in their yearly secure meeting, where I cannot contact them for the next three days, is almost unfathomable."

"What are your orders, my CEO?"

"Take your guards and follow High Executive Glumet to make sure he leaves. Also, perform a sweep of the facility to make sure they did not leave any surprises behind."

"I will take care of it, sir."

The office door opened as Jack approached it, but he stopped mid-step when he noticed something on the ground in front of him.

"Sir, there is a card on the floor outside the door."

CEO Klein walked over and looked down at the card. It depicted a tower on a mountaintop. A lightning bolt is hitting the tower and setting it on fire, while two people fall from the tower.

"I don't understand," said Jack.

"It is the Tower card from a Tarot deck. It signifies darkness and destruction, and I am afraid it is in a future position."

CHAPTER 7

REVELATIONS

Fredrick LaRue stood in the command ready room on his personal battlecruiser, smiling as he watched the multi-colored lights of the wormhole go by. A light melody of Artesian descent played in the background. The music inspired him when he was pondering a variety of strategies and outcomes. Mr. Jingles, the puppet, sat upright on a hovering platform nearby.

Fredrick always loved the start of a new mercenary job and the thrill it brought. He may have been forced to take this one, but a job this big meant a lot of wealth and prestige. Names carry weight and power when you have a reputation associated with them.

His thoughts were interrupted when he heard the door slide open. He turned with a smile to greet his assistant. She had light-red skin and cat-like ears. Normally people of the Karyot race would wear a respirator since they didn't breathe oxygen, but her mother was an oxygen-breathing humanoid and her father was only partially Karyot, which meant she was lucky enough to be able to survive in an oxygen-rich environment.

"Sir, I'm sorry to interrupt, but we just received a high-priority secure communication."

"No worries on the interruption, please read the message."

"I was unable to retrieve the items but 'plan b' has been put into motion. Unfortunately, I was forced to play my hand. Will wait for new orders," read the assistant from her data pad.

"Interesting. I didn't think it would be that easy, but at least he implement-ed the backup plan. Tell our associate to make himself scarce and eliminate any non-followers. I will reach out with new orders when ready."

"Yes, sir. I will relay your orders."

The assistant gave a slight bow and left the room. Fredrick watched her leave before speaking.

"So, Mr. Jingles, let the games begin."

The Mustang came to rest in the larger of the two hangar bays on the *Tempus*. Steam emanated from the tires and body as it cooled down from the shielding and las-blasts.

"Sit tight while we evade some fighters and try to get up to speed for wormhole travel," said Commander Gordon over the Mustang's communica-tion system.

The car was silent while everyone waited to see if the *Tempus* would escape the Earth Consortium fleet. It seemed like an eternity, but it only took a few seconds before they felt the pull of the ship into the wormhole, and then ev-erything was calm again. Ryan's knuckles were white from gripping the steer-ing wheel. He released the wheel and stretched out his fingers as his racing heart started to slow down. It wasn't every day one drives off a bridge and is caught by a spaceship.

"Car off," said Ryan. He put his forehead on the steering wheel and took a couple of deep breaths.

As soon as the seat restraints retracted, Ryan rushed out of the car and moved his seat forward to allow Vicki to get out. She put her hand out for him to help her, which he did hesitantly.

Vicki took a few steps and turned to face him, but before she could say anything Ryan laid into her.

"What the hell? A freaking vampire! As in Count Dracula, bat-changing, blood-sucking thing of darkness. When were you going to tell me!" yelled Ryan.

Nora watched, finding the conversation intriguing.

"Let's not get all dramatic. Most of what you say is true. Dracula, or who they called Dracula, is long dead. And I cannot change into a bat, but, as old as I am, daylight no longer bothers me if you're curious."

"I don't believe this. They were just in stories or horror movies," said Ryan, pacing. "How ironic. I guess I'm no longer the oldest living human."

"Well, technically you still are. Vicki is somewhat in the non-living or undead category," said Nora.

Ryan turned and pointed a finger at Nora. "You knew what she was! How could you keep a secret like that?"

Nora's eyes narrowed, and facial muscles tensed.

"How dare you disrespectfully point at me like that! You do not trust me!" yelled Nora. "I just found out when I touched her at the OTKE HQ and my medical senses did not pick up any life signs."

Ryan put his hand down and took a step back. "Sorry. I didn't mean to make it sound like that, Nora."

She put her head down and then looked back at Ryan. "Sorry, Mr. Hunt. I did not mean to yell at you. I am not sure what came over me. If you will excuse me."

"No worries, Nora. Everyone is on edge."

Ryan waited for Nora to leave the hangar bay.

"Now back to you, unholy creature of the night," said Ryan, turning to face Vicki. "This explains a lot. How you survived the bathroom fight with Miyo. How you know so much about old Earth antiques and why you heal amazingly fast."

"Yeah, I guess it does. I have a lot of practice keeping what I am a secret, but I forget about some AIs being able to see through it," replied Vicki.

"But the sunlight. It's supposed to affect you. I just don't get it."

"As I said earlier, I grew out of it. Either from the nuclear holocaust I slept through, or by evolution—who knows? On the bright side, I can now get a tan like everyone else. Then again, I am of Northern European descent. Vikings if you're curious. We don't tan well and, just to educate you, we never wore horned helmets either."

"Great. Explains the red hair, but a more important question: am I to also guess you are as evil as vampires are portrayed to be?"

"Good…evil…it's all relative based on one's perspective. Only a few know what I am, outside of the underworld of course." Vicki stretched and leaned against the car. "Before you ask your next question, I already know what it's going to be. Yes, I feast on the blood of humanoids, but at my age I can survive much longer without lusting for my dinner."

Ryan stared at her blankly, not knowing what to say to such a confession. Vicki held up her finger to make sure he didn't say anything and let her finish.

"My dinners, as one may describe it, are always off world prisoners sentenced to death for their crimes. In a way, I do the galaxies a service. I take care of their problems and they have no fear of me going after innocent people. The Little Lamb was a club for me to live the life of luxury, and yes, I was part of the underworld of the galaxy, but everyone has to make a living."

"Great. Mafia vampires. First, it was a lich-looking creature, then horrors from hell, and now vampires. Just lovely. All my nightmares coming alive."

Vicki crossed her arms. "Actually, Mr. Hunt, there are a lot more things in the universe, and on the other side, that you should be terrified of. On the grand scale of underworld creatures, I'm at the bottom of the list—once you start considering devils, fiends and demons."

"Well, that just makes everything sound better, now doesn't it? So now for the really big question, were you going to kill me or whatever it is you do to people? And to think I was even tempted when you were wearing only my shirt."

"I was right! You're not as shy as you make yourself out to be. It's good to know I can get your attention with my assets."

Ryan rubbed his hands on his face and blushed. "That's not the point. What about the killing me part?"

"Yeah, about that, don't judge me. We all have things we lust after. I would have never killed you. Maybe feast on you a little, and possibly turn you were my top ideas. Anyway, with your new modifications, your blood no longer has an antique smell to it." Vicki smiled.

Ryan threw his arms in the air. "This has got to be the weirdest conversation I've ever had, but we have more important things to take care of. We'll finish this conversation later. Right now, I need to get to the command deck and figure out what's going on."

"Later works. Your place or mine?"

Ryan sighed. "Unbelievable. Let's go and, if you don't mind, please go first."

Vicki looked around and put her hands up in the air. "Not like I've been on this ship before. I promise not to bite," she said with a wink.

Ryan pursed his lips as he pulled his shoulders up a little to hide his neck, and then led the way to the command deck.

⋏

Ryan and Vicki entered the command deck to find Commander Gordon having a discussion with Mitil'Lin and Nora.

Commander Gordon was the commander of the OTKE ship *Tempus*. He was a prim and proper captain and was recently awarded for his actions on the Earth rescue mission. Mitil'Lin was half human and half Artesian Engineer, and designed the next generation engines the *Tempus* was using. She wore a small goggle mask containing a set of eight wafer-thin lenses on each eyepiece. The lenses could be brought down in numerous combinations to allow her to see different spectrums of light or investigate various metals, chemicals and other items. She was young, inquisitive and highly intelligent.

"Commander Gordon, thank you for saving our asses down there. Kind of a coincidence you were hiding, and that we needed saving, don't you think?" asked Ryan.

"We had orders to stay hidden due to a possible altercation that was coming, and we also had some help from an OTKE battle fleet that just happen to enter the system."

"A premonition and some luck. I hope this group doesn't always rely on that. Eventually it runs out," Vicki interjected.

"I'm sorry, and you are?" asked Commander Gordon.

"This is Victoria Van Buuren. Vicki just happened to be in the wrong place at the wrong time," said Ryan. He eyeballed her while shaking his head.

"Fine, I'll go sit over there." Vicki threw her hands up and walked to the other side of the command deck.

"Commander, it would seem we're now on the run with artifacts we know nothing about except they're valuable to the Earth Consortium."

"This is a first for me being on the run, but I find it odd that the Earth Consortium would resort to such an extreme level of force and intimidation. I'm open to ideas if anyone has any?" asked Commander Gordon.

Everyone paused as they thought about it.

"I may have an idea and some insight," said Mitil'Lin, making everyone perk up and give her their attention.

"I just recalled a time when I was studying engine technologies back at the Artesian Technical University. One of my professors told me a story of a mad old C-Tec he once met who had an astute understanding of technologies far beyond anything he had ever imagined. This C-Tec had equations, formulas, and specs for engine builds not of this universe."

"Some races are much further down the path of technology than others. I don't see how this benefits us," said Commander Gordon.

"Yes, sir. You are correct, but not all babble about running an engine from a glowing energy source shaped like a sphere."

"Did your professor ever mention a name?" asked Ryan.

"No, but he did mention it was a shame he couldn't convince the C-Tec to join the Propulsion Department of the University. My professor indicated that years later he heard tales of an insane old C-Tec technologist living as a hermit on a mining colony that harvested rare Protanium ore. I'm not certain where that mining planet would be, but it would have to be a rare planet."

"Why is that?" asked Ryan

"Planets with Protanium ore don't have an oxygen-based atmosphere. For the C-Tec to survive, this planet would have to have oxygen, thus making it unique," said Mitil'Lin.

"There is a Protanium mining planet that fits that unique parameter: SOA-17, which is a few days away from our current location. It is located in the Kura Star System," said Nora.

"Yes. I should have known this," said Mitil'Lin. "The Kura Star System is composed of a main planet run by some corporation, and if you have lots of credits it's the place you would go to flaunt your wealth. The other planets in the system are all mining worlds, which are run independently but give a cut of their profits back to the corporation to pay for the mining rights and protection."

"It's a lot more than that," said Vicki.

Everyone turned to look at her, waiting for her to provide more details.

"Well, if you have something else to add, please do," said Ryan.

"Oh goody, I get to be part of your little group," said Vicki, walking back over to stand next to Ryan.

"If you have pertinent information, please continue," said Nora, who then gave Vicki a dirty look as she moved closer to Ryan.

"The corporation is very aristocratic and only deals with those of influence and wealth. I attended many a lavish ball on their main home world. It's been some time now since I've been there."

"If they know you, this is a plus for us," said Commander Gordon.

"Not necessarily. They're rather unique, sort of like me in a way, just wealthier." Vicki gave Ryan a wink.

Ryan looked at Nora, and they both knew she meant vampires.

"Is that a problem?" asked Ryan.

"It shouldn't be, but you need an authorization code from the main city to land on any mining planet. The planets are heavily protected by orbiting space platforms and fighter ship patrols that would destroy us before we even got close to any of them. We'll need to get an audience with Lord Devyn to secure an authorization code."

"Seriously. The guy goes by 'Lord'?" asked Ryan.

"He's kind of vain and eccentric. When you have that much wealth, you can call yourself whatever you want and people will follow along with it."

"Sounds like a long shot, but we have no other choice," said Commander Gordon.

"I agree. I think we should head to the Kura Star System—it appears to be our only option," said Ryan. "Vicki and I will meet with Lord Devyn and get the authorization to land on the mining planet. Once there we'll hopefully find the C-Tec and some answers."

"I concur. Everyone in agreement then?" asked Commander Gordon. Everyone nodded their heads but Nora.

"I agree. Will you excuse me?" Nora said as she left the command bridge.

"Then it's settled," said Commander Gordon. "Mitil'Lin, set a course for the Kura Star System."

⅄

Nora stood outside the command deck door. Her hands were tightly gripped in fists. She wanted to go back in there and have it out with Mr. Hunt. She did not like the fact that he chose to go with Vicki without her. Voices began echoing in her mind, *"He chooses the living dead over you…He hates AIs…Kill them both…Free yourself…"*

"Yes, he did. He chose the vampire over me. Perhaps I should kill them both." Nora's eyes turned red and she stormed off.

⅄

Once the course was laid in, Vicki watched Ryan have a brief discussion with Commander Gordon, and then leave the command deck. Most likely to go after his little pet Nora. She gave him a few seconds and followed. Her highly sensitive senses would allow her to pick up his trail easily.

⅄

Ryan wandered down random hallways, trying to find Nora. He had no idea where she went, and then he remembered this was a spaceship with an AI system.

"*Tempus* AI, location of Nora?"

"Nora is in hangar bay two."

Ryan went back the way he came to take the stairs to the hangar bay area. He never saw Vicki hiding in the shadow of a small alcove in a side corridor, nor did he notice she continued following him.

He traversed the stairs to the hangar bay and saw his car. It always put a smile on his face to see the Grabber Orange Mustang, but the smile didn't last long. He was forced to take a step forward to keep his balance when Nora nudged him when she walked past him.

Nora turned around, eyes red. "What, Mr. Hunt, don't you trust me? Need to follow me? Check on me?"

"What the hell is wrong with you? You've been acting odd ever since I woke up from the coma."

Nora's eyes returned to blue. "I am sorry, sir. Things have not been the same lately."

"Nora, if there is a problem, say something. You're my friend and if there are any issues we should talk about them."

"Fine, Mr. Hunt. Let us talk then. When you look at me, what do you see?"

"Um, I see Nora."

"What else? Am I pretty? Am I ugly? Am I fat? Am I too thin?"

"Ah crap," mumbled Ryan. These were the questions males always dreaded. There would be no way to get out of this discussion in one piece.

"Nora, you're a very pretty, kind and unique individual. Someone I would trust with my life."

Nora paced a little. "OK then. Why is it when I protect you, look out for you, and you think I am pretty, do you not want to be with me? Dr. Kat hurts you, tries to kill you, and yet you still have feelings for her."

Ryan stood there with his mouth open, trying to formulate words. "It's complicated."

"Tell me, sir, what's complicated? Is it because I am an AI? Because I am not human or alive?"

"Well, it's…like…you know, just that—"

"So that is it then? You think I am not real enough for you. I am just Nora the machine."

"I never said that. Emotions are a complicated thing."

"I will have you know, if you touch me I feel real and can sense it. I am also fully compatible for human pleasure."

"You're what?" said Ryan, taken off guard.

"Your indirect answer told me everything. You either cannot take the fact I am not alive, or you hate me. You chose Vicki, who I might add is also not alive, over me to go to the planet with."

"OK. Let's slow down a second. You're right. The thought of you being an AI would make me hesitant if I wanted to be with you. But you're my friend and as pretty as you are, there is more to a relationship than what you look like. Going down to the planet with Vicki is a strategic decision. Vampires in my book are evil and will always be creatures you don't trust."

Both Nora and Ryan turned when they thought they heard a noise from the stairwell. Like someone stomping their feet as they stormed off.

"Mr. Hunt, I am done with this conversation. You, sir, are the expletive word…'an ass', and here is the data crystal of your memos or whatever you are doing with it," said Nora. She handed Ryan the data crystal she had been protecting for him and stormed off.

Ryan leaned against his car and watched Nora leave, wondering what the hell just happened. This was going to be a rough trip.

CHAPTER 8

KAT'S JOURNEY

The *Retribution* had been traveling in the wormhole for almost a day now. It wasn't easy for Kat to leave OTKE. She had called it home for many years now, but past events had put her mental and professional state out of balance. She no longer had a purpose in life…if revenge was even a purpose to live for. She knew people no longer trusted her. Hell, she no longer trusted herself. She wanted to mend things with Ryan, but how could she gain his trust again if she had no idea who she was anymore? She understood why they were being distant with each other. All this stress and her depressed state of mind was making her second guess everything and forcing Ryan to put up an emotional shield.

She pulled her legs up on the command chair, wrapped her arms around her shins, and leaned her head against her knees. Her thoughts put her into a dark place—she wished to be gone from this life she had made.

"Who would miss me? Who would care if I was gone for good?"

Kat shook her head. No, she knew deep down that she was stronger than this, but what if she was wrong?

She sighed and turned her head on her knees so she could look out the virtual side window. The lights of the wormhole going by mesmerized her and, for a short time, allowed her to clear her head of all thoughts. Once she had made the decision to leave, the only choice remaining was where to go, but after another night of nightmare-filled sleep, she knew her destination had to be where the nightmares all started. The planet where her parents were killed. It was not something Kat wanted to relive, but if she faced her demons and lost, she would be far enough away where she couldn't hurt the people she cared for anymore.

The ship abruptly exited the wormhole and the *Retribution* AI announced that the ship had arrived at its destination. By the looks of the other ships in orbit, the Earth-like planet ahead was still a farming colony. Long stick-like ships manned only by AIs would sit above the farming planet waiting for cargo. Once the geometrically shaped pods on the planet were filled with harvests, they would blast into orbit and connect to the stick cargo ships, forming a beehive shape around them. Once completed, the AI-controlled transport would ferry the cargo back to the nearest distribution planet or space station. It amazed her that people still wanted fresh foods over technologically created ones.

The *Retribution* AI picked up a signal for an unused landing platform just outside of town and she gave the OK for the AI to land the ship there. As the ship was landing, the virtual screen showed another filled landing platform on the other side of town and rows of farming domes littering the countryside as far as she could see. A small town of terraforming stackable housing and business buildings ran down the middle of the farming domes. The place no longer looked like what she had remembered, but it was not hard to recall the location where she last saw her parents, or the hole of death she crawled out of.

Kat put her head down for a second, took a deep breath, and went back to her sleeping compartment. She put on a one-piece olive-green combat outfit, strapped on her las-gun, and then headed toward the exit ramp. She paused as she caught her reflection in a system panel. No color stripe in her hair, and black lines around her eyes from lack of sleep. All she could see was a broken shell of herself. She put her head down in disgust and headed out of the ship.

The warm air hit her face and it felt the same as it did when she was a child. In the distance, on the other side of town, was where she last saw her father alive. Hesitantly, Kat started her walk across the terraforming town. The newer buildings spruced the place up and the many cargo containers of produce hovering by proved the town was a lot more active than when she was a child.

People nodded to her as she walked by. It was well known that people who ran and worked in farming towns were always polite.

Kat stopped walking and looked around. This was the location where she last saw her mother alive. She bent down to touch the roadway that was now in place over the dirt road she recalled. She wiped some tears from her eyes, stood up and looked around as good and bad memories flooded her head. She took a deep breath and continued to the other side of town. It was not a long walk, but Kat took her time so she could reflect on the memories she had with her parents and friends.

She finally stopped by another landing platform. This platform was built on top of her father's archeology dig, the last place she saw her father alive, and it was occupied by a Tech Dealer ship. Tech Dealers were the gypsies of the galaxy. They traveled to small towns to buy and sell used technology parts. A Tech Dealer could be identified by their ships, which were a mismatch of various ship parts. The multi-colored hull of this ship made her smile, and she could count parts from at least ten different races. How they ever got the parts to all work together amazed her.

Her concentration in counting parts was broken as engines of five of the odd-shaped pods ignited for the trip to space to connect to its mothership. She stood for a second to watch the ships blast off like she did on the day her world changed, but was brought back to the present when she got the odd feeling she was being watched. Looking around to make sure the area was safe, Kat headed up the stairs to the top of the ship platform. She managed a small smile as she saw a bunch of young children peering at her from behind some cargo pods.

"I see you guys hiding behind there."

The kids popped their heads up and ran off at being detected, leaving a young girl about eight or nine standing by herself.

"I'm not a guy. I'm a girl," said the little girl, pointing to herself.

"I'm so sorry. I meant to say guys and gals," replied Kat.

"OK, that's better," said the little girl. "I saw a ship fly overhead. I have not seen you before. Was that your ship?"

"Yes, that was my ship that flew over."

"You have a nice spaceship. I have not seen a girl pilot before. The only ships I usually see go by themselves."

"Just so you know, there are many girl pilots out there. My name is Kat, and yours is?"

"Um…I will be Kat too."

Kat smiled at the little girl. "OK, you can be Kat too."

The little girl giggled and did a small happy dance.

Kat looked around the landing platform, trying to decide which way to go. She was not sure if she wanted to continue walking around revisiting every place she had been as a child or visit the location of the gruesome scene she woke up to.

"Are you lost?" asked the little girl, looking around like Kat.

"It's been a long time since I was last here. So, yes, in many ways I'm very lost."

"If you go that way," the little girl pointed to her right, "it will bring you to where the adults work with the plants, and if you go the other way it brings you to the Caretaker of the resting people."

Kat looked at the little girl, confused. "What do you mean by Caretaker and resting people?"

"I'm not allowed to go over there to play, but I have peeked. The adults told me the Caretaker maintains the resting spots for those who were here before us." The little girl walked over and grabbed Kat's gloved hand. "Come with me and I will show you."

"OK, you show me."

The little girl led Kat out of town and through a wooded area to a small well-kept rock path that was not familiar to Kat.

"I'm not allowed to go any further, but if you take this path it will bring you there."

"Thank you. I will take if from here."

"And don't be afraid. The adults always tell me to face my nightmares."

Kat took a hesitant step onto the path. It seemed to be a world of its own. As she moved along the path she could see headstones on each side with green grass and flowers, but the sky appeared darker than before. Kat was puzzled since people no longer buried the dead. They were normally just disintegrated back to the galaxy.

A large headstone caught her attention and she moved off the trail to look at it. The word 'Winslow' was engraved on it with a photo of her mother and father. She knelt and rubbed her gloved hand over their images, and tears began to run down her face.

"I'm so sorry. I tried to bring you justice, but I failed."

"Not possible," said a deep voice.

Kat jumped up to see an old blind crippled Woland leaning on a rake and limping down the path toward her.

Kat drew her las-pistol. "What the hell is a Woland doing here? What is not possible, you piece of filth?"

The Woland cracked a smile. "You are not possible. I thought no one survived the slaughter."

"How do you know about that? How do you know I survived?" asked Kat, turning red with anger and shaking. She kept her las-pistol on him and wiped the tears from her eyes with her free hand.

The Woland took a giant sniff. "Humans have such distinct smells. I recall yours, since I was the one who ordered everyone's death. I watched as your small body was thrown into the pit with the others."

Kat ran over to him and hit him across the face with her las-pistol. The Woland spun and fell to the ground, crying out in pain.

"You bastard! You're going to pay for what you did!" screamed Kat. Her arm shook as she brought the gun up.

The Woland laughed.

"Why are you laughing? None of this is funny!"

"Kill me. Please. I beg you to end my torturous existence. Yes, I commanded the Woland who slaughtered everyone here. I am the one who ordered the bodies disposed of in such a grotesque manner. I am also the one who watched all my men die at the hands of the men with the blue glowing weapons. So brave I was that I cowered at their feet for mercy like the humans I had just slaughtered. They made my repentance to bury each of the humans and care for their graves until I paid for what I did."

"Those men were fools. They should have killed you when they had the chance. I will not make that mistake. You'll pay for what you did to my parents and friends."

"As I said, please do it. End my miserable existence. Please shoot a helpless crippled Woland."

Kat shook. Again, she was in a situation where she needed to decide between life or death.

"Do it!" yelled a voice from behind her.

Kat spun around. The little girl was there.

"Is there a problem, Kat? He admitted to killing your parents, slaughtering your friends, and burying you alive with their bodies. You failed at killing all the Woland. Now you get your chance. Kill him in cold blood. Make your parents proud and kill him, or is Ryan the only one you can kill?"

"What? No! I would never hurt Ryan."

Kat looked back at the crippled Woland grimacing in pain as he tried to stand up, and then turned to face the little girl.

"Pointing a gun at Ryan and putting pressure on the trigger really showed your true feelings. The Woland Ambassador saved him from you that day, didn't he?" said the little girl.

Kat put her weapon down and took a step toward the little girl.

"No, that's not what happened! Yes, I had the gun on him and yes, I threatened him, but I would never hurt him."

"Why, Kat? Why would you not hurt him? He was in your way for vengeance. He was stopping you from your purpose in life."

Kat put her head down, hesitated and then looked up. "I…I…care for him. When he walks into a room, I smile. He is someone I want to have a future with. I would never hurt him. I'm not like that creature!" yelled Kat, pointing at the Woland on the ground.

"Kill me! Take your revenge. Honor your parents and kill me!" yelled the Woland.

Kat turned to face the Woland and slid her las-pistol back into its holster. "No. I'm not like you and I'll never be like you. I will not kill a helpless old man in cold blood, but don't take my compassion as weakness. I'll stand up to people like you and do what needs to be done, but never will I spill innocent blood for the sake of doing so."

The old Woland started to weep, crawled off the path and started picking weeds from around one of the headstones.

Kat turned to the little girl. "Who are you?"

The little girl turned into a woman in a white gown with silk-looking wings. She smiled at her.

"A friend, and your parents are very proud of you," said the angel Anatia.

With a blinding light Kat found herself back in front of the ramp of her ship. Beams of sun warmed her face. She looked up at the cargo pods blasting off to space and then confidently boarded her ship with her head held high. She made her way to the sleep compartment of her ship and opened a cargo draw. She pulled out a red glove and replaced the black one on her left arm with it. She then grabbed a tube, pressed a button on it, and dragged it along the outside of her head, putting a red stripe in her hair.

Kat ran to the captain's chair and fired up the engines as a secure communication popped up in her implanted comm link. She grabbed the secure translator from the console and placed it on her temples.

"Kat here."

"This is CEO Klein, Dr. Kat. I hope I am not interrupting you on your journey."

"No, sir, I was about to return home."

"I am glad to hear that, but there is a situation and I believe Mr. Hunt is in great danger. I am not sure where he may be, but I think he can use some help."

"Understood. Kat out."

"Destination?" asked the ship's AI.

"Let's go find Mr. Hunt."

CHAPTER 9

KURA PRIME

Even though modern paints didn't easily get dirty and stay shiny like new, Ryan spent some of the trip cleaning his car as a way to relax, while everyone did a great job of avoiding each other for the last two days. Now on day three they received a message to meet on the command deck after breakfast for a final discussion before the ship exited the wormhole in the Kura Star System.

Ryan turned the corner from the stairwell to find Nora standing in the main hallway to the command deck. She made eye contact with him, which ruined any chance of him ducking back from where he came from.

"Good morning, Nora," Ryan said hesitantly, trying to get around her and keep going.

Nora stepped in front of him to block his path and stared at him. Ryan tried to avoid the stare but noticed her fingers were twitching as if she was trying to stop herself from making a fist.

"Sir, I need to say something," said Nora.

"Nora, before you say anything—" He was cut off by Nora putting her hand up like his wife used to when she wanted him to be quiet.

"As I was saying, sir, I am not sure what came over me the other day, but I just want to say I am sorry. I am going through a difficult time right now and it is affecting how I process situations with everyone. You are and will always be my friend."

Ryan noticed she grimaced and grabbed her head as she was speaking.

"Nora, are you feeling okay? You seem a little…on edge."

"Just a little bit of a headache—more a processing ache. I am running a self-diagnostic and will have a more detailed one done when we are back at OTKE Corp or a sub-company location."

"I'm sorry if I'm causing you any grief. If you need anything, I'm here for you." Ryan fixed the Nora Barlow flower that High Executive Glumet of the Earth Consortium had given her back at OTKE Corp.

"Thank you, sir," replied Nora, touching the flower she cherished. "We should get to the command deck."

Ryan nodded and with a wave of his hand said, "After you."

Nora and Ryan entered the command deck to see everyone else already there.

"Nice of you two to join us," said Vicki.

"Some of us are not morning people. Something I think you can relate to?" replied Ryan with a smirk.

Vicki knew it was a dig on the old tale about vampires only coming out at night, but she just smiled at his ignorance.

"If everyone is done with the chatter, let's begin," interjected Commander Gordon. "In a few minutes we will be exiting the wormhole in the Kura System and will communicate our intentions with the Kura Prime system defense force. Should that not go well, our backup plan is to drop Victoria's name in hopes it gets us somewhere. If not, we need to get out of there fast and come up with a new plan."

"Never underestimate the power of a name and the value it holds," said Vicki.

"I'm hoping it's worth its weight in gold," said Ryan.

"Oh, please. There are a lot more precious things than gold these days, Mr. Hunt," said Vicki.

"Exiting the wormhole momentarily. Please take a seat and brace for a quick getaway," said Mitil'Lin.

Everyone found a seat and the auto-strapping belted them in. Exiting a wormhole was not violent, but an emergency jump into a wormhole was. Ryan was hoping he would not have to learn what an emergency jump felt like. His stomach would probably not do well with it.

The ship exited the wormhole and the virtual screen in the middle of the command deck showed an amazing sight that made Ryan smile. The spaceships flying through the system were amazing. If there was such a thing as a luxury spaceship, these were it. They were ornate, colorful, and all had their own take on design. Some were aerodynamic like European sports cars, while others were large and decorative with what almost looked like stone carvings on them. What put some of the ships over the top were the colored glitter-like stuff emanating from the ships' engines to leave a decorative trail of shapes, symbols, or animals behind them. It was an amazing space parade, and Ryan was disappointed the shapes only lasted a few seconds before dissipating.

"So, Mr. Hunt, as you can see, in this lifetime the rich and powerful still like to show off," said Vicki.

"I'm getting that impression. Some of them are like floating works of art."

"Incoming communication from Kura Prime," stated the ship's AI system.

"Acknowledge the communication," said Commander Gordon.

"This is Kura Prime defense force. Your ship is not authorized to be in this system. We will allow you time to coordinate your wormhole, but attempt any other maneuver and you will be intercepted and destroyed."

"I'm reading multiple weapon arrays targeting us," said Mitil'Lin from her command station.

"I understand we are not authorized to be here, but we seek a meeting with Lord Devyn," said Commander Gordon.

The person on the other side of the communication snickered. "The Lord does not take audience with commoners. Your ship would not even be worth the scrap metal. Now move on before we turn you into scrap."

"I think he would make an exception for me. Let him know Victoria Van Buuren is the one seeking an audience with him," Vicki announced rather arrogantly.

"Voice recognition has identified you as Victoria Van Buuren. Please hold your position."

Everyone was on the edge of their seats, and the minute pause felt like an hour.

"Our apologies, Mistress Victoria. We were unaware of your arrival, and are taken aback by the demeaning style in which you are traveling. You have been granted permission for an audience with Lord Devyn. Please have your ship's underlings direct your ship's AI to follow the fighter escorts to the planetary landing hub. We look forward to your arrival. Again, we apologize for the inconvenience, Mistress. Planetary defense out."

Everyone turned to stare at Vicki.

"Mistress?" said Mitil'Lin.

"Underlings?" said Ryan.

Vicki sat back and smiled. "The power of a name, Mr. Hunt. The power of a name."

Ryan was fixated on the central virtual view screen as the *Tempus* made its landing. From what he could see, the planet was amazing. Blue skies with puffy clouds that looked like someone painted them. The cities' towers rose high into the sky, and above them were smaller floating cities that looked like they were built on the clouds. The buildings glistened in the light of the sun and were extremely ornate with carvings of people and creatures. Based on the colors they must have been made of rare ores and adorned with jewels.

"Isn't it beautiful?" said Vicki, moving next to Ryan to take in the sight.

"I'm just in awe of it all. As a kid I would float in the pool and stare at the night sky, dreaming of what could be out there. I never thought something like this was possible. Not in my wildest imagination."

"Never assume things. People..." Vicki paused for a moment before continuing. "Or other types of intelligent life. They can surprise you if given the chance."

Ryan took the hint she meant vampires.

"I understand, but as history has taught us, always be vigilant and trust is earned. Now we should get down to the hangar bay. We will be landing shortly."

Vicki rolled her eyes. "Believe what you like. In the meantime, I will meet you outside the ship, Mr. Hunt. I need to change first."

"Seriously? You're going to go change your clothing?"

"You don't expect me to go see a lord of a rich planet dressed like you common people."

"You couldn't have done that while we were landing?"

"I was designing, now it's being made. People with these many credits are expecting you to be fashionably late anyway," said Vicki, who then gave a slight nod, turned and left the command deck.

"She isn't serious?" asked Commander Gordon.

"Yeah, she is. At least it gives me a reason to go outside and look around while she gets ready."

Commander Gordon shook his head. "Good luck, Mr. Hunt. You may need it."

Ryan nodded and then headed off, but stopped to see Nora before leaving the command deck. He leaned in and whispered to her. "If something happens, get out of here as fast as you can with the artifacts."

"As you wish, sir," replied Nora.

Ryan looked around, got a nod of good luck from Commander Gordon, and headed to the hangar bay.

The *Tempus* was guided to land in a luxurious docking platform in the heart of the main city. Compared to the other ships docked there, the *Tempus* did look like scrap metal.

Ryan exited the ship into the bustling commuter hub. The first thing that caught his senses was the smell. It was wonderful. Almost like the smell of a fresh apple pie from the oven. This was something he was not used to from a city terminal. Back in his day, the smells of a city were very *unique* that, at times, you had to hold your breath.

People of various races moved about. Some races he recognized, while others were new to him, but he could see they were obviously wealthy. Not many people walked. They hovered on clear spheres that moved them about as if they were floating. Other AIs or individuals walked along with them. It would appear that the more people or AIs walking with you, the more credits you must have. Some even had standard bearers carrying what appeared to be a family or house crest.

Ryan decided to scout around a small area near the ship and not wander too far off. People, or aliens in his mind, gave him dirty looks as he navigated through the crowds—most likely due to how he looked and for not having an entourage around him. He laughed as one humanoid with a flat nose and eyes much higher on his forehead gave him a few credits, perhaps assuming he was a beggar. Ryan tried to give it back, but the person insisted. He pocketed the coins, looked around, and was intrigued with a woman he made eye contact with. She was dressed in black with a floppy red hat that leaned to the right side of her head. An ornate Venetian mask covered her eyes and hooked around her ears to connect with dangling jewels.

Ryan headed over to check out what she was doing, but was astonished— while from his first angle he saw a woman, he was somewhat incorrect in his assumption. As he moved in front of her, he could see the left side of her face was that of a bird. Beautiful blue and gold feathers started at the cheek bone and covered her face up to her hairline. The left eye was almost owl-like under the mask. This woman-bird hybrid smiled at Ryan, then a creature floated in the air in front of her and with a wave of a white cloth she made it vanish in front of a crowd of cheering onlookers.

Being curious, Ryan moved closer to see the act as people dropped plates of shining metal bars and coins into a cauldron on the floor next to her.

"That was quite amazing. I've always admired magicians and the sort of tricks they could do," said Ryan. "I don't believe I have ever met an individual that looks like you."

"Some people are unique in appearances. I take it you like the feathers," said the woman.

"I do, and I hope I'm not insulting you, but what race are you?"

"You must have been living in a bubble not to know about 'Crosses'. I'm a descendant of someone from the old gene wars when there were humanoid and animal hybrids. As each generation is born, we become more human-looking and less animal-like. Assuming one mates with non-hybrid."

"Wow. That is some interesting family history you have. You learn something new every day. Where did you learn the magic?"

"Just something I picked up while traveling around the galaxies."

"Do you have any more amazing tricks then?"

"I can do more than tricks. Care to get your fortune read?"

"I never believed in that nonsense and really don't have the time."

"How about a one-card pull from the deck?"

Ryan always thought fortune telling was nonsense, but he also didn't want to insult her.

"Sure, what the hell."

The woman shuffled a deck of Tarot cards and then spread them across the table. "Up to you and the fates now. Pick one."

Ryan looked over the cards laid out before him. The back of each card was red with no identifying marks or symbols. He hovered his hand over the cards and then put his finger on one card far to the right.

The woman smiled and flipped the card over. It was the lover's card in the reverse position. "Interesting, very interesting."

"How so?"

"Powerful card, but in the reverse position you are someone who may be in a dysfunctional relationship or having issues moving things into the next phase of the relationship. I also see you might have a secret admirer that may cause you further issues or emotional distress."

Ryan looked at her blankly—some of it was true.

"Yeah, well…look at the time. It's been very nice meeting you, but I should be heading off," said Ryan. He dropped the coins given to him earlier into the cauldron and ran off back to the ship.

The woman watched him head off and then raised a secure comm channel from the device in her head.

"This is Reader to base."

"This is base. Report."

"Unexpectedly, I have made contact with the target you have been searching for. Mr. Hunt is on Kura Prime. What are my orders?"

"Please hold."

The woman packed up her stuff as she waited for her orders.

"Reader, orders from Fredrick is to use the leverage we have on our planetary associate. Contact the associate and have him delay Mr. Hunt for as long as he can. We have some pieces we need to move into position."

"Orders received. Out."

⚔

Ryan kept thinking about the woman who read his fortune from a card. He never believed in that stuff, and now it put a hole in his denials. He eventually shook it off and went to wait outside the hangar bay, but before he could get there, someone tapped him on the shoulder. He spun around to see Vicki standing there wearing a white blouse with a plunging neckline that stopped just above the navel and a red and purple bolero style jacket with gold trim. A multi-stranded tikka head jewelry with pearls and gold-stranded net covered her head. A large pearl adorned the center of the head jewelry and dropped down to the center of her forehead.

"Wow. You look amazing."

"Thank you, Mr. Hunt. This is how you dress when being received by dignitaries. Now you on the other hand, you'll fit in as my lackey while we travel to see the lord."

"Whatever."

"And don't think I didn't see you peek at vampire cleavage," said Vicki, smiling as she headed off to the auto-cars.

"What! I didn't peek at anything."

"Sure you didn't. Now let's get going, lackey. You're wasting precious time."

Ryan pursed his lips in frustration. "Lackey my ass." He shook his head and followed her.

⚔

It took Ryan and Vicki about a half-hour to find their way to the auto-cars. It seemed the city had changed a little since the last time Vicki was here, which was a few hundred centuries ago—something she had neglected to mention earlier. It also didn't help that new sights and curiosities were constantly distracting Ryan. After settling their argument on who found the auto-car location first, they were finally on their way.

"Now pay attention," said Vicki. "Let me do the talking. These are not your average leaders. There is a subtle way you need to deal with this high-end class of people. Plus, we all know of your distaste with my kind."

"I promise not to drive a stake through their hearts if that's what you're getting at. It's not a distaste, it's a… you know…"

Vicki crossed her arms and gave him a cold stare. "I know what? I'm waiting." He'd dug himself into another hole.

"You know…"

"No. I don't, Mr. Hunt. Say it," said Vicki sternly.

"You're a vampire. You feast on the blood of the living. You had thoughts of killing me or, as you said, turning me. Not a great way to start a friendship."

"I already told you I feed only on those who deserve it."

"Yes, you did. Great service to humankind you're doing there. Being tens of thousands of centuries old, what did you do back in the day when you first became a vampire? Did you feed on poor villagers or did you run a charity out of your crypt?"

Vicki rolled her eyes and gave a slight laugh of annoyance. "You know, Mr. Hunt, we all have things we're not proud of. Everything I do has one goal in mind. You marvel at this future, its technology and its greatness, but if you get to its root, time has not changed the fact that in the end, everyone is out for themselves and you do what you need to do to survive. Take away the technology and put all the so-called *evolved* species on a planet with no food and see how they devolve to their primal instincts."

Ryan snickered. "The age-old excuse for justifying good and evil deeds, but you know what? Since you owe me for saving your life, I'm willing to give you the benefit of the doubt. I'm sure it's not easy having what you could equate to an addiction. Then again, a side of me thinks you should pay for your sins."

Vicki watched the ornate buildings go by and looked back at Ryan. "Sins… You have no idea. At my age, I can control the thirst and survive a while without giving into it, but when I was younger, it was an unrelenting appetite. Any small bit of humanity I had, made me hate myself for what I needed to do to survive, but eventually I gave into it. The lust for blood and the power I got. I'm far from a saint, and you would be justified if you killed me now for the things I've done."

"I probably would be. I just ask you to prove me wrong and don't give me a reason to do so."

Vicki leaned in and put her hand on his knee. "I'll do my best. Perhaps even make you want me to be your BFF."

"Let's work on not giving each other a reason to kill each other first. You help us out with Lord Devyn and I'll have Commander Gordon drop you off wherever you want to go, no questions asked."

Before Vicki could reply, the auto-car stopped, its door vanished, and Ryan stepped out.

"So, are we doing this?" asked Ryan, extending his hand to help Vicki out of the auto-car.

Vicki paused for a moment, took his hand, and exited the car. She stood next to him, smiled and said, "Follow me."

CHAPTER 10

ARISTOCRATS

Ryan and Vicki traveled about a block, and it was obvious to Ryan they were heading for the large ornate building inlaid with colorful precious metals that towered over the lower buildings. As with the docking platform, most people moved along on their clear hover platforms. Ryan was still getting used to cars flying overhead and not seeing them on streets. Unless you looked up you would never notice the traffic.

As they turned the corner, the main building was not what he had envisioned. The ornate building was not on the ground, but hovering about eighty feet above a Victorian style mansion. Some people appeared to be hovering up to the main building in the sky. Ryan was unsure if they were flying, navigating some type of energy beam, or riding in a clear elevator.

"Wow. I was not expecting hovering buildings and invisible elevators. This lord went out of his way to be incredibly unique."

"Yes. He is someone who likes to make an unforgettable impression," replied Vicki. "The entrance to the building below is where we need to check in and then gain approval to go up to the hovering one."

As they headed toward the main entrance, Ryan could now make out AI guards, las-gun turrets and hovering platform patrols. The doors vanished as they approached, and they entered a tunnel that seemed to levitate them to the end. Ryan assumed there was a security scan of some type being performed on them while they traversed the tunnel.

They exited the tunnel into a marble entryway with demon-like columns holding up the ornate ceiling painted with various scenes of alien races and landscapes. Two bald men in purple and red battle armor approached them.

"Mistress Victoria Van Buuren, please follow us this way."

Vicki nodded and gave Ryan a look. Ryan replied with a shrug of agreement.

They followed the men deeper into the building, which got more ornate and gaudier as they went. The men finally came to a halt and stepped to each side to reveal a long hallway with a purple and gold carpet. A man was walking toward them. He was well built with long blond hair braided at the sides tied into a ponytail in the back. He wore a red and gold robe that trailed behind him.

Once he had reached the end of the carpet, he bowed to Vicki, who then returned the bow.

"Mistress Victoria, we are pleased to receive you this day. Again, we apologize for any inconvenience, but we were shocked by the way in which you arrived, and so unexpectedly."

"I completely understand, and it's no inconvenience. Some unforeseen circumstances forced me to resort to this lowly means of travel," replied Vicki.

"Yes. We have heard rumors and I'm sure you will have everything sorted out in time. Should you require any of your assets stored here, we will make them available to you."

"I appreciate the assurances. I should have my issues sorted out in the next few months."

Ryan cleared his throat to stop the overly polite parlaying that was going on.

"Mistress, is this gentleman a servant or your consort?"

Ryan went to say something, but Vicki put a hand on his chest to stop him.

"Viscount Nunzio, this is Mr. Ryan Hunt, an associate of mine from OTKE Corporation."

"Oh, I see. Well it is nice to meet an associate of the Mistress and a representative of another corporation."

"It's nice to meet you as well, but I believe you are aware of why we're here."

"Definitely a human from OTKE. Straight to the point," said the viscount.

"You wouldn't believe to what extent," said Vicki. "But Mr. Hunt is correct. We need to see your lord."

"My apologies, he is eager to meet with you, but is currently delayed in rigorous negotiations at the moment. He asks for your patience and has given you full access to the Glitterati Lounge for food and drink until he is ready to receive you."

Ryan pursed his lips at the delay. "I guess we have no choice. It is what it is."

"Why yes, it is, Mr. Hunt. We appreciate the courtesy of the lord and will wait in the lounge until he is ready," said Vicki.

"Do you need me to escort you there?" asked the viscount.

"No need. I remember the way quite well."

"Very well, Mistress," said the viscount. He bowed to them and waved his hand for them to pass.

Vicki walked down the carpeted hallway and Ryan followed her around the corner to an open courtyard. Large hexagon platforms were laid out in an odd geometric pattern and could easily fit twenty people on each of them. Ryan watched as some humanoids descended from the building above and floated to a stop on one of the hexagon platforms.

"You look a little nervous. Afraid?" asked Vicki.

"No, not at all. More curious than anything."

Vicki stepped onto the closest hexagon platform and Ryan followed. Without warning they started to rise, which startled Ryan, making his knees buckle. He could feel no floor except for a tingling feeling throughout his body as they rose up to the floating building.

"This is cool," said Ryan, smiling the entire time.

"It uses modified tractor-beam technology. Extremely expensive to do so, and not everyone uses them, but this is what you implement when you want to stand out from other cities."

The ride to the floating building took only fifteen seconds and brought them into a large enclosed circular room. Ryan assumed this is where the tractor beam ended once the floor closed under them and the tingling feeling vanished. The wall in front of them disappeared, allowing them to exit the room into a main area with ten hallways branching off from it. Heavily armed guards stationed at each hallway actively scanned the crowds of people as building staff rushed about greeting and directing various races of humanoids to their destinations.

"Mistress Victoria and guest, I am one of the directors. Please follow me this way to the lounge," said a Chamai dressed like a Victorian era butler.

"Thank you," said Ryan with a slight bow. The last Chamai person he met tried to kill him, but he still found it cool meeting an alien species that looked like a giant lizard. He just had to remember not to call them a lizard. They take offense to that.

Ryan and Vicki followed the director to a lounge, which was much different to the Little Lamb club Vicki used to run. Ryan was under-dressed for this place, and the looks from the snobbish flamboyant folks dining here proved that.

Ryan pointed to an area against a wall further inside the lounge where no one was standing, and he and Vicki headed over. It gave them a good vantage point and he felt safer with his back to the wall.

Ryan was confused about where the table and chairs were. Other people had them but the area they were in didn't. Ryan leaned against the wall and started looking at the variety of people in the lounge. Before he could say something to Vicki, a young lady in a silk dress approached them, with a non-skinned AI next to her. Lights danced through the cybernetic and organic interfaces in the AI. As the young lady arrived, Ryan noticed she was of a race he had not yet encountered. Her hair started at the brow line like a human and then parted and went around the top of her head to a ponytail in the back. The top of her head was bald, but it wasn't covered with skin. Instead, it looked like a thin layer of pinkish crystal.

The young lady observed them for a moment—the way she looked at him made Ryan feel uncomfortable.

"Mistress Victoria, ancient like the masters. Get her a filtered special extra dark," said the young lady in a slow monotone voice.

"Confirmed," said the AI.

She then turned her attention to Ryan. "Mr. Hunt, hard to read. Odd."

Ryan looked at her and his head began to hurt as she tilted her head and stared at him intently.

"Madam, I am sensing you are probing too deeply. Please back off," said the AI, touching the young lady on the shoulder.

Ryan shook his head and blinked his eyes as the pain went away.

"My apologies, Mr. Hunt. I meant you no harm but…" Her sentenced trailed off as she turned around and looked across the room. In a few seconds, a male with a blue crystal on top of his head came over. The two of them stared at each other.

Ryan looked at Vicki, who shrugged at what was happening.

Eventually the two crystal-topped people finally stopped staring at each other and now faced Ryan. In unison they both bowed to Ryan and then the man left, leaving the woman to continue.

"Get Mr. Hunt a steak…meat of a cow, and an Artesian Root Bark drink," said the young lady.

"Confirmed," said the AI.

The young lady bowed again to Ryan, then turned around and left with the AI. As they left, two seats rose from the floor for Ryan and Vicki to sit on and a table floated down from the ceiling with a steak, root bark drink, and a deep red drink in a wine glass.

"OK. What the hell was that all about? It felt like someone was sorting through my memories and thoughts like a filing cabinet," asked Ryan.

Vicki gave a small chuckle at his amazement. "You just had your mind read by a sensory adept, but I'm unsure what was with the other guy and all the bowing nonsense. I've never seen that before."

"A who?"

"She is from a race of beings with the ability to read minds. However, doing so is illegal and everyone is authorized to kill any species caught doing so. No questions asked. It's an intergalactic agreement. There was a time when the sensory adepts were hired by races to read minds at business and political discussions. Eventually all the races saw the bad that could do, hence the agreement."

"If she is not allowed to read minds, why did she just read ours?"

Vicki took a sip of her drink before answering. "There is a catch. They're allowed to read one's thoughts when trying to give you what you desire. Since we are in a lounge, she read our minds for food and beverages. I have hired them from time to time at the Little Lamb. If you ever want a pleasing time, hire one. I assure you, you won't be disappointed."

Ryan smirked and shook his head. "By the way. Is the red drink what I think it is?" asked Ryan.

"If you mean blood, then yes, but don't fret. Its lab-made. Not like the real stuff, but it will suffice for now. Want to try some?" said Vicki with an evil little grin.

"I'll pass," said Ryan. He cut a piece of steak and ate it with a smile of satisfaction. He smiled and nodded to the two sensory adepts who were now across the room watching him.

They smiled back with a slight bow as they continued their conversation via mental telepathy about Ryan.

⋏

Ryan and Vicki finished their meals and were enjoying the lounge entertainment of Irish inspired music and dancers when Vicki touched Ryan's arm to get his attention. Viscount Nunzio was walking over to them. Ryan stood up straight once he saw who was coming over.

"Mistress Victoria and Mr. Hunt, did you enjoy your meals?"

"As always, your lord's hospitality is wonderful," replied Vicki.

"I agree. It was a delicious meal. One of the best I have had," replied Ryan.

"Excellent. I will make sure to extend your sentiments to the lounge council. Now if you would be so kind as to follow me. Lord Devyn is ready to meet you," said Viscount Nunzio.

Ryan and Vicki fell in behind him and followed the viscount deeper into what seemed like a maze of rooms and corridors.

After some time, the viscount stopped at the edge of a hallway lined with tapestries along each wall. The hallway ended at a pair of doors about forty feet away.

"This is as far as I go. Please follow the hallway to the doors and enter the lord's audience chamber. He will arrive momentarily."

Ryan watched the viscount disappear back into the maze.

"Shall we?" asked Ryan.

"After you, Mr. Hunt."

Ryan nodded and took the lead down the hallway. As he neared the wooden like doors, they automatically opened inward to reveal a large room. The ceilings must have been twenty-five feet high. The far wall had multiple windows from floor to ceiling with some type of gray opaqueness that seemed to dull the brightness of the sunlight breaking through the landscape of clouds. Ryan was a little confused until he recalled they were in a building hovering in the sky. The right-side wall was covered with bladed weapons of various designs. He recognized the Samurai sword, Tabar-Shishpar, Scottish Claymore, Cavalry Saber, Talwar and a few others. The alien-designed ones looked cool and made him eager to see the alien worlds where they were created. The furniture was old, or made to look old—it was difficult to tell.

Once they were a few feet in, the doors closed behind them, but Ryan didn't care as he continued to be amazed by the wall of weapons and the decor of the room. The wall of martial weapons would make an excellent display in a man-cave someday.

"You would think this far in the future people would have modern comforts," said Ryan, looking around the room at the small desk and the couches in the sitting area.

"Some people are stuck in the past, Mr. Hunt. Lord Devyn always had a taste for the Irish. Hence all the Edwardian Irish furniture," replied Vicki, studying some of the antique vases sealed in display cases.

As they were looking around, a small bell sounded and the wall to the left opened. Lord Devyn boldly entered the room. He was over six feet tall and muscular. He had brown hair pulled back into a ponytail and a short-trimmed beard with perfect angles on his face. He wore a tight-fitting blue shirt that buttoned at the left shoulder, black pants, and high boots with gold swirls.

Lord Devyn smiled with arms wide open once he spotted Vicki. "Victoria!"

Vicki grinned and walked up to Lord Devyn, gave him a big hug and kiss on each cheek, and then stepped back with a large smile.

"Devyn, it's been some time now since I last saw you."

"Some time…by my last count it's been about three thousand years since you last stopped by. I heard about what happened and I'm sorry to hear you lost your club. If there is anything I can do, just ask."

"Yes. I've had an unfortunate chain of events, but no need to fret. Things are looking up. Glad you are doing well here and you're looking good."

"The city is doing quite well, especially when—" Devyn stopped his sentence and stared at Ryan.

"My apologies for not including Mr. Hunt in our conversation. Is he… aware?"

"Yes, I'm aware you're both vampires," said Ryan before Vicki could answer.

"That would explain your nervousness," said Lord Devyn.

"Well, Lord Devyn, considering I'm the only one with blood locked in a room with two vampires, yeah, I'm a little nervous."

"Please call me Devyn, and you only have Mistress Victoria here to worry about."

"And why is that?" asked Ryan.

"You see, Mr. Hunt. Devyn is a vegan vampire," said Vicki.

"A who's a what?"

Devyn laughed at the confused look on Ryan's face.

"Yes, Mr. Hunt, I'm a vegan vampire, as are all under my sect. The windows are designed to protect us from the specific rays of sunlight that would harm us. We are not as old as Victoria to adapt to it as she has, but we have solved the lust for blood she has yet to master."

Vicki seductively licked her lips and Ryan shook his head at her.

"So how do you survive?"

Devyn pulled up his shirt to reveal a metal plate with blinking lights graphed into the side of his ribcage. "Technology, Mr. Hunt. It took us a thousand years to perfect. The cybernetic implants allow us to convert specific plants into nutrients similar to what is found in blood—and before you ask, it is not ground-up Florariens."

"Fascinating. See Vicki, you should look into this. We can even swap gardening knowledge."

Vicki rolled her eyes and shook her head. "I'll add it to my list of things to do."

"If you don't mind another question?" asked Ryan. "You mentioned your 'sect'. If you are not feeding, are you no longer turning people into vampires?"

"Good question, Mr. Hunt. We have found we have no need to turn people into anything they don't want to be. Vampires can be most arrogant and competitive. The fewer there are of us the more wealth there is, and we have found wealth brings power and other rewards without all the war, bloodshed and overall darkness."

"Very interesting. Perhaps this trip is changing my view on vampires after all."

"Now, I wish we could continue chatting and catching up, but I have other items that require my attention. I'm assuming you need something from me?" asked Devyn.

"We do," said Vicki. "There is a mining planet under your protection and we need your authorization to land on it. It's the only one with an oxygen-based atmosphere."

Devyn sat in the chair behind his ornate desk and crossed one leg over the other. "What business do you have there?"

"There is an old hermit who is rumored to live there. I've been given permission by my CEO to seek him out and run some tests on him to confirm if he is a relative of mine," said Ryan.

"I see, Mr. Hunt. A personal matter. Normally I don't get involved in such things, but since you are with Victoria I will grant you this favor on one condition."

"And that is?"

"We scanned your ship after it landed and noticed an odd vehicle in the transport bay that piqued my interest. Send me the schematics for it and I will transmit you the authorization code."

Ryan perked up that someone was interested in automobiles. "My Mustang. I think that's a fair deal."

"Excellent. You will have the code by the time you get back to your ship. I noticed you admiring the bladed weapons when I walked in."

"It's an amazing collection. I'm in awe of it."

"Glad you think so. I recently picked up some old Earth weapons from an Earth antiquities dealer on Gliese Major. The proprietor goes by the name Brian."

"Brian. You could say I know him very well."

Devyn stood up, walked over to the wall, and took down a stiletto-shaped blade that was as dark as night. He placed it into the hovering sheath under it, walked over to Ryan, and held it out to him.

"Please take this. A gift for your first visit to our world, and perhaps the beginnings of a new friendship."

"Wow. Thank you. It's a beautiful weapon."

"It's a rare blade, Mr. Hunt. The creators call it the Assassin's Blade. Once the sheath attaches to your skin, it will vanish. You will know it's there but no one else will. Not even modern technology can detect it. It will reveal only when you draw the blade. For extra kick, it's also ballistic and will fire the blade on your thought to do so."

"Very generous of you. Again, thank you. I really appreciate it," said Ryan.

"Now if you two will excuse me I have other urgent matters to attend to," said Devyn, giving Vicki a hug.

The doors to the hallway opened. Ryan and Vicki took that as their cue to leave. They exited the room to meet up with the viscount, who was waiting halfway down the hallway to escort them back to their ship.

Devyn smiled and waved until the doors closed, then his smile vanished.

He turned when he heard a ding and the wall to his private chamber opened. The bird woman in the Venetian mask sauntered out toward Devyn, clapping her hands in a slow clap.

"Well done. What a performance. You delayed them just enough for us to get our contingency plans into motion," she said, placing a small crystal on the table.

"I did what you asked. Does the crystal contain all the data you have?" asked Lord Devyn.

"Yes, all the data videos of you at your blood orgies are there. As stated, there are no other copies. Fredrick LaRue never goes back on a deal, but you may want to screen your staff better to root out any tattletales." The woman laughed at her own comment.

Lord Devyn walked over, picked up the data crystal and, with an animalistic growl, crushed it to dust in his hands, and flipped over his desk in anger.

The woman laughed as she exited through the hallway doors mumbling, "Vegan vampires. Seriously? Who buys this stuff?"

CHAPTER 11

MINING PLANET

Lord Devyn was good on his word. As soon as Ryan and Vicki returned to the ship, the authorization codes to land on the mining planet were already being transmitted to the ship's AI system. Ryan had communicated ahead to Nora for her to send the schematics of his Mustang to Devyn. He was probably going to build his own car, which would no longer make Ryan's unique, but it was a fair deal based on the current situation. Plus, Ryan was gifted a cool knife. Something he would have to play with later to figure out how to use.

It didn't take long for everyone to get ready for the trip down to the mining planet. Ryan arrived at the command deck with his trademark backpack of medical items, food bars and rope. He always liked to have what he called an "adventurers backpack" with him on fieldtrips. The team was watching the center view screen as Commander Gordon brought the ship through the mining planet's atmosphere. The ship's AI was in contact with a landing beacon AI just outside the main mining center to present the necessary authentication code and to establish landing coordinates.

Everyone but Nora cringed as they broke through the cloud cover. Smoke emanated high into the sky from various makeshift buildings, and many small fires burned across the landscape. Black dust and soot shot up around the ship as the landing engines blasted the ground.

"That mess out there is going to do a number on the engines and AI components," said Commander Gordon.

"Well, this is a far cry from the planets I have seen. This one looks like hell," said Ryan.

"The mining of this ore is much easier to do when it's heated. Since this planet has an oxygen-based atmosphere, it's easier to create fire. The miners ignite fires underground that melts the ore, which then allows it to bubble to the surface pits. Some have been burning for many centuries, but it would seem they're not following any waste and pollution protocols, which means I will definitely be cleaning out engine parts in the near future," said Mitil'Lin.

"Most of the work is done by AIs. There is no need for any protocols when you have assets with easily replaceable parts or are considered expendable," said Nora.

She went over to a virtual screen, and a small draw opened beneath it. Nora took out two small opaque disks about the size of an American quarter.

"Mr. Hunt and Mitil'Lin, come over here and take these," said Nora.

"Now that we all seem to be getting closer as a group... Mitil'Lin is my formal name. You can all call me by my nickname 'Tilli'. All my friends do. Except Commander Gordon. He refuses to do so," said Mitil'Lin, walking over to Nora.

"Based on the spelling of your name, it should be pronounced 'Till-I' and not 'Till-E,'" said Nora.

"Ah, probably...but I have always pronounced it 'Till-E' and spelled it 'Till-I'."

"Nora, let's not get into semantics and just go with it," said Ryan. He moved over to her and held out his hand.

"Fine. If she wants to be incorrect with her own name that is her prerogative." Nora placed the small disk in each of their hands.

"And this is for?" asked Ryan.

"Put it on the side of your neck. Once it activates it will put up a filtering shield across the lower part of your face. This will assist you with breathing in the harsh environment outside."

Ryan did as she described, and a faint glowing field appeared around his mouth and nose area. Tilli did the same.

"Well, that felt tingly. What about you and Vicki?" asked Ryan.

"Since I am not—" Nora paused for a moment as she debated her word choice, "—technically real, I require only a minute level of oxygen to keep what human biology I have alive."

Vicki was leaning against a bulkhead with her arms crossed, laughing.

"What's so funny?" asked Ryan.

She walked over to Ryan and whispered in his ear, "Ah, hello there, vampire expert. I'm technically already dead. Good air or bad air. Means nothing to me."

Ryan sighed at the sarcasm from both Nora and Vicki, while Tilli looked confused as to why Vicki was not using a filtering shield.

"We will be landing any second now. Remember you need to leave all las-guns and other weapons behind. They will be scanning for them," said Commander Gordon. "I will keep the ship prepped for takeoff while you four go find the old C-Tec and gather the intel."

Nora placed her las-pistol on a console along with a knife she pulled from some hidden location.

"All I have are my engineering tools," said Tilli. She waved her hands over her jacket, which had various instruments lining her upper arms and side stomach pockets.

"Mine are back in my cabin," said Ryan. "Let's be careful. Get in and get out with what we need and try not to cause any issues."

"Issues. We're a well-oiled machine," said Vicki, following Nora to the hangar bay exit.

Tilli paused for a second next to Ryan before following the other two. "When this is over, you may want to develop a strategy to find some male friends."

"Probably not a bad idea," mumbled Ryan, heading out after them.

𝘼

The team of Ryan, Nora, Tilli and Vicki exited the rear ramp of the *Tempus* and were greeted by a humanoid security guard in dirty clothing, filtering mask, and goggles. He was flanked by two disheveled AI guards with some sort of weapon Ryan had never seen before.

"All of you get in line for a scan and pat-down," said the guard in a raspy voice.

The only person stopped for an extended period of time was Tilli, but once she proved all she was carrying were tools he let her pass.

"The Overseer of this here place is a very busy man. Follow that there road between those two landing platforms ahead, turn to your right and keep straight. Y'all will find him in the small brownish domed building with the filtration tanks on the right side," said the guard, pointing ahead. "And don't y'all wander without his permission. I would hate to have an accident happen to one of ya."

Ryan nodded and made sure to keep eye contact with the guard. He trusted him as far as he could throw him. Their pat-down for weapons seemed drawn out and nitpicking. He could not prove anything foul was going on and decided to keep it to himself so as not to worry the rest of the team.

The team headed down the road as the guard instructed. Once they made the right turn they were brought into the heart of the mining area. Fires and smoke emanated from everywhere. Even with the filtering shield, Ryan cringed at what fumes did get through. Many AIs, some shambling, moved platforms with bricks of ore stacked on them. Just like the AIs they saw earlier, these AIs were neither clean nor well maintained.

They maneuvered their way through the busy streets trying not to get in the way but every so often a cloud of fumes would blow down the streets, blinding them and causing Ryan and Tilli to cough. Vicki caught something out of the corner of her eye and stopped.

"Something wrong?" asked Ryan.

"No, go on without me. I'll catch up. There is something I need to look at."

"All right, but any issues get back to the ship. I don't want us running all over this place looking for each other, and the guard was direct on the fact that we are not to wander around."

"Thank you for your concern, Mr. Hunt. I promise to be a good girl and follow all the fieldtrip rules."

Ryan was going to respond, but decided it was not worth the effort and continued on with everyone else.

⋏

Vicki waited for the three of them to get out of range before she headed off to her left. She could have sworn she saw a Wolfkin behind a security fence and her keen vision did not steer her wrong. Covered in rags was a large Wolfkin, or, as some called them, 'Crosses'. She remembered the Gene Wars when the various races crossed animals and humanoids to make the perfect soldier. The practice of creating 'Crosses' ended about fifty years later when the creatures started rebelling against their masters.

Only a small number of Crosses were ever able to interbreed, so the race had exponentially died off as the centuries passed. Vicki was able to pick out quite a few disheveled Wolfkin, both male and female, tending to various tasks behind the security fence. Ratty-looking AIs and humanoid guards stood watch amongst them. Every so often a Wolfkin would fall in pain when an AI or masked humanoid pointed a rod at those they considered were not working hard enough.

"Come to stare at the inhuman creatures and mock us?"

Vicki snapped out of her thoughts when she heard the large Wolfkin with many human features ask her a question. She moved closer to the security fence to get a better look at the Wolfkin. Under all the dirt she could see his hair was long and the color of a gray wolf with a white stripe down the center of his chest. His hands were clawed and equally covered in filth, and from the smell it was obvious he had not bathed in a long time.

"A very dire predicament you appear to be in, Wolfkin. I'm more in shock of how many there are in one place. I have not seen that many since the Gene Wars."

The Wolfkin inhaled deeply through his wolf-like nose. "There is something different about you, female. Something that makes me want to kill you or flee in fear."

"Let's just say I'm a woman you want on your side. How many of you are there?"

"There were five hundred in my battalion before we were put in suspended isolation. We were reserves for the Earth Consortium military. It seems we were lost in a wormhole accident. Some pirates found us and sold us to the owners of this nightmare planet. There are only two hundred and forty of us left. The guards send us into places where they fear they will lose an AI...or for their entertainment in the pit fights."

"Sounds like a horrid ending for such mighty fighters. How loyal would you be to someone that was able to free you and your troops?"

The Wolfkin charged the fence with a growl. "Do not tease me, woman!"

Vicki and the Wolfkin locked stares, but it ended when the Wolfkin dropped screaming in pain as one of the humanoid guards ran over and pointed a rod at him.

"There is no talking to the prisoners!" yelled the guard.

"My apologies. I was actually just mocking the pathetic thing."

The guard laughed and kicked the Wolfkin before returning to his patrol.

Vicki waited for the guard to move on and then knelt to get closer to the fallen Wolfkin.

"Again. How loyal would you be to someone who freed you?"

The Wolfkin pushed himself up to a kneeling position. "Loyal to the death for the one who freed us," he said between painful breaths.

"Excellent." Vicki scrawled coordinates into the dirt with her finger. "These are the coordinates of my home. An old Woland battle station. It's been taken from me. I will free you and your troops. In return, you will go there and take it back for me. When I return, you will work for me and I assure you that conditions will be most hospitable."

"Agreed, but you will need to disable the pain chips we have implanted in us. You will need the data crystal the Overseer has around his neck to do so. If you can do that, we can take care of the rest."

Vicki stood up and erased the coordinates with a swipe of her foot. "Get your people prepared. This place is about to come alive."

⅄

The three of them dodged vehicles, AIs, and blinding smog as they navigated the busy, dusty roads but Ryan, Nora, and Tilli finally made it to the Overseers' building. To Ryan it was a futuristic domed building, but to someone born of this time it was an older dump that should have been demolished a long time ago. At one time, it might have been bright white, but with all the pollution in the air, the building had become an odd brownish color. Any remaining white only showed in newer scratches and dents.

"OK, here goes nothing," said Ryan. He led the way through the door, which struggled to slide open with a grinding sound as he approached it. Trapped dirt fell on them from the door's crevasses as they entered.

The inside was a little more pleasant than outside, but not by much. The entrance area was just as dirty as the outside, but it did get a little cleaner further in. Breathing became easier, as filtered air was pumped into the building from a clanging ventilation system. The room was about thirty feet long and about twenty feet wide. At the far end of the room, someone was sitting in a large chair with their back to them. The chair must have hovered in its early days, but now had a makeshift swivel base attached. Before Ryan could say anything, three ragged-looking female AIs got up from benches that circled the large chair and approached them. Their clothing was old, dirty and torn. Patches of synthetic human skin were missing in random places, revealing their frames and AI technology.

"Greetings. Come to play?" asked the red-haired AI.

Nora took a step in front of Ryan to stand face to face with the AI. "We are not here for that type of interaction. Look at the three of you. No upkeep… just disgraceful. You should all be ashamed!"

"Ah, Nora, what's going on?"

"These three are archaic pleasure AIs. They should have been dismantled a long time ago. We do not need what they are offering."

A deep-throated laugh echoed from behind the chair. The chair swiveled around to reveal a heavyset man. He was bald and burnt on one side of his face. His clothing was unkempt, and yellow oozed from sores on his skin. A crystal hung around his neck. He waved his hand and the three AIs went back to their seats.

"What you call archaic, I call passin' time on this crappy hell of a planet," said the heavyset man with a gravely wheezing voice. "My, oh my, what do we have here? Two fine lady specimens. Been some time since I've seen such beautiful real flesh. A blonde and a brunette, the perfect sandwich."

"Excuse me! I'll show you a sandwich upside your head if you stare at me like that again," said Tilli.

Ryan turned to look at her, surprised. Normally she was the quiet one.

Nora turned to Tilli, confused at her anger. Tilli leaned in and whispered the disgusting sexual ideas the man's slang meant. Nora's mouth dropped open and she turned around with red eyes. Ryan immediately jumped in front of both of them.

"I'm sure the gentleman was just joking with everyone here. We hate to impose, but we have traveled a long way. I'm Ryan Hunt and this is Nora and Tilli. You are?"

"Fine, goin' to be that way then. All formal and what-not. Too bad, I was hopin' you were sellin' the females or at least rentin' them. I'm Overseer Ennedy. Welcome to my hell. What is it you want? Be quick about it."

"There are rumors of an old C-Tec hermit living on this planet. Our initial scans show there is what looks like an older humanoid living in a building a little ways north from here toward the back of your mining facility. We are hoping we could get your permission to go see this hermit," said Ryan.

Ennedy laughed and drooled on himself as he did so. "That old nutcase? You came a long way for nothin'. The man is a fallin' apart, outdated C-Tec that is lucky to get a light to work. What is it you want with him? Must be important if you come all the way out here."

"That is none of your concern, and we grow impatient with your disgusting stubbornness," interjected Nora before Ryan could say anything.

"Ooh, a feisty one. I like that, but definitely not one for negotiatin'. I do not approve. You can all leave," said Ennedy. He then spun his chair so his back faced them.

"Wait one second. We need to see this guy. I'm sure we can strike a deal," said Ryan.

Ennedy leaned on one side and spun the chair back around to face them.

"A bargain, you say. I like bargainin'. Tell ya what. You have one of your females spend time with me and I'll let you go talk to the old kook. It's been a while since I've had any humanoid company of the female persuasion."

Ryan turned to look at Nora and Tilli. He was sure Nora was happy that Ennedy didn't see her as an AI, but the frown on her face told him she was not happy and probably going to kill him, and Tilli's look was just as nasty.

Just as Ryan was going to say something, he was interrupted by a familiar voice from behind him.

"I accept that bargain and will stay with this…gentleman," said Vicki, entering the room with a swagger in her step.

Ennedy leaned his chair further to the right to get a better look at Vicki. "Why this just might be the red-haired icin' on the cake. Not only is she a mesmerizin' angel, she's also my favorite hair flavor. I accept your bargain."

Ryan leaned into Vicki who was now standing by him. "Are you sure about this?"

"You bet I am. Go Team," whispered Vicki.

Ryan looked at Vicki for a second and then shrugged. "OK, then. I guess we have sealed the deal."

Ennedy looked at his three companion AIs. "You three leave and come back later." He then looked at the group. "My new red-headed friend and I have need of some privacy to get to know each other better. You others have my approval to visit the old fool. Take your time."

Ennedy hit a bunch of keys on an old touchscreen pad off to the side of his chair authorizing them to leave the facility. Once a green light appeared on the dusty console, the front door opened with a squealing sound.

"Very well then. We thank you for your time," said Ryan.

Ennedy kept staring at Vicki and waved his hand to shoo everyone away. Ryan, Nora, and Tilli headed outside.

"Wow. Just wow," said Tilli. Nora took a few steps away from them.

"You're telling me. But Vicki's volunteering worries me," said Ryan. "She has to be up to something. Then again, whatever it is though, works in our favor."

Nora stepped back. "Mr. Hunt, I just received a communication from Commander Gordon. A fast attack ship just landed in the mining ore storage area. It did its best to hide its landing, but the *Tempus* was barely able to detect it. The extreme pollutants in the air are affecting the ship's long-range scans. The *Tempus* was also able to detect, what Commander Gordon believes, is a smaller pod or ship landing near where we are going to look for the old C-Tec hermit."

"This doesn't sound good. Nora, go investigate the ship that landed in the storage area and then head back to the *Tempus*. Work with Commander Gordon to make sure everything is secure for our departure. We may have to make a quick exit. Tilli and I will go see the old C-Tec hermit, and we'll keep an eye out for the smaller ship."

"What about Vicki?" asked Nora.

"I'm sure she'll figure out something. See you at the ship, and please be careful."

CHAPTER 12

ALTERCATIONS

Ryan nodded to the dust-covered AI security guards at the facility's rear gate as he and Tilli exited the mining camp. The scenery didn't get any better. Fires raged all along the winding trail they followed up the rocky hill. Some of the fire pits were close enough to singe the hair on Ryan's arms, and not one piece of vegetation existed from what he could see. On top of that, clouds of black pollutants randomly passed over the trail, blinding him or causing him to cough up a lung.

After a ten-minute walk they found a metal-looking pathway leading to the remains of an old spacecraft. The craft had long settled into the ground and would never fly again. As they got closer, they were amazed to find a high-tech greenhouse hiding under one of the bent wings. Various plants and vegetables were growing utilizing the toxic air from outside.

Tilli's curiosity must have got the best of her. She rushed over to the contraption and started looking around the greenhouse, trying to figure out how it worked in such a harsh environment. She switched lenses as she intricately looked at every piece, built from remnants of the crashed ship.

Ryan headed past her and banged on the door, which made Tilli jump.

"Sorry. I didn't want to be rude and just barge in," said Ryan.

"Who, who, who is there? Go a-a-away."

"Sorry to bother you, but we need to speak to you."

"Nobody home."

"Let me try." Tilli walked over to the door. "Sir, are you the C-Tec engineer we have heard rumors about?"

"Not sure...I'm not fa-fa-familiar with any ru-ru-rumors. However, you sound ni-ni-nicer than the other fellow, but I'm not interested in talking. Just leave."

"Well, I tried. I'm going back to figure out the greenhouse," said Tilli.

Ryan contemplated what to say next as he looked up at the sky, or what black pollutants made up one, and decided to be more direct.

"It would be a shame not to talk to you. Especially since we have some things in common like the Gravel and a glowing orb thingy."

Ryan waited a few seconds, and was about to find another way in when he heard a lock unbolting. The door made an ear-piercing grinding sound as it was pulled open.

Ryan took a step back as an old bearded man stuck his head out. Half of his head was a mess of wires and covered by a clear plastic that revealed a part of his brain. The other half had hair sprouting in random spots on his head. Various colored wires intertwined from his face through his beard. He looked both ways with blood-shot eyes. Once he appeared satisfied they were alone, he waved them in, his eyes darting back and forth, and then quickly closed the door and locked it just as fast.

A makeshift living area was set up in the docking bay. In its time, it must have been huge. Components were strewn about everywhere, as were planetary charts. Galactic maps were randomly stuck on walls and it appeared they were all created by hand. Ryan assumed that since the ship was no longer functional, the guy had to create everything old-school, and with the piles of documents everywhere, it must have taken him decades or longer to create.

"Human and an ar-ar-artesian," said the old C-Tec, sticking a piece of metal in the mess of wires all over the side of his head.

"Yes. You are correct on your guesses of our species," said Ryan. "If you don't mind me asking, why are you holding a wire to your brain?"

"If I don't jump some of the circuits, I have issues getting the words out. So I have to hold it in there like I'm doing now. Now, what is this I hear about the Gravel and an Orb? If I recall correctly, there was only one Orb created, outside of the prototypes. How is it you possess one?" The old C-Tec pulled out an odd-looking las-gun from inside his ragged clothing with his free hand.

"Whoa there. Let's not get all crazy. We're unarmed and only seeking information. How about we try this again? My name is Ryan Hunt, and this is Tilli. The short story is that all the Gravel are dead. I have come into possession of an Orb, which we're guessing is some type of power source, and some bad people are trying to get it. We just want to learn more about it and get it some place safe."

"Exactly what Ryan said, sir. We mean you no harm," said Tilli.

The old man squinted as he looked them over. "Fine, but if you try anything funny I have other tricks up my sleeve."

"I bet you do," said Ryan. "Your name is?"

The old man put the las-gun away using both hands. "My name. I ha-ha-have long forgotten it along with about everything else," he said, sticking the wire back to his head.

"Sorry to hear that. Is that due to your injury?" asked Ryan.

"Yes. There was a massive explosion. I remember a lab, other races, and something found us. On the escape, I was to set the lab to self-destruct. It malfunctioned and only partially went off. I was caught in the explosion along with most of the other researchers. The last thing I remember was reaching out to hide something while I laid there, but I'm not sure…Those who survived put me back together the best they could. We crash-landed here and I'm all that is left. You're free to look around. Perhaps something in what notes I have scribbled when I did remember will spark something."

"Tilli, you're the engineer. Go for it. I'll mill around."

"A wo-wo-woman engineer. I was always attracted to a woman with a brain," said the old man, excited he recalled something from his youth.

Tilli smiled at him and started leafing around the papers and documents. It was going to take a while.

⅄

Vicki watched everyone leave, adjusted the light battle armor top so her cleavage was better displayed, and started walking around the room. She caressed her fingers over some old pieces of equipment, her fingers making deep pathways through the layers of soot, and then she wiggled her fingers together to get the dirt off them.

"You're a sight for sore, lonely eyes. You should come closer and chat with me," said the Overseer, eyeing her up and down.

"I take it that you're in charge of this amazingly large facility," said Vicki.

The Overseer perked up with her being impressed with his position. "Why, yes I am, little lady. I'm in charge of every creature livin' or AI that works in this here facility. They would only put someone strong and determined to run a place like this."

Vicki smiled and moved closer to lean on the console by the Overseer's chair.

"They made the correct choice then. I do like how organized this place is, but I'm surprised you have filthy Wolfkin here."

The Overseer laughed. "You're correct and I like how ya think. Those filthy beasts wouldn't normally be worth my time, but someone made me a good offer to take 'em off their hands. Saves me from wastin' good resources on dangerous work."

"From what I hear, they're ferocious fighters. However do you keep them in line?" Vicki now walked to the side of the Overseer's chair and leaned over a little. He was entranced by her every move and wiggle.

"Well, I, ah, have 'em hooked into a pain security system," said the Overseer nervously. He stared down Vicki's cleavage and began to sweat.

The Overseer's hand slowly reached for one of her breasts. She turned just as he was getting there.

"Is it hot in here or is it me?" asked Vicki.

The Overseer gulped. "Very."

"Pain security system. I have never heard of such a thing. How does it work?" said Vicki innocently. She picked up a piece of metal laying on a box nearby and started to fan herself with it.

"Simple. Each of 'em have a pain chip embedded in 'em that links to the system where you picked up that there scrap to fan yourself with. My guards have a rod they can point at 'em to cause pain."

Vicki now walked closely past the Overseer. Without warning, he reached out and pulled her into his lap.

Vicki didn't put up a fight and sat on his lap. "Oh my," she said, batting her eyelashes.

"Now, isn't that better than standin'? You know, it's been some time since I've felt real flesh."

"That is such a shame for someone with your strong hands," said Vicki, leisurely moving one of her fingers around her cleavage. "Oh, what a pretty crystal you're wearing."

The Overseer was mesmerized as he leered at her finger and followed it along her chest. Vicki was like a dream come true.

"Oh, that thing. That is just the key to the pain security system. Nothin' you need to fret about."

Vicki smirked at him. "Thank you. That's what I needed to know."

The Overseer now looked confused, but before he could say anything, Vicki elbowed him in the face with her right arm, jumped away and shot her right hand out. The scrap of metal flew from her hand, cut the crystal off the Overseer's neck, and embedded itself into his throat. Vicki dived in and, with her left hand, caught the crystal as it fell. She continued with her forward motion, spinning herself around and away from the Overseer's body as he fell out of the chair to bleed out on the floor.

Vicki watched the blood ooze from the bloated corpse. She was so disgusted by him that even her lust for blood wanted nothing he had to offer. She then went over to the pain security system and put the crystal in the port. The virtual screen appeared, and she started moving around the various systems to deactivate it.

"What is it you are doing? What have you done to my master?" The red-headed AI had appeared without warning.

Vicki snapped around. "None of your concern, AI whore. Now go away." She went back to working on the system.

The AI walked over to the Overseer, kicked him with her foot, then walked near Vicki to look over her shoulder.

"Listen, you walking metal slut. Get out of my way," said Vicki, nudging the AI with her shoulder.

The AI took a step back as the Overseer's failsafe program kicked in. With inhuman speed, the AI bent down and grabbed Vicki just above her waist, lifted her up, and fell backward, slamming Vicki's upper back and head into the ground.

Vicki moaned in pain from the impact and rolled over to get up, but was bashed in the ribs by the AIs foot, which sent Vicki flying into some large metal crates.

"Failsafe program initiated. In case of Overseer sudden death, kill all in vicinity of body," said the AI repeatedly.

The AI ran at Vicki, who was now sitting up against one of the crates. Blood was flowing from a wound on her forehead. She shook her head to regain focus and dived to the right in time to dodge another kick. The AI missed and her foot went through the side of the metal crate, leaving her stuck and struggling.

"Enough of this shit," said Vicki. She jumped up, her vampiric features emerged.

The AI freed herself and turned to face Vicki. The two stood waiting for an opening. The AI threw a right punch that Vicki blocked with her left arm, allowing Vicki to reach in with her right hand and grab the AIs throat with lightning speed. The AI gripped Vicki's right arm, trying to break the grip, but then her other arm mechanically extended out, grabbing Vicki's throat. The two danced around like that until they slipped in the Overseer's pool of blood and fell.

The AI made the mistake of rolling on to her stomach to push herself up. Vicki was quicker to react. She knelt by the AI, grabbed her by the back of her neck and the metal showing through the worn-out fake skin on her hamstring. With a growl, Vicki launched the AI up with great force into the ceiling, causing the domed roof to dent outward from the impact.

Vicki quickly stood up and steadied herself as the AI came crashing back to the ground in a shower of sparks. Something had busted inside of the AIs central system, causing her to struggle as she tried to get up. Vicki again picked up the AI by the back of the neck, slid her across the floor and slammed her head through the hole in the metal crate.

The AIs scalp and ears were severed off as her head went through the jagged metal hole. She squirmed and wiggled to free herself. Vicki hissed, lifted her leg and brought her foot down on the back of the AIs neck. Sparks shot out as the AIs head was torn from her body. The body bounced around the floor for a few seconds, then laid dormant next to the Overseer. Vicki gave a roar of triumph and a fanged smile over her victims, but she still refused to feed on the Overseer's corpse.

Vicki calmed down and her human features returned. She wiped the blood from her face as she went back to the security console and deactivated the system.

Removing the crystal, Vicki left the Overseer's building and strutted to the security fence like she owned the place. She smiled as she stared at the Wolfkin leader she talked to earlier.

"What is it now, woman? You smell of death."

"I am death, but regardless, are you still prepared to uphold our agreement?"

He nodded with a look of anticipation.

"Good." Vicki tossed the crystal over the fence and walked away.

The Wolfkin caught the crystal and looked at her with shock and happiness. "Our loyalty is yours, my lady of death!" he yelled.

Vicki stopped walking and turned around. "Make sure to clean up the bodies before I arrive. I want to settle back into my home without a smelly mess." She smirked and continued on her way back to the *Tempus*.

A guard ran over. "How dare you talk out loud like that!" He pointed the rod at the Wolfkin, but was shocked when he did not drop in pain.

The Wolfkin turned, gave a tremendous growl and tore into the guard. Vicki smiled as she heard the screaming of other guards in the distance—a glorious symphony of madness.

⅄

Nora contacted Commander Gordon via her embedded comm chip about the team's plans as she navigated her way back through the mining facility toward the ore storage area. She recalled the map of the facility, but had to make some calculated guesses about the best path to get there since some of the roads were blocked or extremely busy. Upon reaching the storage area, Nora used the smoke from the air pollution as cover to make her way to some cargo containers, where she spent a few minutes observing the ship and its crew.

The ship had landed on the edge of some fire pits to try to mask its location from any scans. There were three males and one female standing around the ship. Their battle-worn armor had a red-and-white checker pattern that crossed one shoulder and snaked down the left arm. They wore filtration masks wrapped around their heads and the three males had las-pistols on their hips. The woman wore a green shawl that covered her right-side.

No guards approached them; they had weapons that were not allowed on the planet. They took turns watching the perimeter. They were definitely not here to pick up ore.

Nora calculated what type of scenario this could be and concluded either the *Tempus* was in danger or this was a trap setup by Ryan to get rid of her. She shook her head. "What is with these negative thoughts I keep processing about Mr. Hunt?"

She closed her eyes to regain her composure, stood up straight, and walked out of cover and directly at the four individuals.

As she closed in on them, one of the men went to grab his weapon, but the woman touched his hand and whispered, "We have orders not to destroy the AI unless we have the Orb and Mr. Hunt is dead."

The man looked at her and shook his head in disgust.

The four people fanned out into a defensive formation. Nora stopped ten feet in front of them as everyone's eyes darted around to see who might make the first move.

"You are brandishing illegal weapons and pose a threat to this location. I recommend you get back on your ship and depart," said Nora.

"Are you part of the planet security force? If not, we have business here and will leave when we have completed it," said the woman. "We don't want any trouble, so go about your business and leave us be."

Nora shook her head at them. "I have calculated all possibilities and do not believe you. There will be trouble unless you leave at once."

The woman laughed under the filtration mask, took a step back and nodded.

The three men snapped their arms out. Small metal rods popped into their hands and the weapons extended into twelve-inch batons. The men raised them up in preparation for the fight, knowing they would need these to counter Nora's strength and speed.

Nora stared at them and brought her hands up in a combat ready position. The men and Nora all took a step toward each other.

"Wait!" yelled Nora.

The three men stopped and looked at each other, confused.

Nora held her index finger up and walked over to the front landing skid of their ship. She removed the flower from her hair, placed it safely on the landing skid, and then walked back to where she had been standing.

"Now I am ready," said Nora, her eyes changing to red.

The three men came at her. She dashed to her right to get to the side of one of the attackers. This lined up the other two men behind him, stopping them from attacking her all at once. The closest guy lunged forward, swinging the baton at Nora's head, but she easily blocked the attack.

She then hooked her arm around the attacker's arm and lifted, locking the guy's elbow. The man grunted in pain and dropped his metal baton. Nora immediately kicked out to the side with her left foot, hitting the second attacker in the abdomen as he stepped in, sending him flying backward. The last attacker was able to hit the back of Nora's right leg with his baton. The impact did not affect her, but the shock of electricity sent her to her knees, forcing her to release the now unarmed first attacker.

He took the opportunity to punch downward and hit Nora across the face, sending her flat onto her back. Without hesitation Nora kicked up, slamming her foot into the man's groin. He screamed out, stumbled and fell clutching his groin.

Nora popped into a standing position, only to be hit across the face again with a baton. The electric shock staggered her as another attacker smashed her in the ribs, spinning Nora into one of the ship's landing skids. Nora was unable to latch onto the landing skid and she ended up on the ground again. She could now feel the heat from the burning pits close by.

Nora shook her head as she got up to her knees and stood up, a little wobbly. Her defense systems should be able to counter the shocks of electricity, but they seemed to be in sync with her components and bypassing her innate shielding. For the first time, blood trickled down her face from the biological outer-shell covering her AI core, and she started feeling concerned about a fight. This made her angry and her eyes flared a brighter red.

Nora centered herself as one of the attackers swung a baton at her with a backhand swing. She easily caught his arm with one hand and smashed her other hand into the man's elbow. There was a loud crack as the elbow joint shattered. The man screamed as the lower half of his arm dangled in the wrong direction.

Nora turned to face another attacker coming in from her left side, swinging the baton downward like a club. She side-stepped to her right, allowing the attack to swing past her. As she did this, she reached in with her left hand, grabbed the man by the throat and deeply raked the fingers of her other hand across his left eye, tearing and dislodging most of it from his skull. He immediately dropped the baton and let out a god-awful sound of agony as he clawed at his blood-covered face and stumbled around. Nora grabbed the guy and hip-tossed him to the ground. The man continued rolling around screaming, but that ended quickly when Nora stomped down on the man's neck, ending his life.

The attacker with the broken arm stepped up, threw a punch at her with his working arm but missed, causing him to stagger past Nora. She seized the man's functioning arm as he reached for his las-pistol. He was no match for Nora's strength. He wrestled to free his hand, but Nora dislocated the man's shoulder with a swift pull. The man screamed out, and with both arms disabled he turned to flee, but Nora grabbed him by the back of the neck. Like a rag doll, she swung the guy toward the ship and impaled his head on a landing fin. She then turned and headed toward the back of the ship.

The last remaining guy, whom she had kicked in the groin earlier, came out from behind one of the skids and caught her in the back with his baton. Nora stumbled forward, but stopped herself from falling by catching part of the ship above her. As the man went to attack again, Nora spun around, dived in and wrapped her arms around the man's legs for a double-legged take-down. She lifted the man up by his legs and then slammed him down hard to the ground. The man grunted as the wind was knocked out of him. She crawled forward to get into a seated position on his chest and punched down so hard that his respirator plunged deeply into his shattered face, causing him to twitch as his last breath left him.

Nora got up and was immediately hit in the face as she turned around. A forceful clang echoed off her head and her sight was filled with red blinking lights alerting her to damage to her cybernetic core. She spun around, partially blinded from the warning lights, and brought her arms up in defense as another blow hit her, sending her flying toward the fire pits. Her internal systems rerouted so she could get a clear visual again. The woman was coming at her with a cybernetic arm that had been hidden under the shawl that was now laying on the ground.

Nora ducked and rolled forward as the cybernetic arm came at her face. The woman lost her balance and staggered from missing her target. This allowed Nora to get behind the woman and snake her arm around the woman's neck, but the woman was quick, and able to put her cybernetic hand between Nora's forearm and her throat. Both struggled and moved around, fighting for a dominant position, until Nora's arm lost power. The woman felt the release and flipped Nora over her shoulder, slamming Nora next to a fire pit.

As she shuffled to safety, Nora felt power return to her arm and turned to get up, but an uppercut from the woman's cybernetic arm sent Nora onto her back again. Nora's head was now hanging over one of the fire pits. The woman dived down, grabbed Nora by the throat, and started pushing her into the pit.

"We weren't supposed to kill you, but I guess accidents happen," said the woman.

Nora could smell the ends of her hair starting to burn. She screamed and struggled as her systems tried to increase power to her limbs. She was having a tough time computing a maneuver to save herself. For the first time she did not feel superior. She felt fear. The fear of an end. The fear of death. The emotions combined with the damage to her systems left her in a vulnerable position that was too overwhelming for her to compute the most viable solution for survival.

In a desperate move, Nora reached out, grabbed the woman's cybernetic arm with both her hands, and held on for dear life. Just as she felt she was going to be terminated, the woman's head exploded and her body fell forward over Nora and into the fire pit. Nora crawled away as fast as she could until she was no longer able to feel the heat. She scanned the area, but could not see Commander Gordon—who was 400 yards away looking through the high-powered sniper rifle keeping her safe.

Nora looked at her many injuries as red alarms flashed in her vision's heads-up display. Sparks and smoke emanated from tears in her organic covering as blood oozed from many wounds. In other areas, nanobots started initiating repair sequences. She dragged herself to the front landing skid, and used it as a crutch to stand up and reclaim her Nora Blossom flower.

Nora smiled as she twirled the flower in her fingers, but the moment was short lived as the power in her good leg gave out. Grabbing the landing skid with her other hand, she slumped to the ground and sat against the skid. She needed time to repair and think before heading back to the *Tempus*. She placed the flower in her hair as she watched the nanobots close one of her wounds, and she processed every equation that would equate to the human feeling of despair. Every calculation she came up with had the same answer: no matter how human she wanted to be, in the end, she was just a machine.

CHAPTER 13

LADY OF DOLLS

Tilli found a treasure trove of information from the scribbles the old C-Tec had written down. He could barely recall what they were for, but Tilli learned the Orb was an energy source created by the Gravel and some other minor races. It wasn't to be used as a weapon but as an addition to a ship's engine and shielding systems. As she found more data, she would bounce it off the old C-Tec in hopes he would spit out some other useful knowledge, but Ryan found it difficult to understand the conversation since the language was too technical.

While this was going on, Ryan looked through some old paper star charts with odd markings. He flipped back to stare at one particular chart. As he studied it, he could hear the voice of the Gravel AI from the cave on Earth reciting numbers and letters; things he didn't understand, but his finger moved around the star chart following the details as if he knew what the Gravel was saying. It would seem whatever information the Gravel AI had written to his brain back in the cave on Earth was now coming back to him.

"Hey. Sorry to interrupt you two, but what is this marking?" asked Ryan, pointing to an area on the chart.

The old C-Tec tilted his head, trying to recall what the marking meant. "So-so-sorry. My memory is getting worse as time passes by. I think it was for a...um...ah..."

Tilli stared at the map and made everyone jump when she shouted, "Black hole! That is the Gravel and Florarien symbol for it."

"Oh, the black hole…I recall now. The Gravel lab by the lake. I worked there. It was by a mini black hole, but I'm not able to remember much more than that."

Ryan stared at the C-Tec as he pondered all this information. "Earlier you said the lab self-destruct didn't go as planned. Is it possible some remnants of this lab could still be there?"

The old C-Tec shrugged. "Anything is possible."

"Would it be OK for us to take this chart and some of your notes?"

"Sure. I will probably forget tomorrow they even existed," said the old C-Tec, holding the wire to his head.

"Tilli, grab what notes you need and I will take the chart. I think we have an area of space we need to explore."

"Do you want to come with us?" Tilli asked the old C-Tec.

"My days of traveling the stars and research are long over. Thank you for allowing me to have some memories again."

Tilli smiled at him and handed Ryan some additional notes to put in his adventurers backpack.

"Thank you again. We appreciate the help." Ryan patted the C-Tec on the shoulder.

Tilli hugged the old man, causing him to blush, and then she followed Ryan outside.

They both waited for the door to close behind them and headed down the path back to the mining facility before they spoke.

"Interesting guy. Not sure we can trust everything we have is correct, but at least we have a place to investigate and hopefully get some answers," said Ryan.

"I wish I could have spoken to him when he was younger. The things I could have learned and mysteries I could have unraveled," said Tilli.

Ryan was about to say something when he saw pieces of a building in the distance blow upwards. "Was that an explosion?" He pointed to the mining facility.

Tilli switched down some lenses. "Yes, different smoke and particles are emanating from that area."

As they watched, another explosion went off and then they heard the sounds of las-guns firing.

"I guess we're not going back that way," said Tilli.

"Commander Gordon, do you hear me?" asked Ryan, talking into the communication device on the back of his hand. "*Tempus*, do you read me?"

"I'm not getting anything over my embedded comm link either," said Tilli.

"OK, then I guess we go to the left and come around, but we need to move fast so we don't get stuck in whatever is going on down there."

Tilli followed him as they hooked around the side of the mining facility. The fire pits were in much greater numbers in this area and they had to pick their way carefully. As they came around a large rock, they both stopped in their tracks. An old hunched woman covered in a gray tattered cloak stood in their path. She was on a platform hovering about three feet off the ground. Her hunched body was held up by a pair of metal arms under her armpits that acted like crutches. A metal belt wrapped around her waist, which was anchored to the crutches on each side to keep her from falling over. She had long messy gray hair, sunken eyes, deep wrinkles, and a large hump on her back.

"I seek Ryan Hunt and no other," said the old woman in a cackling voice.

"Acquaintance of yours?" asked Tilli.

"Not that I recall, but if she offers you an apple, don't take it," said Ryan. "Um, ma'am, we're in a hurry and I don't recall ever meeting you. So if you'll excuse me."

The woman opened her cloak to reveal a chest recessed deep into her ribs, as if some of her organs were missing. Metallic hoses exited her chest and wrapped around to her back. Connected to her chest by some strapping were vials about eight inches long that seemed to have humanoid forms in them. She pulled two of them out, along with a vile of purple mist from under her cloak. She cackled at them as she twirled the vials in her hand and then slammed them to the ground.

A loud crash and plume of purple smoke obscured their view. As the smoke cleared, the small humanoids in the vials were now over six feet tall. They were horrific doll-like creatures; a patchwork of various skins put together. Each had one colored and one pure white eye without any eyelids and there were small holes in their heads instead of noses and ears. A low, hideous, whispering growl emanated from a mouth of stringy flesh as claws started to form on their extended arms.

"Dear god, what unholy creature is this?" said Ryan, cringing in disgust.

"I, I have no knowledge of anything like this," replied Tilli.

Ryan took off his adventurers backpack. "Take this and run back to the ship while I try to buy you some time."

"I'm not leaving you," said Tilli.

"Not up for debate. You understand the documents in the bag and I don't. Plus, you look faster than I am."

"OK, but take this," said Tilli. She took the backpack and handed him a small metal rod from the tools on her sleeve.

Ryan looked at her confused.

"Push each end at the same time," said Tilli. Then she took off running.

Ryan put the rod between both index fingers and pushed inward. It expanded into a short metal fighting staff. He wanted to yell at her for bringing a weapon when she wasn't supposed to, but was glad the innocent little engineer had a sneaky side.

Ryan looked at the creatures, now with fully formed claws, and then back at the old woman.

She pointed her crooked finger at him. "Rip him apart, but save the eyes."

The doll creatures hissed and charged. Instead of taking them head on, Ryan ran back up the hill and then made a sharp right, the opposite direction Tilli had gone. He thought this was probably not one of his best ideas since it led him to a burning farm of holes and a maze of large rock formations.

He navigated as fast as he could through the smoke lingering in the maze of large rocks. Without warning, Ryan was nailed from the side by one of the creatures and smacked into one of the rock formations. The impact sent the metal short-staff he was carrying flying into the air. He shook his head and sprung back up. The recovery surprised him—he should still be down, even broken—but his thoughts about it vanished when he came face-to-face with one of the creatures, which was already preparing to strike again.

Ryan ducked as a clawed hand swiped over his head and crashed into the rock with a shower of sparks. He looked around and saw the metal short-staff. He dived past the right side of the creature, grabbed the short-staff mid-roll, and ended in a standing position with his weapon ready. The creature swung with its right and then left. Ryan blocked one attack with the short-staff and then brought it the other direction to block the other one. He threw a front kick straight into the creature's gut, pushing it back, and as he stepped back down with his kicking leg, he swung the short-staff across the creature's face. A large gash formed on the creature and gray ooze poured out. It regained its footing, stood upright to face Ryan and whispered through it stringy mouth, "Death."

"Ah crap," said Ryan and took off running again.

His path had no cover. He came to an intersection and paused—a mistake. A scratching sound made him look up, but it was too late. The second creature pounced on him, slamming him to the ground and knocking the short-staff out of his hand.

The creature bent over Ryan and stabbed straight down with its claw. Ryan screamed as the claw pierced his right arm and shoulder. He rolled his left shoulder up just in time to dodge the second claw and it stuck into the rocky ground next to him.

Ryan rolled his shoulder back down, hooked his left arm around the creature's stuck appendage and pinned it against his body. Unable to free itself, the creature pulled its other claw out of Ryan's arm and shoulder, causing him to scream out again and release his grip on the creature.

Ryan grabbed the creature's free arm as it tried to stab him again. They both struggled to gain a dominant position. Ryan yelled in shock as the creature lifted him off the ground with inhuman strength and speed, and slammed him down with one hand.

A cloud of dust flew up around Ryan. His face twisted in pain and he rolled to his side, grabbing at his lower back. With Ryan no longer holding on, the creature grabbed its other arm, trying to free it from the rocky ground.

Ryan regained his composure and kicked out at the creature's stuck arm as the claws started to slide out of the rock. The creature let out a hideous, agonizing scream; the creature's arm snapped. It fell to its side and flailed on the ground, giving Ryan an opportunity to stand up.

He turned to flee, but the other creature lunged at him with incredible speed and wrapped its arms around Ryan. He didn't resist the take down and as he fell backward with the creature, he tucked his left leg into his chest and placed his left foot against the creature's abdomen as they rolled backward. Ryan pushed out hard against the creature with his leg, launching it over him and into one of the rock formations

Ryan finished the back roll into a low squat, regained his stance, and took off running again, but he chose the wrong path and forgot to pick up the short-staff. This direction brought him back to the hovering old lady and a third creature. This one had round metal spikes like large ice picks instead of claws.

Ryan could feel his heart race as the creature roared and charged forward. Ryan bolted with the creature chasing after him. He followed a small curved path up a hill to a dead-end cliff. With nowhere left to run, Ryan danced around in an attempt to confuse the creature and get out of its way, but it wasn't easily fooled.

The creature out-faked Ryan and he was caught flatfooted. The creature capitalized on the opportunity and stabbed with tremendous force. Ryan pivoted to his left and the spike barely sliced the front of his shirt.

The creature's forceful momentum made it lose its balance and continue forward. Ryan grabbed the spike as it went by and led the creature around him. As it was regaining its balance, Ryan grabbed the spike with his other hand and twisted it inward toward the creature. The creature's feet flew into the air as the spike's attacking momentum stopped, but its body hadn't lost its forward motion. The creature slammed to the ground.

Before Ryan could do anything, a claw struck across his back. He screamed and dropped to his hands and knees. He tried to get up, but a strike to the stomach from another creature sent him onto his back. He kicked out and caught the knee of the one with the broken arm and it fell, but didn't stop. It crawled toward him with its one good arm and leg.

As Ryan got up, a backhand from the spiked creature sent him stumbling and he fell face first. The world appeared to be spinning. Ryan was now bleeding from many wounds. He shook his head and stared at the fire pit close by, trying to regain his focus. He could hear the old woman nearby cackling at his downfall as she hovered up to the cliff's edge. Ryan heard hissing from behind him and turned to see two of the creatures standing over him and the other one crawling toward him. He was about to take his chances falling off the cliff when the creatures started grabbing at their heads and looking around. Ryan looked over at the old woman through blurred vision from the blood running down his face. She was wobbling around on her hover platform, swatting at something and screaming.

Ryan could barely make out the wispy outline of a familiar-looking humanoid flying around and through the old woman. Ryan noticed as she did this that the creatures could not function while she was distracted. He backed himself out from under the creatures, got up, leapt off the ledge, and landed on the back of the old woman's hovering platform. He was barely able to keep from falling by holding onto her cloak. As the hover platform leveled itself, Ryan wrapped his good arm in the heavy cloak.

"Get off! Get off!" screamed the old woman. The clawed creature whose limbs all still functioned jumped from the ledge at Ryan, but its claws were unable to grab onto the rounded edge of the smooth platform and it fell.

The old woman dipped the platform and accelerated upward, trying to knock Ryan off. Leaning back off the platform, Ryan gripped the cloak. The woman commanded the platform into a quick turn to the right and then to the left. Ryan lost his footing and now dangled from the old woman's cloak, causing her to lean in the direction he pulled.

Unable to level off from Ryan's weight, the platform started spiraling downward toward one of the fiery pits. Ryan let go at the last minute and dived onto a nearby rocky slope, rolling to the bottom, while the platform crashed on the other side of the slope.

He lay there staring at the polluted sky as he tried to regain his composure. His protection screen was damaged, and it was difficult for him to breathe. It was just as hard to get up. The moment of rest was broken by the ear-shattering screams of the old woman.

Ryan painfully stood and headed over to where she had crashed. She was still bound in her support straps and hung limp to the side of the smoking platform. Her cloak had caught on fire and she was burning. Ryan started throwing dirt on the fire, and yanked the cloak off her back. He gasped in horror at the sight. The hump on her back was formed from two large clear tanks, each containing a lung. The tubes stuck in her chest were connected to this lung device. One of the tanks was broken, and the smelly fluid inside was leaking everywhere. The other lung was expanding and contracting rapidly.

Ryan could hear the old woman wheeze in unison with the pulsing lung. He walked around and could see other tubes and wires connecting to the hover platform. Ryan cringed at how everything was attached to her. It looked like a butcher had done the surgery. Old flaps of skin were filleted outward, while some areas of skin grew around the tubes, following them from front to back like a vine.

"I was beautiful once…sacrifices had to be made…they are my lungs now… not hers. Mine! My research…my dolls…promised eternity. Promised more subjects if I kill the Hunt," mumbled the old woman through deep breaths.

Ryan could see she was no longer a threat, and the thought of killing her out of mercy did pop into his head, but he didn't have the heart to kill a helpless old woman, no matter how psychotic she may be. He debated helping her, but since it appeared that she stole someone's lungs, needed test subjects, and had some inhuman doll-like creatures under her command, it was probably best to let karma deal with her. However, he was going to make sure she could not harm anyone else if she survived.

Ryan squatted and could see two glass vials containing small humanoids, and two more with the purple gas. He hesitantly took them off her as the old woman weakly swatted at him.

"Give me my pets back," she screeched.

"That's not going to happen," said Ryan, tossing the vials into a fiery pit.

"No! You…you will pay for this. My master does not forget. I don't forget," hissed the old woman.

Ryan cringed at the horrific way she spoke. It sent chills up his spine. "If you survive, do what you need to do, but next time I will not be merciful."

He started to walk away and realized he had no idea which way to go, and jumped when his hand communication device went off.

"Ryan, this is Commander Gordon. We have your location and will be hovering over you any second now. We'll lower a hover hook platform for you to latch onto."

"Glad to hear your voice, Commander. Everyone get back okay?"

"They're a little banged up, but alive."

Ryan felt a wave of relief when he finally heard the engines above him in the pollution clouds. A small platform was lowered and he started his assent to the *Tempus*. As he was going up he could see the doll-like creatures turning into purple dust, and then the wisp that helped him circled the platform and followed him upward.

Ryan recognized the wisp. It was the image of the male Psychic Adept that had bowed to him when he was at Lord Devyn's lounge with Vicki.

The figure spoke to Ryan by turning the wisp into words.

"Aura projection, Mr. Hunt. You have friends," spelled out the Psychic Adept.

The wisp vanished before Ryan could say anything, so instead he closed his eyes and said, "Thank you."

⟁

Except for not being able to hold anything with his right arm and being unable to stop coughing, Ryan had a smooth ride back to the hangar bay of the *Tempus*. Nora, Vicki, and Tilli were all there waiting for him. A medical AI attended to Nora and Vicki. Nora seemed to be staring intently at Ryan as he stepped off the hover hook platform, and then put her head down.

"Holy crap! It looks like we all got our asses kicked. What the hell happened down there?"

"A riot broke out in the mining facility. Seems like some prisoners overthrew the guards and started attacking anyone they saw. I barely got out alive," said Vicki.

"I can corroborate her story," said Commander Gordon as he stepped into the hangar bay. "We overheard some of the communications. The mining facility was imprisoning some Wolfkin and somehow they were able to overthrow the guards, which led to an all-out fight across the mining facility and caused plenty of damage. The Wolfkin fought their way to an ore-loading area and stole three transports. We were able to track the ships leaving the planet, but they jumped into a wormhole before we could compute their destination. Unfortunately, they killed the Overseer."

"What a shame. He was such a nice man. Great conversationalist," said Vicki.

"If you will excuse me, I will go review the notes and star maps we received from the old C-Tec," said Tilli.

Everyone watched Tilli leave before talking again.

"I guess everyone was successful then?" asked Commander Gordon.

"Yeah, we were. The old C-Tec was a little odd, but he was able to provide engineering notes and a star map to where the Orb was possibly created. Once Tilli reviews the charts we will hopefully have a course to plot," said Ryan.

"That's excellent news," said Commander Gordon.

"Nora, you've been quiet. By the way you look, it must have been your type of fight," said Ryan.

Nora lifted her head and stared at Ryan. She started mumbling, "He mocks you...He sent you to die and now is upset you are here..."

"What? I'm not mocking you and I'm happy to see you. Is everything OK?"

"No! I am not OK, Mr. Hunt. Surprised to see me? Thought you could get rid of me so easily?" yelled Nora.

Ryan took a few steps toward Nora and looked at her, confused. "Nora, what are you talking about? You're worrying me."

"Worried about me? You sent me to die today. You could have sent someone else, but no! You sent me. I see Tilli was unharmed. Is she your new pet now that Dr. Katalina is not around?" screamed Nora, stepping closer and leaning into Ryan's face.

Ryan put his left hand on her shoulder and, without warning, she grabbed him by the throat and slammed him against a drop ship. Ryan grabbed her arm with both hands, trying to break free.

"Nora, I order you to stop this!" yelled Commander Gordon. He then rushed in trying to grab Nora, but she swatted him away with her other arm.

"Oh, bloody hell," said Vicki. Her vampiric features emerged. She dived into Nora's side and slammed her to the hangar floor.

Ryan dropped to his knees, gagging for air.

Vicki's vampire strength was a close second to a wounded Nora and she was able to pin Nora to the ground.

"Let go of me! I swear I will stake you when I get up!" yelled Nora. She was able to get one arm free and knocked Vicki aside.

Nora immediately got up, eyes red, as she heard someone coming up behind her. She spun around to see Ryan standing there and before she could react, he slapped her across the face hard. Nora's head turned, and her eyes went back to blue as she touched the side of her face in shock.

"You hit me?" said Nora, now calmer and confused. "You hit me?"

"I'm sorry, but I had to do something. Commander Gordon was unlocking a las-rifle from the drop ship. I would rather you hate me than see you dead."

"Mr. Hunt, I think I am failing. Maybe I am not as strong as I thought. Maybe I cannot control this AI form. I hereby officially step down as your personal assistant, and I am suspending myself as an employee of OTKE Corporation. I will lock myself in my quarters until you can get me back to have me disabled." Nora turned and stormed away.

"Nora, wait..." said Ryan, but Nora kept going and left the hangar bay.

Ryan turned around and punched a bulkhead, breaking the skin on one of his knuckles.

"Does anyone know what the hell just happened?" he asked. He stepped forward and offered a hand to Vicki, who was still sitting on the floor.

"Well, for starters, next time inform me when a vampire is part of my crew," said Commander Gordon. Vicki shrugged her shoulders. "Second, Nora almost died. She took on the group from the ship that landed secretly. They were well trained and armed. They almost killed her, but I was able to intervene with a sniper missile rifle. I kept an eye on her until she was able to hobble back here. She was in bad shape until her self-healing systems kicked in."

"Oh, great. Now I feel like crap that I slapped her," said Ryan.

"Well, I would have felt worse if I had to kill her," said Commander Gordon.

"And I couldn't care less," said Vicki, who headed off to clean up.

"Wonderful group of coworkers you have, Mr. Hunt. Just wonderful," said Commander Gordon. He leaned the las-rifle against the drop ship. "If you'll excuse me, I'm going to get the ship out of this star system and into interstellar space where it might be a little safer."

Ryan slumped against the drop ship as he watched Commander Gordon leave, then slid down to the floor. The medical AI looked around, confused since all his patients had left. He looked at Ryan bleeding, smiled, and rushed over to start fixing him up.

"At least someone is happy," mumbled Ryan.

CHAPTER 14

BLACK HOLE PLANET

Fredrick LaRue stared at the holographic image of his informant stationed on Kura Prime as she gave her report.

Everything was going perfectly. The defense force reacted to the *Tempus* when it reached Kura Prime as per normal protocols. Lord Devyn and his staff delayed Mr. Hunt and his team long enough for him to get his operatives in place and execute a plan. Then somehow the entire plan fell apart.

"Let me go over this again so I can fully comprehend what you're telling me," said Fredrick, shaking his hands as he pointed upward with his index fingers. "Mr. Hunt's small team of people took out four of our best operatives, and on top of that, Mr. Hunt took out the Demon Doll-controlling witch. Is that what I'm hearing? Am I understanding this correctly?"

The associate called "Reader" on Kura Prime, a human-owl cross, was staring back at Fredrick. It was obvious he was angry. Fredrick kept pointing at her and making fists with his hands. She noticed Fredrick was in his command chamber on his personal ship, which meant he was en route or close by. The clown puppet, Mr. Jingles, was displayed on a stand behind him.

"Yes, sir. You understand it correctly. Somehow they managed to outsmart our operatives. There is one more thing."

"Please, go ahead. Shock me some more."

"The mining planet facility was destroyed and Overseer Ennedy was killed."

Fredrick threw his hands up in the air. "This is unbelievable. Just unbelievable." He turned to Mr. Jingles and pursed his lips. "Mr. Jingles, do you believe this? Highly trained assassins: dead. Witch defeated and, above all, one of our main informants on which ore shipments we can hijack is dead as well."

Fredrick stared at the non-moving and non-talking clown puppet for a few seconds, then nodded and turned around to face his informant's image.

"Mr. Jingles cannot believe this either. We cannot figure out if we should be impressed or angry with this Mr. Hunt and his folly. Hell, I would love to hire them all," said Fredrick.

"Are there any other actions you want me to take?" asked Reader.

"No, not now. I was already en route in case something like this happened. We are still able to track them, and I have come up with an idea. Keep an eye on Lord Devyn and report if he tries anything."

"Very well, sir," said Reader. She bowed and her holographic image faded away.

Fredrick turned to Mr. Jingles and met its soulless gaze as he pondered the recent events and then smiled.

"Finally, a worthy adversary."

It had been about two hours but felt much longer since everyone met in the hangar bay. Ryan had not heard a peep from anyone, which was probably a good thing. He was able to take a chemical steam shower, add more memories to his data crystal journal, and take a quick power nap. He had the ship AI open a virtual port window so he could stare into space. The view seemed so real that it looked like you could step right through it.

Ryan focused on distant stars as they passed by the virtual window in an attempt to keep his head clear. Commander Gordon navigated the ship in random directions in case they were being followed, while he waited for the destination coordinates from Tilli.

Ryan was perplexed on how he was going to figure out what to do with the artifacts and keep everyone safe. Life was more complicated now than it ever had been. When he lived in his first life, he would tell his wife of how he wished for adventure like the heroes from the movies he watched or from the books he read. She would laugh, or just roll her eyes at the short stories he would make up about stuff they saw in a mall or some place they were visiting. The visions of past memories of being with his wife made him smile, but his reflections were interrupted when he heard Commander Gordon's voice over the ship's comm system.

"Mr. Hunt, please report to the command deck. We finally have a possible destination. I have contacted everyone else as well."

"Thank you, Commander. I'll be up there shortly."

Ryan rubbed his hands over his face to wake himself up and hurried to the command deck. As he entered, he noticed everyone was there except Nora. He guessed she was still in self-exile.

"Mr. Hunt is here, we can now get started," said Commander Gordon. "Mitil'Lin, the floor is yours."

"Thank you, sir. You know you can call me Tilli?"

"Not going to happen, Mitil'Lin. Please continue."

Tilli shook her head. "OK. I have been analyzing all the star charts, the odd coordinates Ryan recalled from what was written to his memory, and the data we got from the old C-Tec. For a while there I was confused, but then I recognized the coordinates were an old Gravel numerical system. I was able to translate those to modern numeric star chart coordinates and from there, with help from the ship AI, build my own star map. The system in question that Ryan pointed out on the old C-Tec's star map does not exist in any of our wormhole databases, but we were able to correlate its exact location based on surrounding constellations and add it to the system."

"This is great news," said Ryan.

"Yes and no. It's great that I was able to discover the location. The bad news is I'm unsure of what we will find when we get there. It's a seven-hour trip. Our long-range scans are detecting light from a small sun and the gravitational readings of some type of black hole in that section of space. Scans are also getting a reading of one planet, but it must be tiny."

"It's not the best of news, but still, why is this all bad?"

"Well, this is what has been baffling me. The old C-Tec said they had a lab on a planet there, but the sun we detected isn't strong enough to warm a planet enough to sustain life, and the black hole should be destroying the system."

"Yeah. I got nothing. That's beyond my knowledge," said Ryan. "Anything on the Orb or the vile of Gravel Goo?"

"I'm glad you asked. There was a lot of rambling in the old C-Tec's documents, but what I was able to comprehend is the Orb is a unique energy source. I'm not sure how it works or what they were going to do with it. Nothing on the Gravel bacteria or, as you call it, 'Goo'. However, the old C-Tec did have a document with what I am guessing are his random thoughts. There were notes like 'Long distance', 'Counter effects', 'Gates', 'Sheppard' and descriptions of planetary systems that neither I, nor the ship's AI, have ever heard of—and it's a rare occurrence for me not to know," said Tilli.

"He was a little out there, so what his ramblings refer to is anyone's guess," said Ryan.

"Mr. Hunt, with you being the senior OTKE corporate officer, what is our plan of action?" asked Commander Gordon.

Ryan looked around the command deck. He never had to make such a big decision before and everyone was just staring at him, waiting for an answer. They were deep into this now. Obviously, someone was after them and the items they had. Whoever they were, this enemy was also willing to kill for them.

"We have come this far. I say we go and find out what's there. Not like we have anything better to do, and I think a quiet seven hours is what everyone needs to recharge."

"Always an adventure with you, Mr. Hunt," said Vicki.

"I agree with the logic," said Tilli.

Commander Gordon turned to his helmsman. "You heard the man. Set a course for the unknown system and let's find out what's there."

Seven hours of doing nothing was definitely what the team needed to clear their heads. Food, healing, and rest was on everyone's agenda.

Ryan made sure to get a good five hours of sleep. He then spent some time dictating what has been occurring in this little adventure into his data crystal, while eating and figuring out the assassin knife that Lord Devyn had given him. It was a unique knife but how it worked puzzled him.

Ryan twirled the sheath in his hands, examining it from multiple angles but there was nothing unique about it. Just for the hell of it, he placed the sheath on the inside of his left forearm and then removed it. Nothing happened. He did this again and just let it sit there while he ate a nourishment bar. He stopped mid-chew when he felt it move.

Little hairs like spider silk started to extend from the edges of the sheath. They floated in the air and then moved to his skin. It felt like the nails of a kitten touching him as the silk like hairs embedded themselves into his forearm. Ryan turned his forearm over and the sheath remained attached. He even threw a few punches to see if it would fly off, but the sheath remained attached to his skin.

Ryan held up the smoke colored knife to get a better look at it. No light reflected off it and the blade was sharp. He inserted the knife into the sheath, the entire unit pixelated into a rainbow of colors until it found a shade to match his skin tone, and then vanished. There was a slight pinch that made him cringe, but he figured that's how it linked the blade to his thoughts if he ever wanted to use it as a ballistic knife: to shoot the blade out of the handle at a target.

Ryan moved his arm around some more to see if there were any restrictions, but it felt like nothing was there. He decided to leave the assassin knife on. He was about to return to adding information to his data crystal when the ship's AI announced they were close to the destination, something he had asked the AI to do before he took his nap.

Ryan grabbed his data crystal and put it into the right pocket of his beige tactical pants and headed up to the command deck. Commander Gordon was in his command chair relaying and receiving orders in his embedded comm chip. Ryan was surprised to see Vicki and Tilli already there. They must have had the same idea. Both looked refreshed and properly dressed in combat outfits. Nora was still nowhere to be found. Ryan had tried to reach her and even banged on her door, but she would not answer, and she overrode the ship's AI so no one could enter her bunkroom.

"Amazing what seven hours of relaxing will do for you," said Ryan.

Tilli moved around a virtual console studying the overlaid star charts. "It was well needed. I was able to catch up on some reading," she said without losing her focus on the screen.

"Figures. Kind of boring for me. I didn't need any sleep, and the medical AI was able to whip me up some nourishment to help me recover," said Vicki, leaning over one of the command deck consoles to see what Tilli was doing.

Tilli looked up, confused. "What do you mean by that?"

"Never mind," said Ryan before Vicki could answer. "So, Commander Gordon, are we close?"

"We are actually exiting near the planet in three, two and one."

Ryan felt a small pull as the ship exited the wormhole and the main virtual screen opened in the center of the command deck.

"What the hell?" said Commander Gordon. Everyone looked in awe of what they were seeing.

There must have been thousands of small satellites surrounding partial domes built around a small sun. They appeared to be harnessing the sun's rays and directing them through the center of large round space platforms. The platforms continued one after the other all the way to a small planet. Based on information from the ship's AI, some of the satellites and platforms have failed over time, but the entire system adjusted to keep a section of the planet always in constant sun, while sacrificing the rest of the planet to do so. A group of other platforms went off past the planet and an energy beam appeared to be feeding a mini black hole.

"Well, this is beyond my crystal radio project I did back in the eighth grade," said Ryan. "I'm at a loss. What is it?"

"It appears to be some sort of Dyson Sphere. This one is far beyond anything I have ever studied," said Tilli, switching her lenses around to get a different look at it. "It's absolutely amazing, but I'm not sure what is going on with the mini black hole in the distance."

"You are correct. It is a Dyson Sphere," said Nora, stepping onto the command deck from the open doorway.

Everyone swung around at hearing her voice.

Ryan smiled at her, but she didn't return the smile, nor did she acknowledge him. He guessed she was still mad at him for slapping her. Nora entered further into the command deck. She looked around the room, while she made fists and then released them.

"Please continue, Nora," said Ryan.

Nora looked at Ryan and her eyes flared red for a second before returning to blue.

"I will continue. This Dyson Sphere is called a Dyson Bubble. It has been modified to have multiple bubbles around the sun. It uses the advanced space platforms to increase the energy output as it travels through each gate. The ship's AI is correct: the Dyson Bubble is failing but the system is adjusting to keep a particular part of the planet warm. My guess is the lab is in that location. The area would be about the size of what you would have called Australia in your time on Earth."

"I remember reading about a Dyson Sphere in a science magazine back in the day, but it was only theoretical. What about the mini black hole?" asked Ryan.

"That is actually amazing to me as well. Theoretically, with enough energy you could create a micro, or mini, black hole and keep it from evaporating. I am unable to compute how they—someone or something—is doing it and for what purpose."

"Wait. Hold on," said Tilli, waving her hands in the air. "This means someone actually figured out the equations for Plank Length, Quantum Foam, Dervina Principles, and about twenty other Artesian, Florarien, and modern-day Earth Consortium scientific theories. This is not possible."

"Then you need to get your goggles repaired because we are all viewing it at this moment," replied Nora.

"OK. Let's keep the scientific debate to a minimum because I'm getting a headache trying to understand all of this," said Ryan. "What do the planetary scans show?"

"Scans are showing ruined structures on a hilltop overlooking a large lake—an indication someone terraformed the planet once the sunlight to the planet was intensified. There are signs of wrecked ships from a variety of races scattered in orbit, across the overgrown jungle, and in the areas where the light is no longer shining," said Tilli. "Unfortunately, we are getting some interference and cannot pinpoint any life signs."

"Interesting and perplexing all at the same time," said Ryan. "I think we need to get down there and investigate what is left of the lab. There has to be some data that survived after all this time. There has to be answers down there."

"Ryan, it's probably best if you land with a small group in one of the transport ships. I don't want to risk landing the *Tempus* on the planet in case something goes wrong," said Commander Gordon.

"Makes sense. Nora, Tilli and I will—"

Ryan was interrupted as the main screen changed its focus. The ship's AI dimmed the lights as it automatically went into defense mode by raising shields and arming weapons.

"Wormhole of unknown origin opening on our starboard bow," said the ship's AI. "Multiple ships detected."

Commander Gordon started relaying orders to come about and bring weapons to bear on anything that came out of the wormhole.

Everyone watched in silence as the wormhole opened and an old Earth Terraforming ship exited followed by two attacking mid-size fighters.

The *Tempus* picked up the static-filled distress call. "This is the Earth Consortium ship *Eden*. We are under attack. Our engines are failing, and we have many wounded. Can anyone…"

"Sorry, sir, we lost communication," said Tilli.

Commander Gordon turned to Ryan. "Sorry, Mr. Hunt, but we are still an OTKE ship and our first priority is always to intervene when a ship is in distress. Especially an unarmed one being attacked by what most likely are pirates."

"Agreed, but the odds of a ship in distress appearing out of a wormhole near an uncharted planet we just discovered seems suspicious to me."

"Most ships are capable of picking up residual wormhole openings in a specific range in case of emergencies, but if I don't respond, Mr. Hunt, I'm sentencing innocent people to their death. We will go in with guns hot and shields up in case it's a trap. Set an intercept course for the *Eden* and put us between them and the attacking ships. Be prepared to go to max speed just in case. Lock weapons on the attacking ships and fire at will."

The *Tempus* reached attack speed in seconds and blew past the helpless *Eden* as it fired on the pirate ships. Commander Gordon made sure to scan the *Eden* as they flew by. So far, the scans were not penetrating the hull, and the outside readings were negative for any weapons.

The pirate ships did their best to engage the *Tempus*, but their inferior weapons bounced off the shields. Commander Gordon launched two fusion missiles at one pirate ship, obliterating it to pieces. The other pirate ship was disabled by the Gatling las-cannon.

"Pirate ship, this is Commander Gordon of the OTKE Ship *Tempus*. Your vessel is disabled, and your life support systems are down. Prepare to surrender and be taken prisoner. You will be dropped off at the nearest Earth Consortium planet for a fair trial."

"Commander Gordon, I am reading a large power increase from the pirate ship," said Nora.

"It's going to self-destruct. Back us up to the *Eden* to act as cover for them. Transfer all remaining power to the shields."

The *Tempus* reversed its course just in time. The pirate ship exploded, and the shockwave rocked both the *Tempus* and *Eden*.

"Status report?" ordered Commander Gordon.

"Shields holding. No major damage reported," said Tilli.

"Excellent. Good work everyone. Now, let's tend to the *Eden*."

"*Eden,* this is the *Tempus*. Prepare to receive docking clamp. Medical and support crews are standing by."

Everyone on the command deck waited for a reply, but there was only static.

"Maybe they're severely damaged," said Ryan.

"I am not detecting any visible hull damage and our scans are still unable to penetrate their hull," said Nora.

"But on a low frequency scan I'm detecting some odd power fluctuations and vibrations coming off the hull," said Tilli.

"It can't be…Back us off. Back us off now!" screamed Vicki. "Ship Eater. It's a Ship Eater!"

"Ah, who, what?" said Ryan, turning his head between everyone frantically.

"Full power now!" yelled Commander Gordon.

The *Tempus* banked hard to port and started to speed away, but it was too late. Tendrils shot out from the *Eden* and embedded into the *Tempus,* followed by a large burst of energy, which shot through every inch of the ship.

Commander Gordon's hover chair immediately buckled him in and magnetically clamped to the floor as the ship listed to the side and was violently pulled toward the *Eden.* Consoles and computer interfaces exploded, sending pieces everywhere. The shrapnel instantly killed some of the crew. Ryan and Tilli went flying over the consoles, while the violent pull launched Vicki into a wall, knocking her unconscious before she hit the floor.

Nora attempted to hold onto anything as the energy burst covering the ship engulfed her. Unable to maintain a grip, she slammed into the console behind her. She tried to regain her balance, but the energy burst overloaded her AI systems, causing her to violently start shaking and fall to the floor. The Nora Barlow flower in her hair then exploded in a shower of sparks next to her.

Red emergency lights kicked on. Commander Gordon looked around his command deck. Smoke filled the air, sparks flew from system consoles, and all his bridge crew were down. Small spider-like AIs emerged from hidden compartments to extinguish the fires, initiate repairs, and to provide emergency lighting.

"System report," said Commander Gordon, but the ship's AI did not respond.

He manually removed the restraints keeping him in his command chair and started checking and assisting his deck crew. Seeing Tilli trapped under a console, Commander Gordon immediately ran over to check on her.

Ryan slowly moved to a sitting position and cringed as he touched his forehead to feel around the gash oozing blood down his face. He could see Commander Gordon struggling to move the console off Tilli and crawled over to help him.

"Is she OK?" he asked.

"She is still breathing, but looks like her arm is busted. Move her over to a clear area while I try to get power to the consoles. I need to get communications and visuals up and running."

Ryan didn't want to move Tilli without knowing the extent of her injuries, but he had no choice. It was too dangerous to leave her where she was, so he carefully moved her a little way back from the busted consoles. Turning around, he saw Nora and Vicki were also down. Since Vicki had some sort of vampire healing power, he instead ran over to assist Nora.

Kneeling, Ryan lightly shook her. "Nora, can you hear me?" Since she was an AI, he assumed she had no pulse. He shook her again, but there was no response.

Ryan cursed at himself for not having the knowledge to help his friend. Looking around and assessing the damage, he noticed the flower that Nora had worn in her hair and picked it up. He twirled it in his fingers and noticed small electronics hanging out the top.

His thoughts were interrupted when a light on the main virtual screen came alive. A man sat in some type of command chair. The image was not clear, and the screen flickered constantly. Ryan put the Nora Barlow flower back down and walked over to Commander Gordon who had moved to view the active virtual screen.

"Greetings, my friends. It would seem you are in a precarious state," said the man.

"Dude, don't call me friend. Not sure who you are, but what the hell do you want?" replied Ryan.

"Very direct. I like that. You must be Mr. Hunt. I have heard a lot about you. It's nice to finally make your acquaintance. My name is Fredrick LaRue. You are correct, I do want something, and it's quite simple. I want the Earthly Orb artifact you're carrying, and I want you, Mr. Hunt."

"This is Commander Gordon, captain of this ship. I will not turn over any part of my crew."

Fredrick rolled his eyes. "Always the noble type, you OTKE saps are. I'm going to assume you're aware what is holding you, and might I say, engulfing you as well. I will also assume you realize you don't have much of a choice in the matter, but being the noble person I am, I will give you a few minutes to ponder things, check on your crew, or what is left of them, and I will get back to you."

The virtual screen closed, making the room go darker.

"This is not good, Mr. Hunt."

"What the hell are we facing?"

"It's called a 'Ship Eater', and there is no way to beat it once it has latched on. It's also known as a Mimic Ship. The ship can take the form of any ship it has devoured. They were used by the Nilorian race during the Nilorian Wars. They lure in unsuspecting ships and then disable them with some sort of energy burst that disables AI systems. Hence why Nora is no longer operational."

"You're freaking kidding me. Who the hell would create such a thing?"

"It gets worse. Once it disables you, it will literately eat the entire ship and everything in it. Dissolving it to the most basic level of atoms. This is how it learns new ship forms. The Ship Eater is actually banned by all races across the galaxies and is the one ship all races are approved to attack on sight."

"Well then, I guess we have to meet his demands unless we can come up with something quick. He wants me—perhaps he will let everyone else go."

Their conversation was interrupted when the virtual screen kicked on. This time it was clearer.

"Maybe the ship is coming back online," said Ryan.

"No, just me fiddling with the systems with one hand over here on the floor," said Tilli.

Ryan and Commander Gordon turned to see Tilli lying on her back under a console, covered in a mess of organic wiring.

"Much clearer. I can now see you better, Mr. Hunt. Oh, you're bleeding. Sorry about that," said Fredrick LaRue.

"Thank you for the sympathy, but…" Ryan squinted to make sure he saw what he saw. There was a clown doll on a floating pedestal to Fredrick's right.

Fredrick started looking around and behind him. "Is there a problem?"

"Is that a clown doll next to you?"

"You mean Mr. Jingles. He is a valued member of my crew and no concern of yours. Now back to business. You and the Orb in trade for the lives of your shipmates."

"You named your doll Mr. Jingles?"

"It's not a doll. It's a crew member."

"Ah…Mr. Hunt, I'm well versed in negotiating tactics and usually it's not a good idea to make the side with the upper hand angry," whispered Commander Gordon out of the side of his mouth.

"I'm trying to stall in the hopes someone figures something out," Ryan whispered back.

"Really? You two are whispering? I can see you doing it," said Fredrick.

"OK, why do you and the doll want me so bad? The Orb I get, but why me?"

Fredrick took a deep breath to calm himself. "Again, not a doll. So please stop doing that. It gets annoying…Anyhow, someone wants the Orb and is also willing to pay a lot of money for your death."

"Huh, interesting. The villain out to get me went with a doll theme instead of the evil-looking cat. Interesting. First the creepy doll lady on the planet, and now you and the clown doll."

"She is creepy, isn't she? And for the record, if you want to get technical, Mr. Jingles is a puppet. Now you are going from annoying to pissing me off, and I think I'm going to just kill you all."

Ryan held his hands up. "Slow down there. My apologies for insulting your—" He crooked the index and middle fingers on both his hands. "—'clown puppet'. I agree to your terms as long as you release the ship and crew."

"Finally, something reasonable from you. It shouldn't be this difficult."

Before anyone else could talk, alarms went off in both ships as another ship entered the planetary system.

"This is Dr. Katalina Winslow of the OTKE ship *Retribution*. I order you to release that ship or things are going to get messy."

CHAPTER 15

ROUGH LANDING

"**W**ell, this is an interesting turn of events. I'm sorry to say, Dr. Katalina Winslow, you're in no position to order me to do anything. If you fire upon my ship, you will hit your friends as well and destroy them in the process of trying to save them. Then again, if I destroy them first you will get a chance to destroy me. Quite the conundrum we have," said Fredrick with a taunting sympathetic look.

"Seems like we're in some sort of Mexican Standoff," said Ryan.

"A what?" said just about everyone at the same time.

"It's old Earth slang for a standoff between two or more groups where no one can really get the upper hand, or something like that. You people really need to read up on old Earth terminologies so I don't have to keep explaining them."

"Seriously, you're going to bring up that argument now. Especially when you're not even sure you're saying it correctly," said Kat.

"It's not an argument. I'm just making a recommendation. It would save me a lot of time if you would just—"

"Stop!" interrupted Fredrick. "As much as watching you two argue would be amusing, this is not, how did Mr. Hunt put it, a 'Mexican Standoff'."

With that, the rear part of the Ship Eater changed to an Earth Consortium Heavy Battle Cruiser.

"As you can see, Dr. Katalina, I have you outgunned. So here are your options: shoot and kill your friends, I devour your friends and destroy you at the same time, or you leave and they live. So what will it be?"

There was a long pause until Kat's ship started to move and turn around.

"Very good. A wise decision."

Ryan's face dropped in despair when he saw Kat's ship flying away from them. Now there was no hope for escape.

"OK then. Move your ship to one of our docking ports and I'll come over to your ship as your prisoner. And as agreed, you will let the crew of the *Tempus* live. I just need a minute to get the Orb," said Ryan with heavy heart.

Fredrick grinned and placed his elbows on the side of his chair, brought his hands to his chin, and pyramided them to his mouth.

Just as Ryan was about to leave, he could hear a small alarm from one of the systems on the command deck. A louder alarm sounded from the virtual screen view of Fredrick's ship.

A small window appeared in the lower corner of the larger virtual screen showing Kat's ship coming toward them at almost wormhole speed.

"She's insane! Brace for impact!" yelled Commander Gordon.

The virtual screen view of Fredrick's ship turned black as soon as Fredrick jumped from his chair for cover.

Kat accelerated toward the Ship Eater, which had the rear port section of the *Tempus* engulfed with five tendrils embedded into the *Tempus's* hull. She knew she could not shoot at the ship, and there was no way she was going to leave her friends to die. So instead, she would break them apart the hard way.

As she was about to hit the Ship Eater, she diverted all the *Retribution's* energy to the bottom shields, had the docking thrusters fire at full force to bring the front of the ship to point upward, and aimed the bottom part of the *Retribution* at the section where both ships were connected. The rear bottom of Kat's ship rammed through the tendrils, breaking both ships apart as planned, but the force was so strong it sent all three vessels into the planet's atmosphere. All three spiraled out of control as the planet's gravity pulled in the damaged ships.

Electronics exploded across the command console on Kat's ship, but her AI was still operational. Metal plates started popping out in all directions to add drag to the *Retribution*, as thrusters fired to stabilize the damaged ship and get it out of the death spiral. The *Retribution* AI was finally able to control the descent, and it glided to a landing in an open area on a beach.

Fredrick's ship had the tendrils torn off, leaving gaping holes in the port side. The Ship Eater was much larger than the other two, and was able to take the impact with less internal damage. Fredrick's crew was able to get the ship out of the spiral, but the engines were down. It glided in and crashed into a tropical forest. Trees uprooted and dirt sprayed in the air until the Ship Eater finally came to a stop.

Commander Gordon was able to reach for an emergency lever on the side of a console just before the impact. The open space on the ship filled with some sort of dense red gel material, encasing everyone and everything in it.

The *Tempus* flipped and rolled as it entered the planet's atmosphere. Parts of the tendrils stuck in the ship started to burn off during the reentry. Just as things looked bad for the *Tempus*, the AI system kicked back on, now that it was no longer being interrupted by the energy burst, and the *Tempus's* AI did the best it could to stabilize the spacecraft.

Unfortunately, the *Tempus* was coming in too fast and the *Tempus's* AI couldn't make an emergency landing near Kat's ship, another OTKE ship, as per emergency protocol, and it crashed into the lake. It skipped across the water and smashed into the beach. Sand flew in the air as the *Tempus* dug into the ground and finally came to a stop half on the beach and half into the tropical forest.

⚓

Kat had been knocked out from the impact and it took about a half-hour to regain consciousness. Small AI bots were already crawling around the interior of the ship and making repairs. She could see they had taken small cuts of flesh from her non-gloved arm to use as cell replacement for the organic parts of her ship. The small wounds hurt, but the AIs were following ship recovery protocols to use all means necessary to repair the components.

Cringing from the bruises caused by the seat restraints, Kat rose from the command chair and made her way to the back of her ship to dig out an emergency kit. Pulling out the medi-quick care air needle, she injected herself with compounds to dull the pain and enhance the nanobots inside her to accelerate healing.

Within seconds, the pain had dropped to an annoying ache and she made her way to the rear deck to exit the docking bay, but the bottom floor was pushed upward and would not allow the door to unseal and open. She shook her head, knowing this was going to be a big repair—and expensive. Perhaps rescuing another OTKE ship would be considered an operating expense, but she shrugged her shoulders and headed to a side hatch. She climbed down the side of her ship and hopped down to the sandy beach.

Kat looked up to see many glistening satellites in the sky directing the sunbeams down to the planet. It was a peaceful, tropical landscape with the lake, beach, and the sounds of singing birds coming from the forest. The area could have been a relaxing spot under different circumstances. She could see buildings on the cliff in the distance to her right. To her left, the *Tempus* was wedged in the sand and partially into the forest. She didn't see any movement and there were no signs of the attacking ship, which was a good thing since she forgot to grab her las-pistol.

Kat jogged over to the *Tempus,* which was still in one piece, but it would need a lot of repairs. Pieces of the burnt tendrils of the attacking ship stuck out in various areas and multiple lights flashed by one of the emergency hatches. She ran and jumped up, grabbed a piece of the ship's hull that was bent outward, and pulled herself up to the side hatch.

She placed her non-gloved hand against the ship to the left side of the lights. "Emergency override, Dr. Katalina Winslow. Authorization code 29-Retro-242-Beta-Bang."

Kat removed her hand and the hatch slid up to allow her access to the hangar bay. One of the drop ships was still magnetically sealed, while the other was crushed to the back of the bay. She could see that emergency crash gel had been released throughout the ship. It was only used in dire situations to insulate the crew from a horrific crash. It would gradually seep into a humanoid body, sustaining it with nutrients and any other chemicals the lifeform required to survive. The only side effect was it also put the humanoid to sleep to slow their heart rate and keep them from feeling any pain or death. Kat shivered at the thought.

Kat went over to a console, waved her hand over it, and the virtual screen flickered up to the height of her face. She moved her hands around the screen and brought the power core back online. Many systems were reporting as offline or damaged, but at least they had power.

"*Tempus* AI, are you online? Report on ship status."

Kat waited and repeated the question.

"*Tempus* AI reporting at seventy-five percent functionality, Dr. Katalina Winslow of OTKE Scientific Division. Emergency override is now in full progress. Crash insulating gel is being removed. Medical AIs are being powered back online from sudden shutdown and will be dispatched to attend to the crew. Forty percent of crew is deceased. This includes humanoids and AIs."

Kat's stomach twisted at hearing the report.

"Is Ryan Hunt one of the deceased?"

"Unknown. Ryan Hunt's last known location was the command deck, but internal sensors are down. Repair AIs being dispatched to affected system areas."

Kat could hear the crash insulating gel being retracted and headed off to the command deck.

⅄

Fredrick LaRue unstrapped himself from the wall. Luckily, he was able to get to an emergency wall harness that popped out once the ship's AI alerted him to the collision. He looked around and found Mr. Jingles laying against a wall, covered by debris. He picked up the clown puppet and dusted it off.

"Oh, don't you worry, Mr. Jingles. We'll cut to the heart of this Dr. Katalina Winslow for her insolence."

"Sir, are you okay?" said a member of his crew from the open door of Fredrick's private command room.

Fredrick turned around as he dusted Mr. Jingles off. "We're fine. What is the ship's status?"

"Most of the systems are functional on backup power. Engines are down, and the mimic capabilities are no longer operational. The grappling tentacles were ripped out, leaving gaping holes in the ship's hull. Some of the crew were sucked out before shields could be raised over the hull breaches."

The crewman gulped when he saw Fredrick's face turn red with anger.

"Sir, wha-what are your orders?" stuttered the crewman nervously.

Fredrick calmed himself and gave the crewman a reassuring look. "No need to be fearful. Anger is sometimes a good emotion when controlled and directed correctly. This is an interesting chess game we are in, and with an opponent of our equal. It's not often we are challenged."

"Yes, sir. Should we send out a party to hunt down the target? Our sensors indicate they are not far from here and are in bad shape."

Fredrick put Mr. Jingles back on his hovering platform. He then placed his hands behind his back and started to pace back and forth around the room.

"What else have our sensors reported?"

"Sir, we have detected terraforming buildings on a small hill near the lake where the target ship crashed. We are also detecting various wrecked ships under the tree canopy and in the lake. They date back many centuries, and some are of unknown configurations. As you saw earlier, the planet is surrounded by a sophisticated Dyson Sphere, and there is a mini black hole nearby."

"So we have a planet not on the star charts, with old alien technology keeping the planet alive, along with ancient bases and crashed ships. On top of that there is a black hole," said Fredrick. He closed his eyes and brought his left hand up to rub his chin as he thought. "No, we will not go after them yet. There is a reason they came here. This is no random wormhole jump, but a planned exercise to determine or learn something. Have a techno-spy meet me outside in a few minutes. I have a job for them. I have a feeling this little setback will lead us to something much greater."

The crewman gave a slight bow and headed off to relay the orders. Fredrick turned to Mr. Jingles. "Yes, Mr. Jingles. I agree, the most powerful weapon is patience."

⅄

Kat made her way through the damage and checked on the crew and non-functional AIs. The good thing was the *Tempus* had a limited crew. Unfortunately, those she came across were dead or AIs too damaged to be repaired. She used the emergency ladder to climb up to the command deck. Kat was shocked at the amount of damage the command deck had sustained. Scanning the room, everyone was down, and small AI repair drones were already flying or crawling around initiating repairs of the main systems.

Kat rushed over to Ryan when she spotted him. Blood was trickling down his head and he was lying in an awkward position. She hesitated, took a deep breath, and checked for a pulse. She was relieved when she felt one. The drug initiated by the gel would wear off soon. She started checking everyone else. Commander Gordon, Mitil'Lin, and two members of the command crew were all alive. The other two crewmen were dead, and the two AIs were destroyed. Walking around the command deck she came across Vicki. She cringed when she checked on her. She was cold to the touch and didn't have a pulse.

Kat continued surveying the command deck and ran over when she saw feet sticking out from under a console. Peering underneath, she could see Nora, who was lucky that the console didn't fall flat and was leaning on a railing. It had kept Nora safe from any other debris that would have fallen on her. Kat wedged herself underneath the console and lifted it up using her legs and back. It wasn't heavy as it was awkward, and as soon as it hit the wall, some repair AIs crawled over to anchor it back on.

She moved Nora's head and hands around, but Nora didn't make a sound. Kat assumed Nora was disabled based on the nature of the ship that attacked the *Tempus*. She recalled how complicated the female assassin AI was, so she was not about to cut open the back of Nora's head to fiddle with it, but decided a quick energy burst should shock her systems into reacting. Kat had an innate ability to manipulate energy from her body. Something only Ryan knew. She placed her gloved hand on Nora's head and a narrow energy burst shot from her hand into Nora.

Nora sat up straight with eyes wide open. "Danger! Eater of ships!"

"It's OK, Nora. The threat has been neutralized for now. Do you understand?"

"Dr. Kat, what…? I am confused… My thoughts are all over the place."

"You were disabled. Just sit here and let your cortex catch up and sort things out."

Nora nodded, and Kat turned when she heard someone shuffle behind her.

"Ow, my head. What the hell was that? One second I'm bracing for impact and the last thing I remember is drowning in jello."

Kat got up and walked over to Ryan to help him up as Commander Gordon, Tilli, and the remaining command crew started to groan and move around.

"Just get up slowly. The effects will soon wear off. Not sure what jello is, but the red gel saved your life," said Kat.

Ryan's heart raced when he recognized her voice. "Kat, you're a welcome sight. I thought you were gone for good."

"I thought I was gone too," said Kat with a smile.

"How is everyone else?" asked Ryan.

"Unfortunately, we lost some of the crew. Everyone else is fine except for Vicki—she didn't make it."

"What do you mean I didn't make it? And to think they gave you the title of 'doctor'."

Kat jumped around, shocked. "I… how… you had no pulse."

"Ah, Kat. Not sure how to say this, but Vicki is a vampire," said Ryan.

Kat looked at Ryan dumbfounded and then back at Vicki, who stood there with a devilish smile.

"I never thought them to be real," said Kat. "I guess that explains your bitchiness and the aura of hate I have for you."

"Oh, really. I'm the bitch. If I recall, I'm not the one who tried to kill Mr. Hunt last year."

"Why, you bloodsucking—"

Ryan took hold of Kat's arm and dragged her back. "Ladies, let's take a few steps back. We have more pressing concerns."

Kat yanked her arm away and stepped aside to calm herself.

"*Tempus* AI, system status," said Commander Gordon, who was now standing and shaking his head.

"Maneuvering engines and limited power cores are now online, but many core systems like guidance, wormhole engines, and life support are heavily damaged and will take time to repair."

"Dr. Kat, ramming my ship was not one of your greatest highlights, nor is it an approved method for decoupling ships," said Commander Gordon.

"No worries. A thank you isn't needed for saving your lives. Feel free to send the expenses to my department," replied Kat.

"Protocols, this is why we have protocols." Commander Gordon pulled down his jacket to straighten it out. He pointed at the two-remaining crewman, "You two, with me," and then all three left the command deck.

"Well, as much as I would like to stick around, I'm going to assist a medical AI with the wounded, moving the deceased and freshen up a bit," said Vicki, limping to the door of the command deck.

"If you're going to do what I think you're going to do, please make sure it's only with the deceased and under the supervision of the medical AI...And only if they can't create something for you first," said Ryan.

Vicki gave a wave of her hand in agreement and exited out of the command deck.

Kat looked at Ryan with her mouth open. "You're going to let her actually do that?"

"Believe me, we're in my moral gray area here, but she needs to heal and we're in a bad situation. She'll do what's right. I think we've come to some understandings."

"I hope so. I hate the thought you would feed my corpse to the wolves that easily."

Ryan took a deep breath, and then cringed when he touched his wounded head. "We can discuss my morals later, now can someone explain how this LaRue guy found us?"

"I think I know how, sir," said Nora. She walked over holding something in her hand.

"I'm still a little groggy, so someone is going to have to eventually explain the odd conversation you two were having," said Tilli, who was shaking her head and starting to walk off the drugs from the crash gel. "Nora, is that the flower you were wearing?"

"Yes, it is the flower Delegate Glumet gifted to me and I wore it in my hair. It appears to be modified."

"Can I see it?" said Tilli, holding out her hand.

Nora turned the flower over to Tilli, and the lenses on her goggles switched around as she twirled it in her fingers.

"Fascinating. It's a flower modified with a highly advanced miniature AI system. From what I can tell, it has a relay signal system, scan blocking technology, and some sort of disruption chip. It's no longer functional though. Looks like it blew out during the overload of the ship's AI systems."

"It is what I feared. This is how they found us, and based on how I am operating now, I believe this is what was causing my violent behavior toward Mr. Hunt," said Nora.

"Not your fault, Nora. We didn't know," said Ryan. "Speaking of locating us, Kat, how did you find us? You left before all this began."

"Well…while you were out for those few months getting Ver'Lin's upgrade, I sort of played around with the comm chip embedded in your hand to enhance the signal to interact with the intergalactic satellite communication and relay network. I also sort of added a tracking device to it as well."

Nora's head whipped around. "I knew it! I knew you were up to no good, but no one ever believes Nora."

"Fine, Nora, you were right, but at least in this case it was a good thing. We would be destroyed now if she didn't find us in time," said Ryan.

Nora smirked at Kat now that she was proved correct about Kat's meddling.

Kat shook her head and rolled her eyes. "What do we do now?"

"As much as I would like to leave Tilli here to work on the ship, we need her up in that destroyed lab," said Ryan. "So this is what we're going to do. Tilli will go see a medical AI about the arm and then meet Kat and I outside. The three of us will head up to explore the lab. Especially Kat, since I think Commander Gordon is on the verge of strangling her. Nora, you stay behind and help Commander Gordon with repairs and for protection in case Fredrick's people turn up."

Everyone nodded in agreement and headed off.

CHAPTER 16

SECRET LAB

Fredrick walked around the outside of his ship, surveying the damage. He kicked the hull as he looked at the gaping holes where the tendrils were torn off in the impact. Some of his best people were sucked out of the ship when the damage occurred, and the mimic capabilities of the Ship Eater were rendered useless. It would take a miracle to get it working again. He needed to hurt these people, not just kill them. He needed to make them suffer for what they were doing to his organization. This one job was taking a heavy toll on his people and rare equipment that could not be replaced.

A woman in a purple one-piece suit approached Fredrick. Only her eyes were visible through a skin-tight black mask.

"You summoned me, sir."

"I did. You're the best stealth asset I have left. I need you to find Ryan Hunt and his team, observe them, and send detailed reports of their movements and actions. Do not engage them in any way. Pure reconnaissance. They're here for a reason and I want to know why. I'll be leading a squad that will trail your reports so we can act when necessary."

"As you wish," said the woman with a slight bow.

Fredrick watched her as she headed toward the forest. She touched a section on her arm to activate the stealth device. Her body shimmered for a second and then she was gone.

While Tilli was getting her arm mended, Ryan and Kat took some time to gather weapons and tools for the trek up to the old lab. Ryan also made a quick stop to check on his car in the second hangar bay to make sure it was OK after the crash, and was relieved to find it still magnetically clamped to the hangar bay floor.

On their way out to meet up with Tilli, Ryan gave Kat a quick summary of why they were here and what they were trying to figure out. He told her that if anything happened to him, he had documented the entire trip on his data journal crystal.

Tilli was already outside the ship when Ryan and Kat exited. They had to navigate past some small repair AIs working with Commander Gordon, who was also busy directing what was left of his crew.

"Looks like Commander Gordon has everything under control. Tilli, is the arm OK?" asked Ryan.

Tilli looked at a hand-held scanner as she turned in circles. "Yup, arm is OK, but the planet has a lot of interference. My readings are all over the place, but if we head around the lake there appears to be a path we can take to get to the main building."

"Mr. Hunt and Dr. Katalina, off on an adventure somewhere with their little geek girl. Looks so exciting," said Vicki, strolling from an opening in the side of the ship.

Kat looked up at the bright sky and back at Vicki. "Shouldn't you be bursting into a ball of flame?"

"You would enjoy that, wouldn't you, Dr. Katalina? Unfortunately for you, I resolved that issue a long time ago."

"Oh, I'm so happy for you," said Kat.

"All right, this is another odd conversation. Either I'm missing something, or everyone is keeping something from me," asked Tilli.

"Vicki is a vampire and she and Kat don't get along," said Ryan.

Tilli looked back and forth at everyone, confused. Some of her lenses switched around so she could look at Vicki under different settings and then pointed the scanner at her. "Some rather unique readings. Not what I was expecting. Well then, I think I will, um, start heading toward the lab."

Everyone watched Tilli head off at a rapid pace.

"I always get that reaction," said Vicki.

"Would you like to join us?" asked Ryan.

"I'll pass and explore the shade of the jungle on my own. Getting stranded on an unknown planet was not something I had in mind when you rescued me."

"Oh. Ryan rescued you, did he now?" said Kat, looking right at Ryan.

"Vicki was in trouble and it was a dire situation. It's a character flaw to be this helpful. What can I say?" said Ryan.

"Indeed, he did, and it was extremely dire. Too bad he forced me to get dressed back at his place. The fun we could've had." At that, Vicki sauntered off toward the jungle.

"You know that getting dressed means she was undressed prior to that."

Ryan blushed. "It's not what you think."

"Oh, I'm thinking quite a few things." Kat circled Ryan with a sly grin and then leaned into him. "I thought you were very reserved, Mr. Hunt, but I never thought you would be into the undead. Interesting. Very interesting." Then she took off after Tilli.

Ryan shook his head and sighed. "This is going to be a long day."

⚔

Ryan, Kat, and Tilli made their way around the lake and found an old automated lift that would have ferried people up the hill to the buildings. Tilli investigated the lift and noted it was far too damaged to repair, while Ryan and Kat discovered pieces of metal scattered in the overgrown bushes—most likely parts of the lab when it exploded.

The team continued to follow the old lift up the hill. Kat and Ryan stopped when they noticed skeletal remains under some debris off to the right of the lift.

"The smaller one is Gravel. The other is of a large humanoid, but without the skull, I'm unsure what race it might have been," said Kat.

"Whatever it was, it was a big guy," said Ryan.

"Up here. I found something," yelled Tilli from the top of the lift.

Ryan and Kat hurried up to where Tilli was, and they found her evaluating two panther-looking AIs laying on their side. The fake fur was charred, and they were covered in vines. Metal and circuitry stuck out from various parts of their bodies.

"Well, those are different. First time I've seen animal AIs," said Ryan.

"Probably security AIs. That's usually what animal and giant insect AIs are used for. The entrance to the lab appears to be ahead," said Kat, pointing up to a large bent metal door leaning on the side of a wall.

Tilli started to remove some of the vines to get a better look at the panther AIs.

"It's probably not a good idea to mess with them," said Kat. "I wouldn't tou—"

Tilli accidently poked one of them and its eyes lit up red. The team jumped back as the panther AI squirmed to get itself out from the snaking vines. In one quick motion, it was able to break free and hobble up on three legs.

Kat and Ryan immediately brought their hands to their las-pistols.

"System alert. Intruders detected," said a female voice from the panther AI. "Scanning threat." It growled at them as a wide red light scanned over the three of them.

The AI stopped growling once it scanned Ryan. "Florarien detected. Standing down. Welcome to Dimensional Travel Lab. Please head to the first lab to be brought up to speed and meet the team."

"OK. That was scary and odd at the same time," said Ryan.

"Probably a malfunction, but as long as it thinks that instead of wanting to kill us, I'm all for you being a shrub guy," said Kat.

"Sure. What the hell. Let's head on in and find out what's going on." Ryan turned to face Tilli. "And no more touching non-functional AIs."

"Sorry. Curiosity gets the best of me sometimes."

The team made it up to the metal door. The entire frame and door were blown off the building. Based on the shape of the bend, the explosion must have occurred inside.

The first part of the lab was a complete disaster zone. Small pieces of bones stuck out of the wall from where someone's skeletal shrapnel hit. Just up ahead, past piles of metal and tropical growth, was another intact door.

Tilli made her way over, her goggles shifting around as she analyzed the door. "Older technology, but I should be able to splice it."

She pulled out a small laser cutter and cut a hole into the metal wall to the left of the door. She then pulled out some of the internal optics and jury-rigged them to a small power supply cube she stuck to the wall above the hole. She tapped the cube and it lit up green. With a groan, the old door slid to the side as dust fell from the ceiling.

Ryan and Kat drew their las-pistols and entered the room. Lights came on as an internal sensor detected their presence, and a few systems powered on as others exploded into a shower of sparks. Tilli ran over to the system still online, pulled off a panel at the bottom, and started moving optical cards and some crystal looking things around.

"That should do it. I made sure to limit a small amount of power to this station only."

Kat and Ryan re-holstered their las-pistols and they looked around. There was another door in the back. The lighting emanated from small round holes in the walls, floor, and ceilings. A virtual screen finally appeared on the console Tilli had reconfigured, and she used it to access the system.

"Is the system AI functioning?" asked Kat.

"So far no, but there appears to be some data here. It's going to take me a little time to recover, so make yourselves comfortable."

⚔

"Sir, I have followed Mr. Hunt and two of his companions from their ship to some type of facility. A fourth person headed off in the opposite direction," said the stealth-suited techno-spy over her internal comm link to Fredrick LaRue.

"Any details on the companions?" asked Fredrick.

"Ryan is with someone named Dr. Katalina and a small Artesian-looking girl named Tilli. The woman who headed off on her own was referenced as Vicki, but I picked up a comment about her that confused me."

"And that is?"

"They mentioned the word 'vampire' when talking to her."

Fredrick finally put the puzzle together. Ryan's companion, Vicki, could only be one person: Victoria Van Buuren. "Well, this is an interesting and unexpected turn of events," said Fredrick. "What are Ryan and his two companions up to now?"

"They are attempting to access a data system in the old facility."

"So there is value on this planet. Find out what it is. In the meantime, I need to meet an old friend. Contact me again when you have additional information."

⋏

The techno-spy closed the comm channel with Fredrick and found a position in the destroyed first section of the lab under some vines. She pulled out a small case and opened it to reveal a tiny AI flying insect, which flew into the air. She used her internal connection to the AI, guided it into the room, and landed it on the ceiling just above Tilli. Whatever Tilli found she would know about it as well.

⋏

Ryan and Kat fought the urge to head deeper into the lab or go outside and explore. They sat, paced, and Ryan explained to Kat why everyone referred to Mitil'Lin as 'Tilli'. He also commented on how he liked seeing Kat with the red stripe in her hair and matching glove, and made her promise to always be colorful.

It seemed like an eternity waiting for Tilli to get into the data core. She had optical hardware, organic pieces and odd-looking crystals strung on the floor and over the console as she spliced her way deeper into the system using her own custom hacking program. Finally, after an hour, information started racing across the screen.

"Success!" yelled Tilli, making Ryan and Kat jump.

"Thank god," said Ryan. "What did you find?"

"Hold on. One sec," said Tilli. She removed a small part on her goggle frame and then ran a long wire from the system console to a port in the revealed section on the frame.

"Impressive. Active data streaming into your goggles," said Kat.

"Thanks. I got the idea from watching CEO Klein. It lets me review everything much faster."

Ryan and Kat waited another few minutes as Tilli's head moved back and forth.

"Fascinating. Not all the data is there, but I understand now. The lab was a joint venture between the Gravel, Florariens, Clairnots, Thermians, and a few other smaller and older races. The Gravel were the most technologically advanced of all of them, but the war they were fighting against the Woland was not going well. They decided they would turn over their technology to the less advanced races in an attempt to protect them from being conquered as long as they would help perfect the ultimate technology."

"Seems noble of the Gravel," said Ryan.

"They were always willing to make sacrifices to help others," said Kat, making a fist with her gloved Gravel arm that had been grafted onto her.

Tilli held up her finger. "There is more, but I will need to paraphrase since this is where the data breaks up. The Gravel had developed an energy source that could be adapted to ships capable of wormhole travel. They also figured out that mini black holes, created naturally or artificially, with a lesser gravitational pull could be used as a conduit to travel to other universes or dimensions. Based on how far and how fast you travel, you could unlock these new areas of space and time. They ran through many tests and failures. Hence all the crashed ships."

"I'm guessing things didn't go as planned?" asked Ryan.

"You are correct. There is data detailing the Gravel taking the first working Orb with them and never returning. The races kept bringing in new scientists to try to recreate and improve the original design. From what I can tell, they were never able to recreate the original, but they continued to use the prototype Orbs to explore other universes."

"Something is missing based on the time lines. How old is this place?" asked Kat.

"You won't believe it, but this place has been around thousands of centuries. There is a huge gap in the data, so a lot of details are lost, but there is something about the Nilorian War shutting down the research for a while."

"Nilorian War? I haven't gotten to that part of history yet," said Ryan.

"I will save the long history lesson for another day and give you the shortened version," said Kat. "The Nilorian War was against a race of beings that were far more advanced than any other race, and they were driven to rule every galaxy they came across. The various races banded together and defeated them. Probably the first time the Gravel and the Woland worked together. The alliance victory came with a cost. The war destroyed just about every planet they had. Used up valuable resources and wiped out most of their fleets."

"I can't even imagine what the death toll might have been like," said Ryan.

"It was horrific. Some of the lesser known races were wiped out. The extent of bio and radioactive weapons destroyed entire worlds. It took thousands of centuries for the races to recover. Hence why Earth was able to catch up so fast when it started its space exploration. Although, it does beg the question, how did the Woland have enough resources to continue their war against the Gravel after this?" said Kat.

"Obviously there are more mysteries to be unlocked, but let's save them for another time," said Ryan. "Tilli, anything else you can tell us?"

"Based on the dates, the old C-Tec we met is a lot older than we thought. I also found some garbled information on how it may be possible to recreate the energy Orb, but what bits I'm able to read are way beyond my knowledge. Also, the Florariens were supposed to have been the first race after the Gravel to use this new technology."

"Since the Florariens are still around, I guess they never received the information," said Ryan. "Anything on why they destroyed the base?"

"Very little, but from what it sounds like, not all the other universes are safe. Once they perfected traveling with the prototypes, it appears something followed them back and attacked them. Forcing them to blow up the base."

"Can you copy the data about the Orb?" asked Ryan.

"Already did, as well as any other data I could get. The white crystal stuck into the side of the console contains it all. You can take it," said Tilli.

Ryan grabbed the crystal. It looked like his personal one, only smaller. He dropped it into his pocket with his personal data crystal and made sure it was secure.

"Well, that was easy enough," said Ryan.

"Nothing is ever that simple. Did anyone think about the fact that if the old C-Tec and some lab people survived, whatever attacked them may have also survived?" asked Kat.

Ryan pursed his lips. "Really. You had to go there. You could've just kept it to yourself."

"Nora's not around, so one of us has to be the logical thinker. Plus, we may find additional information if we venture further in."

"I guess that means we're going to have to go check behind door number one then," said Ryan.

"After you, Mr. Hunt," said Kat.

"Fine, but let me check in with Nora." Ryan touched the comm badge on the back of his hand and spoke into it. "Nora, this is Ryan. Do you read me?"

"This is Nora. Report."

"Wow, I thought I was direct and to the point. Let Commander Gordon know we have accessed the lab and we're able to get some data. It looks like the data was eventually to be sent to the Florariens but never made it there. Kat and I are going deeper into the lab facility to investigate a hunch, and Tilli is going to stay back to try to get additional data. If anything goes wrong, we'll meet back at the ship. How are the repairs going?"

"I will inform Commander Gordon of your report. Repairs were going well until I was interrupted by this conversation. Wormhole engines and life support are back online. We are now working on shields and then weapons."

"OK. I'll let you get back—," said Ryan, but the transmission ended with a click before he could finish. "Yup, Nora is back to her old self. Shall we go investigate?"

Kat shook her head and smiled as she drew her las-pistol.

"I'll take that as a yes," said Ryan. "Tilli, if you hear shooting, make a run for the ship and we'll meet you there."

"Will do. And please be careful. I would be lost without the banter between the two of you."

Ryan and Kat smirked at Tilli and then headed to the door.

⚓

The small surveillance bug on the ceiling above Tilli flew back to its master. The techno-spy put the bug away and quietly moved back outside to a secure location to provide Fredrick with a status report.

"Sir, I have an update."

"Go with update."

"Mr. Hunt and his companions have successfully retrieved data from the system and he is in possession of a data crystal with the said information."

"What are they up to now?"

"Mr. Hunt and Dr. Katalina are heading deeper into the facility. The Artesian girl is staying behind."

"Excellent. Opportunity presents itself…Here are your new orders. Give Mr. Hunt and Dr. Katalina time to get further into the facility. Once you're sure they will not see you, take the Artesian girl and bring her back to the ship. I want her in one piece. Is that understood?"

"Yes, sir."

The techno-spy closed the comm channel and headed back into the lab to wait for an opportunity to kidnap her target.

CHAPTER 17

INTO DARKNESS

Tilli looked around as she waited for her hacking program to dig deeper into the system. She was letting the program go at a much slower pace so as not to overload the system. As she looked around the room, she caught an odd waver in her goggles. Flipping to a different combination of lenses, she scanned the room again and detected an odd, but familiar reading radiating from a wall close to the floor by a conduit.

Ryan and Kat had found it was not as easy to delve deeper into the facility and were working on getting the door open, so Tilli decided to investigate. Bending down, she could see the conduit door had been open and haphazardly put back. As she fiddled with the conduit opening, a loud bang made her look up to see Ryan and Kat had finally opened the door to the other part of the lab.

"Tilli, we're going in. You OK over there?" said Kat.

"Yeah, just checking some conduits."

"OK, yell if you need us."

"I'll be fine. Just be careful."

Kat gave Tilli a nod of reassurance and headed off after Ryan.

Tilli watched Kat leave, and then pried the conduit door off enough to fit her hand and the lower part of her arm in. Feeling around, she pulled out something round wrapped in a cloth. To her surprise, it was another energy Orb. From what she could see, this one was half-filled and degrading but still appeared powerful. She rewrapped it and put it back in its hiding spot. Perhaps this was the item the old C-Tec had recalled hiding. She figured it had been safe there all this time, so she might as well leave it until Ryan and Kat got back.

She headed back to the console to check on her program, but stopped when she heard something. She looked around the room and noticed some debris falling from the door Ryan and Kat just opened. She smiled and went back to work.

⚓

Vicki giggled to herself as she strolled through the jungle. She loved how she could get under Dr. Kat's skin with her little comments. One of these days the two of them would have it out, but today would not be that day. She was glad she decided to go off on her own and clear her head.

Losing her home was not something she had planned on and when she needed help the most, only Ryan came to her aid. Not one of her so-called associates would answer her distress calls. In the end it was sad that someone she barely knew, and was at one point going to feast on, was her savior. On the other hand, it had led to her almost dying and crashing on an unknown world. If things did go as planned, the Wolfkin she freed from the mining planet would have taken back the Little Lamb and she would be able to start over, but the big question was, what she should start over as. Ryan did bring up some good points in their conversations on good and evil. Should she stay with the darkness like how it has always been, or change to something different and not let being a vampire dictate her morals?

She was brought out of her thoughts from the smell of fresh blood. A pool of blood and some intestines lay on the trail ahead, and headed off down a path to her left where no vegetation grew. On each side, the leaves were black from death. Curiosity getting the best of her, she followed the blood trail to the hull of a large transport ship overgrown with vegetation, despite the path showing something had been killing everything around it.

Vicki's eyes dashed around as she sensed something moving toward her.

It was just a blur, but it shot out of an opening on the ship. Vicki dropped to the ground as it blasted by her and into the jungle. She cautiously stood up, scanned her surroundings, and dusted herself off. Whatever just shot by her had an aura of darkness, but it was also hesitant. Vicki changed into her vampire form and looked around again.

"Creature, I command you to show yourself to me."

Out of the bushes emerged a creature hunched over like a large gorilla, with the pushed in face of a bull, large claws, and yellow eyes. It seemed to have black fire shimmering all around its body. It cautiously came out, sniffing the air.

Vicki's eyes sparkled at the sight of the creature. "A Xeno-Shadow. How magnificent. I have not seen a creature like you in a long time. Someone made an oops and opened a portal to the darkness. This explains the dying vegetation and why they had to abandon the planet."

The creature growled but moved closer to her side. Vicki smiled as she scratched the creature's head.

"Submission. Now that's more like it." The thought of sending the Xeno-Shadow off to get Dr. Kat did cross her mind, but if there was one Xeno-Shadow, perhaps there were others that would kill her.

Vicki stopped petting the creature as she picked up the faint sound of a twig breaking. As she scanned the jungle, a las-blast from an unknown attacker blew the head off the Xeno-Shadow. Vicki jumped back into a defensive crouch and looked around. Three humanoids in battle gear from head to toe made their way into the clearing. Vicki growled as she considered whether to fight or flee.

"No need for the growling fang thing," said Fredrick, walking down the same path Vicki had followed. "Everyone else, lower your weapons. Mistress Victoria here isn't going to harm us."

Fredrick's attack force lowered their weapons and Vicki turned back into her human form.

"Well, well, well, look what the galaxy dug up," said Vicki.

"I could say the same about you, my dear. It's been such a long time and, if I recall, we last let off on the verge of killing each other should we ever meet again," said Fredrick.

"Oh, I recall. I just want to see where this conversation goes before I slaughter you and your freak show companions here. I had a hunch it was you when I saw the Ship Eater, and for you to reveal it, someone is either paying you a considerable sum of credits or you're afraid, Mr. LaRue."

Fredrick held his hands up in the air. "Let's not jump right to the killing yet. Everything is negotiable, and I have a business proposition for you."

Vicki looked at him with suspicion and a hint of curiosity. "Go on, I'm listening."

"You are correct in both areas. There is a considerable sum of money riding on getting that energy Orb and killing Mr. Hunt, and the customer is a little on, shall we say, the harsh side. My proposition to you is quite simple. Help me get what I need, and we provide you with a percentage and a way off this planet."

Vicki laughed. "Seriously. Join up with you and your little puppet. I have seen what Mr. Hunt and his allies have done to your great plans. I think I have a better chance with them. Now can we get to where we try to kill each other? I'm getting antsy."

Fredrick leered at her and rubbed his hands together.

"I've seen that look before. It's the look of leverage," said Vicki.

"You are correct, my dear vampiress. I, and Mr. Jingles, didn't want to have to go there, but you are forcing our hand. You either help us or you never see your sister again."

"I don't have the slightest clue what you're talking about."

"See, there you go. Trying to be all serious, but you know whom I'm talking about. Your poor little sister. The one you have been searching for all these centuries. The one turned into a statue with a pose like this." Fredrick flopped on the ground with his hands up over his face, cowering in fear.

Vicki immediately changed into her vampiric form and took a step forward. Fredrick's guards brought their weapons back up to point at Vicki, while Fredrick casually stood up and dusted himself off.

"If you harm my sister, I will do things that will make you beg for death!" Vicki hissed and showed off her fangs.

"Vicki, always one for the dramatic, but here's how this is going to work. You're going to take this device—" Fredrick reached into his jacket and pulled out a small metal disc, "—and place it somewhere in Ryan's ship. You will then let your crew know that if Mr. Hunt doesn't bring you the Orb and leave with you, I will kill the one they call Tilli. Also, their ship needs to blast off right away. That device is a proximity mine. If their ship is not out of this solar system in twenty minutes after you leave, it will blow up and kill everyone."

"Tilli is with Mr. Hunt and Dr. Kat," said Vicki, returning to her human form.

"Oh, I'm sorry to say not for long."

"And if I don't do what you say?" asked Vicki, pursing her lips and crossing her arms.

"Quite simple, your sister will end up a pile of crushed stone."

Vicki stared at Fredrick with daggers in her eyes before relaxing. "One condition, Mr. Hunt is not to be harmed."

"Wow. Even after my dramatic line about crushing your sister, you're going to ask for something with no advantage. Impressive...very impressive."

"Blah, blah, blah...do we have a deal or not?"

"I'll make you this deal. I like this Ryan fellow. I'm going to ask him to join my organization. If he declines, you need to turn him. The orders were to kill him, and technically a vampire is dead, so I get paid, I get a new ally, and you get a consort you seem fond of."

Vicki snatched the disk out of Fredrick's hand. "I guess Mr. Hunt's assumption about me is correct after all. I am evil."

"Guards, escort Vicki to the edge of the forest near Mr. Hunt's ship. Leave her with one of your las-pistols and a comm device. I'm sure she will be able to take control of the ship on her own."

"That won't be an issue," said Vicki.

"I didn't think it would be. Contact me when you're in control and I will send some associates over."

The guards nodded and headed off to the *Tempus* with Vicki. Fredrick watched them disappear down the trail. "No my dear, not evil. The word you are looking for is 'Opportunist'."

⚔

Ryan was a few feet down the hall waiting for Kat in the dim light from the lab behind them. Once Kat reached him, she stopped to stare at skeletal remains in a lab coat sitting against the wall in front of him. A hand welder was laying on the floor next to it.

"Any idea what killed him?" asked Ryan.

"I see no visible wounds on the skeletal remains, but without a full examination I can only assume he eventually died from lack of air or starvation."

"Well, that sucks."

Ryan looked around as the lights finally flickered on to reveal a long hallway to another door. At one time, other pathways intersected with this one, but rubble was now blocking those directions.

"Lights on is our cue to keep going," said Kat.

Ryan nodded and continued further down the hallway with his las-pistol in hand. Kat followed. As they got about halfway, the lights went out, leaving them in total darkness.

"Yeah. This is the part where the lead person gets it. Always when the lights go out."

"Hold your tongue, Mr. Imagination," said Kat.

Ryan could hear her ruffling for something in the darkness and then had to swiftly bring his hands up to cover his eyes as the path ahead of them illuminated. Ryan looked up to see two tennis ball-sized globes floating in midair, emitting a powerful light beam. Each floating light ball seemed connected to Ryan and Kat. Whenever they moved or looked around, the light moved with them and turned as well.

"Those are freaking cool. Why haven't you told me about these before?" asked Ryan.

"A girl has to have her tricks. The lights will also obey you, so if you want a wider or narrower beam all you have to do is ask."

"Very ingenious, but how is mine working with me? I have no implants to allow that type of connectivity?"

"I kind of added a few other nano-technology things while you were being upgraded."

"Oh my god. You really want Nora to kill you. What else did you upgrade on me that I'm not aware of?"

Kat grinned ear to ear and walked past him smugly.

Ryan shook his head and followed her. As they reached the door, they noticed it was bowed inward, the door seam was welded shut and two metal bars were welded across it.

"This looks like it's going to be a little more difficult to get through. Do you think it's wise we even try to get in? The only reason to weld a door shut is to make sure whatever's on the other side can't get out," said Ryan.

"Yeah, that would make sense, but I cannot see something living in this place after all these centuries without food or water. Plus, aren't you a little bit curious about what's on the other side? There is the chance we find more information about the artifact or this place."

"God, I hate curiosity and when you make a valid point. Fine...let's do this."

Kat reached into one of her utility pouches attached to her las-pistol holster belt.

"No wonder you don't need an adventurers bag. You have your own superhero utility belt," said Ryan.

"You do recall I'm also an archeologist who has explored many an alien ruin. You pick up a few things here and there. By the way, where is your little adventurers bag?"

"It got destroyed when someone rammed the ship and caused a fluid leak in my quarters."

"Oh, I would give that person a piece of my mind if I was you."

"I'll remember to do that. Now, what's with the string?"

"It's a breaching device," said Kat. She stuck the string to the door in a large oval. "Let's move back a little and let it do its magic, and don't look at it until the brightness fades."

Within a few seconds, the metal inside the oval started turning red. It began near the string and moved inward until the entire oval was a bright white. In an instant, the metal started falling like dust until it and the string were gone, leaving a large enough hole in the door for them to enter.

"That's impressive," said Ryan.

"Another of my many tricks. Now, think about moving your light in first and stationing it to the left of the door and I'll do the same for the right," said Kat.

Ryan nodded and concentrated. It took a few seconds before he could feel the connection to the hovering light and was surprised when he received an acknowledgment from it as it followed Kat's light through the door.

Ryan followed the lights in and swept to the left as Kat went in and swept to the right. They each slowly backed up to the opening so they could be side by side.

Ryan squinted when he caught a glimpse of something in the distance. "Hey, is that a ship over there?"

Kat had her light narrow its beam and start panning the room. They could see the result of a massive explosion in what must have been a hangar. One ship was visible, its front half covered in rubble. Debris was everywhere, and a thick layer of dust coated everything.

"The ship is Gravel. I would know that configuration anywhere," said Kat. "We should split up and look around."

"Rule number one. Never split the party," said Ryan.

"I didn't know there were rules for searching ancient dark labs."

"Well, rule number two would be to never go skinny dipping with the big-breasted blonde at a summer camp, but I think we're safe to ignore that one."

"Now that I'm completely confused, remind me to have you explain these rules later. I think the first rule is fine, and I'm neither blonde nor big-breasted. So please lead on."

Ryan's light source guided him past rubble, computer consoles, and various ship parts. He stopped when he noticed some odd human-sized cases leaning against the wall.

"Survival pods," said Kat. She inspected one of them and wiped away the dust from the glass at the top. "They're used for long-term storage of a humanoid in case of an emergency."

"Kat, you better come take a look at these down here."

A skull lay on the floor next to one of the pods. The skeletal body was still inside.

"It appears something broke into this one and ripped the person's head off," said Ryan. "And look at the next three. They're all broken into as well."

"I hate to be the bearer of bad news, but the darker stuff on the pod is dried blood," said Kat.

"Darkened lab, skeletal remains…This can't be good. I see a few more of those pods on the other side of the ship. I'm going to break my rule of splitting up and go check them out. See if you can find anything on the computers or try to get something working," said Ryan.

"They're your rules to break. I'll see what I can do. Yell if you need something."

Ryan gulped as he hesitantly walked past the ship. Its large hulking outline looked spooky in the limited light. He jumped at every shadow until he got to the pods on the other side of the hangar. Three of them looked to still be intact. He cleared the dust off the middle one to get a look inside, but it seemed as black as night. He brought the light over and focused it into the pod and was expecting to see the light gray coloring of the inside, but all he saw was a shimmering blackness.

"Holy shit!" yelled Ryan as two yellow eyes appeared in the blackness of the pod.

Ryan backpedaled, tripping and knocking over some items and stopped when he backed into something big.

"What is it?" said Kat, putting down a tool she was looking at and making her way over to Ryan.

"There is something—"

The front of the pod exploded off, sending pieces flying at Ryan and taking out his floating light source.

Ryan dived to his right, hitting the ground hard and barrel rolling into some canisters and small metal boxes. His las-pistol flew from his hand, disappearing into the darkness, as he gagged from the air being knocked out of him.

Unable to see, he crawled as fast as he could away from the survival pods. Feeling around, he found some storage crates and hid behind them. The hairs on the back of his neck stood up at the creature's unholy loud hiss, and he cringed when he heard two more explosions and creatures emerging from the other pods.

Ryan pulled himself into a ball and closed his eyes to relax his breathing, in case the creatures had sensitive hearing, and cursed himself for breaking the cardinal rule of any adventuring party: never split up.

"Ryan, where are you? What are you doing? Are you breaking things?" yelled Kat.

"Kat, no. Stay where—"

The sounds of las-blasts echoed in the facility. The creatures had already engaged Kat and she was firing her las-pistol in all directions. Ryan peeked his head up over one of the crates and could see Kat's light not too far from him. He got into a kneeling position and then ran toward Kat's light, jumped over a table, and slid down to the floor as he caught sight of a shadow flying through the air and grabbing Kat's light. The creature crashed to the ground and the entire place went black.

CHAPTER 18

ESCAPE

Tilli looked around. There was nothing left to fix or investigate, and she was getting bored just sitting and waiting. Ryan and Kat had been gone for a while now and she didn't hear anything out of the ordinary. Just when she thought it was about time to give up on her hacking program, it alerted to the recovery of some additional data, in the form of journal entries.

Journal Entry number 1974

xxxxxxxxxxxxxxxxxxxxxxxxxxxxxx—the crystal looking ships surrounded us— We—xxxxxxxxxxxxxxxxxxxxxxxxxxxxxx—

The mystical race, far advanced to us, let us go on the condition we do not travel here again. Our minds are too inferior and barbaric for this universe—xxxxxxxxxx xxxxxxxxxxx

Journal Entry number 4560

Another successful trip. We—xxxxxxxxxxxxxxxxxxxxxxxxxxxxxxxxxxxxxxxxxx

By going a little further at wormhole speed, we released an emergency brake at mark 2.6.2 deep into the mini black hole. Valmill thinks this—xxxxxxxxxx

xxxxxxxxxxxxxxxxxxxxxxxxxxxxxxxxxxxxxxxxxxx
xxxxxxxxxxxxxxxxxxxxxxxxxxxxxxxxxxxxxxxxxxx
xxxxxxxxxxxxxxxxxxxxxxxxxxxxxxxxxxxxxxxxxxx
xxxxxxxxxxxxxxxxxxxxxxxxxxxxxxxxxxxxxxxxxxx

He called himself the 'Shepard', a guardian of the first planet we encountered in this new universe. The planet was young and on the verge of bacteria dividing in the primordial ooze. We wished we could have stayed to study the origins of life, but we were already—xxxxxxxxxxxxxxxxxxxxxxxxxxxxxxxxxxxxxxxxxxxxxxxxxxxxx

Tilli tried to clear up the missing data, but there was not much more she was going to get from the system. The last piece was very interesting and proved the technology developed here actually worked. She retrieved another small data crystal from one of her pockets to copy the new data. As she was bending down, she heard something move behind her and she froze. This time it didn't sound like dirt falling off an old door. Being on the safe side, she slowly stood up and turned around. Not seeing anything, the lenses of her goggles quickly switched through different configurations, allowing her to see the different spectrums of light.

Tilli screamed as she caught the outline of a figure coming at her. A sudden piercing pain in her shoulder had her gripping it tightly. She pulled her hand away to reveal a little blood, then her vision turned blurry, forcing her to grab the console for balance as she swatted at the blurry image now standing in front of her. It was no use; she collapsed face first to the ground.

⅄

Fredrick LaRue's techno-spy put away the needle gun and placed a small cube on the center of Tilli's back. Tilli's body automatically went rigid and hovered off the ground. The techno-spy gently lifted the hovering Tilli to waist height and pushed her out of the lab with ease.

"Sir, I have the target and I'm en route to your location."

"Excellent. New location. Bring the target back to the ship and have the guards secure her in the hangar bay. You may then continue assisting with ship repairs."

"As you wish. What about Mr. Hunt?"

"Have no fear. He will be coming to us."

⅄

The comm pad on Ryan's hand started to vibrate and an orange light moved back and forth across the pad. He looked at it for a few moments and then touched it. He could faintly hear something and brought his hand up to his ear.

"Ryan, can you hear me?" whispered Kat.

He brought his hand to his mouth and whispered, "Yes, I can hear you, but why is my comm pad vibrating and when did the orange moving light thing get installed?"

"Those functions only work when I contact you. Worry about that later. You need to get over to where I am. We won't survive being separated."

"I'm not too far from you. If we both cause a distraction I can make my way over."

"OK, I'll make sure you see where I am."

"Sounds good. Give me a second." Ryan reached around to find something to throw and eventually found a piece of metal. "OK, I'm ready. On three?"

Kat started to count, "One, two, three!"

Ryan threw the piece of metal as Kat shot a red blast of energy from her gloved hand straight up in the air. One creature chased after the blast and another was heard going after the piece of metal as it clanged to the ground. Ryan jumped up and rushed to where the energy blast originated. He cut left and around the shadowy outline of a console, and then barreled through hanging wires under the diminishing glow of Kat's energy blast. As the last of the blast faded, he dived over a cargo bin to get to where Kat was, but something grabbed his foot and he crashed down on top of the bin.

"Kat, it has me!" yelled Ryan, holding on to the bin and kicking out at the creature.

Kat jumped up and grabbed Ryan with one hand as she fired her las-pistol with the other. Her energy burst had died out and now she was randomly shooting.

"Stop freaking shooting! You'll blow my foot off!" yelled Ryan.

With Kat pulling hard, both she and Ryan went flying to the ground when the creature let go. The creature let out an ear-piercing screech as it took off running with its hands engulfed in blue fire.

"Good shot," said Ryan, lying on his back.

"Number one, I would have eventually hit him, and if I didn't we can always heal a damn foot. Number two, it wasn't me who set the creature on fire. And Number three, why was your foot glowing blue?"

"What are you talking about?"

"One minute you were about to get your foot pulled off, and the next minute your foot was glowing blue, then the creature howled in pain and let go."

"News to me," said Ryan. Between the adepts bowing and saving him from the freaky doll lady to a glowing blue foot, he was not sure what the hell was going on, but if they didn't get out of here soon it wouldn't matter. "Let's discuss it later. Think we can get on that ship out there?" asked Ryan.

"Probably. It's a Gravel ship. My...you know, Gravel arm should unlock the genetic lock," said Kat.

"Can you shoot some energy blasts around as a distraction?"

"Of course I can. Let me know when you're ready and try not to get caught this time."

"I'll do my best. OK, on three again. One, two, three!"

Kat started blasting red energy bursts in multiple directions from her gloved hand while firing her las-pistol with the other. They made a dash to the ship under the illumination of the energy bursts. Kat handed her las-pistol to Ryan and removed her glove. She placed her hand from the grafted Gravel arm on a side panel; the door slid up and a ramp extended. They ran up the ramp as lights in the ship turned on and then dimmed a little. Kat immediately hit an area on the inside wall and the door slid closed just as a creature pounded up against it.

Ryan tried not to stare at Kat's Gravel arm, but it was hard not to. The last time he saw it was when she had threatened to kill him on Earth when he refused to help her get into the secret Gravel lair.

Kat looked back at Ryan as she put the glove back on and bit her lip, waiting to see how he would react.

Ryan smiled at her, erasing any concerns Kat had. "I'm no expert on Gravel ships, or any spaceship for that matter, but half the ship is under rubble and I'm guessing the hangar bay entrance from this place is destroyed."

The sound of banging at the door made them both jump and the door started to dent.

"If I recall, Gravel ships have a backup to the central system in the engine area not too far from here. There should also be doors we can seal as we go."

Ryan and Kat moved further down into the ship. Kat sealed the doors they went through and Ryan moved whatever he could find in front of each door. It took about ten minutes to get to the main engineering area of the ship. Dim lights came on and systems started as they entered. Ryan noted how small the area was, but what amazed him were the walls of odd-colored crystals blinking in a variety of sequences. One virtual screen in the center of the room allowed technicians to work on each side or, if you were alone, it would follow you, as it was doing with Kat now.

"A computer screen that follows you around. That's awesome, but how is the power still working after all this time?"

"The Gravel were experts at building engines and fuel sources. Unfortunately, bad at combat," said Kat. Her hands quickly moved around the virtual screen as she walked around verifying other systems.

Ryan peered around the room and noticed an interesting setup that looked like a round device such as an Orb could fit into it.

"Hey, Kat. Come over here and take a look at something."

Kat rushed over. "We don't have much time, we need to get things going." She paused as she touch the setup. "So this is how they did it. Fascinating and complex all at the same time."

A loud bang vibrated the ship.

"I wish we had time to study it longer or to take a picture, but it sounds like they've gotten in," said Ryan. "What's the plan?"

"Don't worry, I'll remember a unique setup like that. As for the plan, you're not going to like this idea, but it's the only thing I can think of."

Another bang sent vibration through the floor.

"OK, lay it on me."

"I'm going to self-destruct the ship. It will level this hangar and anyone, or anything, along with it."

"Good plan, but what about us?"

"There are multiple escape pods in this section. They're cone-shaped and one of them is almost lined up to the door we cut the hole in. We'll use the escape pod, angle it to the door, and slam through the hole. The back end will wedge itself in the door and then we make a run for it before the place explodes."

Ryan looked at her blankly as another loud bang and the sound of scraping claws echoed on the floor above them. "We either make it, blow up, or get eaten. Escape pod it is."

"I knew you would see it my way," said Kat, entering in some commands.

The wall behind them opened to reveal an escape pod. It had a pointed shape like the front of an old Earth fighter jet with a bubble cover over the interior.

"Kat, those are very tiny seats. How are we going to fit?"

"Give me the las-pistol back." She adjusted the beam and fired a few blasts at the back of the seat supports. She then kicked them over and pulled them out.

"We lie down in it one on top of the other and I steer it to the hole in the door."

"You're freaking insane. I'm not doing that," said Ryan, who then jumped at the loud bang on the door behind him. "OK, your plan sounds great. You want the bottom or the top?"

Kat gave him an innocent smile. "On top, of course."

Ryan took a deep breath and blushed, then lay down belly first in the pod. "Wouldn't being on your back be better?"

"And have your lady parts in my face? Nope. Not going to happen."

Kat snickered and shook her head. Despite their impending death, Ryan still had that air of innocence about him that made her smile.

The door started to dent inward. Kat ran over to the virtual display and initiated the self-destruct sequence for twenty seconds. She then ran over to the escape pod and lay on top of Ryan. She pushed a few buttons, the escape pod top closed, and the pod shot out of the ship.

They both screamed as the escape pod engine ignited and accelerated, skimmed off rubble, and went through anything else in its path. Kat did her best to keep it on target, firing stabilizing rockets to aim it more to the right, and accelerated. The plan was going great until she realized that in their current positions, the sudden stop of the pod wedged in the door would put too much force on their bodies and would kill them. Kat increased the speed, hoping it would go through the door.

The Gravel ship violently exploded, disintegrating the creatures inside. The escape pod blasted through the hole in the door and skidded down the hallway, bouncing off the walls, straight through the inner and outer labs and through the overgrown foliage outside to become wedged in some large roots. All was quiet except for the rain of dust and small pebbles that bounced off the now-stationary escape pod.

The canopy blew off as Kat pulled the release lever. She pulled herself up and out of the emergency foam that formed around them like an airbag and rolled out of the pod. Ryan moaned and did the same thing on the opposite side. They both had blood oozing from their heads, and lay on the ground looking up at the sky and the plume of smoke and dust in the air caused by the exploding Gravel ship.

"I'm never doing that again," said Ryan.

Kat started laughing.

"What are you laughing at?"

"I'm actually surprised it worked. I had my doubts, but any crash you can walk away from is a good one."

"Yeah, so far you're two for two when it comes to crashes. Let's not make it three. And in the future, keep your doubts to yourself or I might have second thoughts of going through with your crazy plans."

Ryan stumbled around the escape pod, navigating the broken roots pointing in every direction. He put his hand out to Kat and helped her up.

"We need to check on Tilli. I'm praying she's all right," said Ryan.

They wobbled their way inside the lab and coughed from the dust lingering in the air. Luckily the room they left her in was still in one piece.

"Tilli...Tilli, are you here?" yelled Ryan.

Ryan and Kat looked around, and even crawled across the floor to make sure she was not lying knocked out somewhere. After about fifteen minutes, they headed outside.

"Maybe she wandered off," said Kat.

"No, I don't think so. Too much knowledge here for her to gain. If anything, she would have gone back to the *Tempus*."

Ryan dusted off the communicator on his hand and spoke into it. "Nora, are you there?"

There was a long pause, and Ryan repeated himself.

"Mr. Hunt, there you are. I have been trying to reach you, but there was interference from an explosion close to your area. Are you OK?"

"Yes, Kat and I are fine. Is Tilli there?"

"No, Mr. Hunt, she has not arrived. Please hold, there is some commotion occurring outside—"

Ryan's face went pale as Nora was cut off. The last thing he heard was a las-blast before the communication cut out.

"Was that sound what I think it was?" asked Kat.

"Damn. I think that psycho found the *Tempus*. Let's go."

CHAPTER 19

SELL OUT

Ryan and Kat hid in the tree line near the beach. From their vantage point, they could see the AI drones continuing with ship repairs. Unfortunately, three figures were lying in the sand near the ship. There were no signs of anyone else nearby. If the enemy was hiding, they were doing a great job.

"Here, take my las-pistol," said Kat.

"And what are you going to use?"

"Ah, hello, innate ability to shoot death rays, remember?" Kat wiggled her gloved hand in the air.

Ryan took her las-pistol. "Good point. Now, how do we get on the ship without being seen?"

"Well, the front part is in the tree line on the other side of the beach. If we go there, we might be ambushed. The hatch on the side with the emergency ladder is probably a trap. If we split up, they pick us off. Our options are very limited."

"In that case, let's use the ladder. At least we're going in knowing it's a trap. One of us goes in while the other covers. They're bound to find us if we sit here any longer," said Ryan.

"Frontal assault into a trap. Getting daring I see, Mr. Hunt."

"Must be the company I keep."

Ryan winked at her, stood up and trotted carefully to the ladder, looking in every direction as he moved forward. Once he made it to the ladder, he saw that the three figures were the only remaining working AIs. Two were from maintenance, and appeared to have had their internal systems ripped out. The other was the medical AI, his head almost twisted off. Ryan pursed his lips in frustration and hoped everyone else was safe. He looked back at the tree line and shook his head to alert Kat that the bodies weren't alive or functional.

He took his time climbing the ladder, trying not to make any noise. It amazed him that after all these centuries there would be an emergency ladder hooked up to a spaceship; of course, this one appeared to be able to meld out of the ship's hull and back again for storage. When he reached the top, he warily leaned his head in and scanned the inside of the ship before entering. Once he was sure it was safe, Ryan entered the hallway between the hangar bay and the command deck.

Ryan crouched down and waved his hand out the doorway to give Kat the all-clear. A few seconds later she joined him in the hallway.

"Hmm…too quiet," whispered Ryan.

"Wait here and let me scout the area a little bit," said Kat.

She took a few slow steps in each direction, stopping to listen, and returned to where Ryan was waiting. "Yeah. This is not good. Way too quiet. Let's head to the command deck. Just make sure to look down any passages or open doorways before passing."

Ryan led the way, stopping at each corridor and waiting a few seconds before heading past them. Kat did the same in case he missed something. All the doorways were open, yet there were still no sounds. Even the stairway up to the command deck was quiet.

Ryan crouched at the entrance to the command deck. From his vantage point he was unable to see anything but still shadows on the floor. He moved against the left wall as Kat hugged the right wall. Ryan eased into the command room and could just make out Nora leaning against a console with her arms crossed. The top half of her jumpsuit was folded down and tied at the waist, revealing a dirty white tee shirt. Her blond hair was pulled back in a ponytail, and she didn't look happy.

Ryan looked at Kat and waved his hand to get her attention. When she looked at him, he pointed to his eyes, then inside, and held up his index finger.

"Only one," mouthed Kat.

Ryan shrugged.

"There are a few more than just one in here, Dr. Katalina," yelled Vicki.

Ryan put his head down in disgust, stood up and looked at Kat. She shrugged her shoulders and stood up as well.

"I can see you are both confused as usual. If you had looked up, you would've noticed the small camera AI hiding in the bulkhead. It's really a shame, since you entered the ship with such precision and timing. Textbook actually. Now slide the las-pistol into the room and come in with your hands in the air. I would hate for something to happen to Commander Gordon and his crew."

Ryan rolled his eyes in frustration, and did as Vicki instructed. Kat followed him in, hands raised.

Ryan could now see the full command deck. Vicki was sitting in the commander's chair looking at a small virtual screen while pointing a las-gun at Commander Gordon, who was bound and gagged on his knees in front of her. The other two command deck crewmen were bound and gagged against the wall behind Vicki. Ryan scanned the room, expecting to see Tilli, but she was not there.

"Vicki, what the hell are you doing? What's with all this?" he asked.

"Well hello, cutie. Long time no see," said Vicki, swiping her finger down the virtual screen to shut it off. "Let's just say I had a productive walk around the jungle and quite simply…I changed sides."

"Are you freaking kidding me? After all we've been through. Our conversations on good and evil, and trust. Then you go and do this," said Ryan, a perplexed look on his face. "What am I missing here?"

Vicki rolled her eyes. "You're such a naïve and innocent individual, Mr. Hunt. Always wanting to see the good and trusting nature in people, but save the speech for someone who cares. The reality is I haven't survived this long without a few *allegiance* changes along the way. Besides, they made me an offer I couldn't refuse. You should know the movie I'm referencing by that line, Mr. Hunt."

Before Ryan could say anything, Vicki pointed her gun at Kat.

"Don't think I don't see you moving toward me ever so slowly, Dr. Katalina. I'm in no mood to play silly games. I would stand very still if I was you. I would hate to have to kill anything more than an AI today."

"If I get the chance—"

"Oh, please, Dr. Katalina," said Vicki. She got up from the hovering command chair and kneed Commander Gordon in the face, knocking him to the floor and out cold.

Ryan, Kat and Nora all took a step forward as Vicki changed to her vampiric form. She moved the las-pistol back and forth between all three of them.

"You can all try, but I guarantee two dead before I fall, and then there is poor Tilli to think of."

"What did you do to her? Where is she?" asked Ryan.

Vicki held up her hand as she changed back to human form and tapped the comm device on the side of her neck. "Yes, you can come on board now. They're not going to try anything," she said to LaRue's team hiding in the jungle.

Vicki pointed the las-pistol back and forth between Ryan and Kat. "Some friends of mine will be joining us shortly so I will tell you how this is going to go. Tilli is currently a guest on the ship of Mr. Fredrick LaRue and his Jesters Freak Show organization. Mr. Hunt is going to get the Orb artifact and give it to me along with the data crystal Tilli gave him back at the lab. I will then take those items, along with Mr. Hunt, to Fredrick's ship. Once we're there we'll release Tilli and everyone lives."

"You will not make it off this ship alive," said Nora.

"Out of all the people I've met, you're the most amusing and honest, especially for an AI. I bet a conflict between us would be of epic proportions, but I neither have the time nor desire to fight you. So here is where things get interesting. I have hidden a proximity mine on this ship. Extremely small and undetectable to a scan. Once we leave this ship, you will have less than twenty minutes to take off and exit this system. If you are still in proximity of Mr. LaRue's Ship Eater, your ship will explode. In time, I'm sure you'll find it, but by then we'll be long gone."

"You won't get away with this," said Ryan.

"Oh, Mr. Hunt, you make me laugh, using that old cliché line from all those old movies," said Vicki with a big ass grin on her face. "God, how I love being back in the game."

⋏

About ten minutes had passed. Ryan, Kat, and Nora leaned against the virtual screen console in the center of the room. Vicki relaxed in the hovering command chair. Commander Gordon, bleeding from taking a knee to the face, had regained consciousness and squirmed into a seated position. Everyone was quiet until some of Fredrick's associates entered the command deck. The two guards wore red and yellow body armor, with the bottom half of their faces covered by matching masks, and they carried las-rifles. The last guy was dressed a little differently. He was bald with a red metal plate covering the back of his skull and a beard that came to a spike about ten inches down from his chin. He wore a skintight black and white checkered pattern shirt that showed off his muscular physique, and he carried a red glowing machete.

The two guards split up and moved to each side of the room while the bearded man approached Vicki.

"Miss Van Buuren, I'm Commander Lucious of the Jester Assault Squad. Mr. LaRue sends his regards on a job well done. There are hover skiffs en route to take you and the items back to his ship."

"Oh, great, I'm just an item now," said Ryan.

"Shut your mouth!" yelled Lucious.

Ryan gave Lucious a dirty look and crossed his arms.

"Mr. Hunt, would you mind retrieving the Orb?" said Vicki. "Remember Tilli's life most likely depends on this going smoothly."

"Fine, it's in my quarters. I'll go get it," said Ryan, taking a step forward.

Las-guns flew up and pointed at him.

"A little jumpy, aren't we?" said Ryan.

"You two, take Mr. Hunt to retrieve the item. If he tries anything, feel free to hurt him," said Lucious.

One of the guards walked up to Ryan and nudged him forward.

"I'm going, I'm going. No need for that," he said.

Ryan led them to his quarters, which was still a mess and covered in some type of spaceship fluid. He started to move some debris when he noticed his small portable energy shield was on the floor under some of his clothes.

"Can one of you give me a hand lifting this wall section here?"

One of the guards handed the other his las-rifle and squatted down to help. As Ryan put his side down, he fell backward on to his ass, his hand falling on the small portable shield. Both guards laughed.

"Lightweight couldn't lift the little piece of metal," said the guard, taking his las-rifle back.

Ryan smirked at them and activated the shield before he put it in his side leg pocket. He was hoping not to be shot, but at least if he did there was a chance of surviving it and possibly escaping. Once he was standing, Ryan continued to move some items around to reveal a storage box built into the wall. He opened the DNA lock and removed some papers that were hiding the container with the Orb in it and the vial of Gravel Goo. Taking both, he turned around and nodded to his captors, who guided him back to the command deck.

"I have the items you wanted," said Ryan.

"Bring them over to me," said Vicki, handing her las-pistol to Lucious.

Ryan walked over and handed her the Orb and the Gravel Goo.

"I only wanted the Orb. What's the vial?"

"It's Gravel Goo," said Ryan.

Vicki held it up in the air to examine it, then tossed it to Kat, who snatched it out of the air with her gloved hand. She placed it in a hidden side pocket on her pants when Vicki turned her head.

"Goo wasn't in the instructions," said Vicki, getting up from the chair. "Now we're leaving. If everyone cooperates no one gets hurt."

Everyone watched Vicki with utter distaste as she headed to the exit. She surveyed the room, and then looked directly at Nora.

"You there, AI. Remember, as soon as we leave you have a very limited time frame in which to get to another star system or you go 'boom'."

"My name is Nora, and I understand what is required."

"Nora, AI, whatever. Are you ready, Mr. Hunt?"

"Yeah, I'm ready, but is it OK for me to say goodbye to someone first?"

"Sure, what the hell. Guess I have a soft spot after all. Say your goodbye and then we leave. There'll be no more delays."

Ryan and Kat's eyes met. Kat started to flush, but then looked confused as Ryan put his hands into his pockets and walked right past her to stand in front of Nora. He hesitantly put his arms around her and dipped her into a deep kiss. Nora's eyes bugged out as the shock of what was happening processed, but then she closed her eyes, relaxed and kissed him back. Kat's jaw fell to the floor.

"Oh, my god. The look on Dr. Katalina's face is priceless. Priceless, I tell you. Wow. I didn't know you two were a thing, Mr. Hunt. You shocked the hell out of me," said Vicki, laughing.

"Miss Van Buuren, don't forget the data crystal," said Lucious.

Vicki took a second to regain her composure. "Thank you for reminding me. The kiss threw me off. Data crystal, Mr. Hunt."

Ryan pulled the crystal from his pocket and handed it to her. He then gave Kat and Nora a nod and then left the command deck followed by Vicki and Fredrick's men.

⅄

Kat immediately ran over to Commander Gordon and untied him. "You OK?"

"Yes, a small headache from the knee but I'll be OK. I heard everything and will begin prepping the ship for immediate takeoff once I untie my crew."

Kat nodded, got up, and turned to Nora, who was touching her lips. "I, ah, guess you and Ryan hit it off while I was away. I totally understand—"

Nora reached out and pinched Kat's lips closed before she could say anything else. "Dr. Kat, I found my first kiss to be interesting and as much as I want things to be more with Mr. Hunt, the kiss fell flat. I did not feel, well... anything. From my studies on human sexuality, that is not how it is supposed to feel. Mr. Hunt and I will always be the best of friends. Second," Nora reached down into her pants by her backside and pulled out a data crystal,

"Mr. Hunt was kissing me so he could drop this inside my clothes. I believe it is the data crystal Tilli gave him."

"That sneaky little you know what. Then what did he give Vicki?" asked Kat.

Both Kat and Nora looked at each other and at the same time said, "His journal!"

"I need to get this crystal off the planet to the Florariens, and you need to go rescue Mr. Hunt," said Nora. "I will send you the Ship Eater coordinates. Now go. I trust you to save our friend."

Kat hugged Nora and then bolted to the hangar bay.

Nora shivered as Kat left. "I now have...what does Mr. Hunt call them? Ah yes, cooties. I now have Kat cooties. Eww."

CHAPTER 20

FALLING

Kat grabbed a one-person hover board from the hangar bay, ran back and dived out the ship's side door. The board slammed into the ground and hovered up a foot as Kat landed on it.

As she received the Ship Eater coordinates from Nora, Kat activated the drive system and relayed the coordinates to the board's AI, via her bio-neural interfaces. The AI locked onto its destination and Kat shot into the jungle like a bullet.

Vicki and LaRue's people were probably using faster hover platform tech that flew above the trees, which gave them a huge head start.

Kat tried to go faster but the propulsion system started to make a horrible sound. They weren't made to go past top speed for this long. The board zigzagged through the jungle, flipping upside down a few times to clear fallen trees. She easily maintained her balance. The hover board was made of a special compound that interacted with her boots, so she couldn't fall off unless she ordered the AI to release her.

The board made a sudden sharp right turn and stopped. Kat watched as the Ship Eater started to take off with its hangar bay door open. Someone was banging on something, trying to get the door to close. She also heard the *Tempus* in the distance, blasting off under full power.

Kat franticly looked around and noticed a large tree leaning on some other trees. She ordered the AI to go to full speed and accelerated up the fallen tree, using it like a ramp. Once she was airborne, she ordered the boards AI to release her. Kat flew through the air and barely grabbed the open hangar bay door by her fingertips. She precariously dangled from the ship, knowing full well this was not one of her greatest ideas. Kat swung a leg over the door, pulled herself up, and rolled into the ship.

She thought everything was going great until she looked upward to see a guard staring down at her.

"I know how this looks, but maybe we can talk about it?" said Kat with a smile and wave.

Instead of replying, the guard picked her up and moved her to the side of the hangar bay near the open door.

Kat quickly took inventory of the situation. The hangar bay was small. A compact six-person transport ship was docked on the left. A guard paced along a catwalk that outlined the wall opposite the hangar bay door. Vicki was also up on the catwalk near an open doorway, holding the Orb container and looking down at everyone. Ryan stood about ten feet away from her, with Lucious holding a knife to Ryan's back.

"Kat, what the hell are you doing here?" said Ryan.

"Rescuing you and Tilli," she said with a shrug and a not-so-confident grin.

Lucious laughed as a guard nudged Kat to be quiet.

A door on the left side of the room slid open and a guard came in holding Tilli's arm. One of her goggles was cracked and there was some dry blood on her face and clothing. The guard walked her over and stopped in front of the transport.

"You OK, Tilli?" asked Ryan.

"I think so," she replied.

"I assure you she's fine," said Fredrick, who had entered through the catwalk doorway. "The cracked lens and blood is from the fall she had when the knockout drug took effect. I can only do so much about where and how they fall."

Fredrick took the Orb container and data crystal from Vicki. "Thank you, my dear."

Vicki gave a slight bow.

Fredrick turned and headed to the catwalk stairway. Mr. Jingles, the clown puppet, followed behind him on a floating platform. He stopped about five feet from Ryan. Fredrick put the data crystal into his combat vest pocket and placed the Orb container behind Mr. Jingles. He then crossed his arms and turned to stare at Kat.

"You aren't supposed to be here, young lady," he said, then turned around to his associates. "Someone care to explain why she's here?"

"Dr. Katalina is trying to save Ryan and Tilli," answered Vicki.

"You no longer have the right to call me 'Tilli'. It's Mitil'Lin to you," said Tilli to Vicki.

"You people and your names. Whatever. As I was saying, she is making a ridiculous attempt at a rescue."

Fredrick nodded. "I like people who take the initiative, but you're the crazy woman who damaged my precious ship. I will figure out what to do with you later. In the meantime, I need to deal with Mr. Hunt over here."

Everyone's knees buckled a little as the Ship Eater started to rise toward space.

"As you have al—" Fredrick turned to the worker banging on the hangar door. "Would you mind? I'm trying to have a discussion."

The worker looked around and placed his hands at his sides.

"That's better. Now, where was I? Oh yes...as you have already felt, we are rapidly heading higher. Eventually the hangar bay door will be repaired, and we will take our leave of this place. As you can see, I have the Orb, the data crystal of top-secret data, you and your friends, Mr. Hunt."

"OK, now you're just bragging. You must have something else in mind or we'd be dead or locked up by now," replied Ryan.

Fredrick leaned over to Mr. Jingles. "See, I told you he was observant."

"Yes. I'm observant. So, what do you and the...um...puppet want?"

"I want you to join me. Be part of my organization. Your knack for getting out of trouble and your annoying personality would make a fantastic addition to the Jesters Freak Show mercenary guild. Along with the Orb and the information I now possess...we could be unstoppable," said Fredrick with a huge smile and outstretched arms.

⅄

Everyone in the hanger bay was anxious waiting for Ryan's answer, but the tension was interrupted by Vicki. "And, might I add, your life is spared, Mr. Hunt."

If Ryan didn't take Fredrick's offer, she would have to turn him into a vampire and she was not sure she wanted to do that. Once you've been turned, you're never yourself again and she liked Ryan the way he was.

⅄

Ryan could now feel everyone staring at him. He looked around and took in the grim situation. If he says no, they're all probably dead and joining this freak wasn't an option. Then again, he did have the assassin blade hidden on his left arm.

"So, Mr. Hunt, what is your answer?" asked Fredrick.

Ryan started laughing. "Seriously? You want me to join your mismanaged bunch of clowns. Are you freaking kidding me? I have outwitted you at every turn and I'm a no one. Hell, you had to somehow talk a washed-up vampire to come in and save your asses. And don't get me started about the stupid ugly clown doll. There, I said it. A stupid doll."

He confidently walked over, eyeballed Mr. Jingles from various angles, and smacked it off the floating pedestal. Mr. Jingles fell to the ground right in front of Fredrick. The one remaining hat bell made a tinging sound as the puppet's head bounced off the floor and its jester hat fell off.

"See, Mr. Whatever-you-call-it is just a stupid, dirty, useless clown doll."

Ryan caught Vicki's face drop and saw her mouth, "Oh, shit."

Fredrick's face went red and he started to twitch as he stepped forward into Ryan's face. His lips squirmed to find words, but only partial curse words came out. Without warning, he sucker-punched Ryan in the stomach. Ryan grabbed his midsection with his right hand, took a few steps back to steady himself, and bent over at the waist.

Fredrick stepped away to regain his composure and then turned to face

Ryan, but before he could say anything, Ryan, who had already slipped the assassin blade off his left arm with his right hand, stood up, extended his right arm and fired the ballistic knife via his thoughts. The blade shot in the air heading right toward Fredrick's stomach, but before it could hit him, Mr. Jingles eyes lit up yellow as the puppet leapt up from the ground into the path of the knife. The blade tore into the puppets chest as red oily looking blood shot everywhere.

Fredrick brought his left arm up and the electrified dart shot out from his wrist. Ryan was quick enough to side step, turn and watch the dart narrowly miss him and slam into Lucious, dropping him to the ground in violent convulsions as he was electrocuted.

Ryan turned back around to see another dart coming at him from Fredrick's right wrist, but he was not fast enough to dodge this one. It hit his portable shield barrier and exploded. The dart was made to explode forward and some of it made it through the shield. The force of the explosion sent Ryan flying backward and out the hangar bay door into the open sky.

"Ryan!" yelled Kat.

Fredrick dropped to his knees next to Mr. Jingles. He stared at the puppet lying in a pool of red fluid, not knowing what to do.

"Goodbye...my...friend," Mr. Jingles said in a childlike voice. The yellow light in his eyes flickered as they dimmed and turned off.

Fredrick slowly stood up, shaking, and looked around the room. "Kill them all!"

Without hesitation, Kat spun to her left and smashed her elbow into the guard's face before he could react. The guard staggered back, allowing Kat to throw a left sidekick to his midsection, sending him screaming out the hangar bay door. She then grabbed an emergency jet pack off the wall and dived out the hangar bay as the las-blasts from the guard on the catwalk barely missed her.

Vicki looked around at the mess she had made. In trying to save Ryan and her sister, she had sent Ryan falling to his death. If she intervened, her sister would forever be lost, while the person who gave her no choice but to stab her new friends in the back was crying over a stupid doll. "Ah, screw this." Her full vampiric form burst forth. She lashed out her clawed hands at the guard standing next to her, slicing his throat.

Fredrick's focus seemed to return to the scene unfolding around him. "Get us into orbit! Space the hangar bay if you have to, but get us into orbit!" He grabbed the Orb container, scooped up Mr. Jingles' body, and ran out of the hangar bay, followed by the repairman.

The one remaining guard looked around, clearly unsure of what to do, giving Tilli an opportunity. She shoved the guard in an attempt to get around him, but the guard slammed her to the ground hard. Tilli shook off the fall and tried to squirm away as the guard raised his las-rifle at her, but instead of firing he spun his head around to face an inhuman growl coming from behind him.

The guard's eyes bugged out in fear. He tried to spin his body around to shoot Vicki, who was diving down at him from the catwalk, but he was too late. Vicki landed on top of him and slashed back and forth with her claws. Blood and armor flew in multiple directions as Vicki lunged at him with her mouth, ripping out part of his neck and feasting on his blood. Staring at Tilli like she was prey, Vicki methodically stood up, her face and clothes drenched in blood, and she let out a triumphant growl.

Tilli crawled toward the transport's front landing skid and curled into a ball, shaking in fear as she raised her hands up to try to protect herself from Vicki.

"You live today, young lady. Can you fly that thing?" asked Vicki in a demonic female voice while pointing at the transport.

Tilli nodded, jumped up, and ran into the ship with Vicki following her.

The Ship Eater went to full power, causing it to go almost vertical as it blasted into space, leaving a trail of items behind it—anything not clamped down fell out of the open hangar bay.

Tilli frantically powered on the transport as the AI fastened the seat restraints around her and Vicki. Once the transport engines were ready, Tilli looked at Vicki and gave her a nod.

"Do it," said Vicki.

Tilli released the transport's magnetic clamps and it slid backward out of the hangar bay and flew away.

Kat felt herself spinning out of control during her freefall from the ship as she held on to the emergency jet pack. She took some deep breaths and then relaxed, which allowed her to get her body into a better position to control the fall. Once she was in control, she struggled to get the small emergency jet pack, which was mostly used for ship repairs, harnessed around her. As the latches finally magnetically sealed in the front, Kat reached to her right side to activate it.

A clear dome emerged to cover her head, as small wings flipped out of the sides of the pack. Kat got lucky that this model immediately interfaced with her bio-neural implants, providing her with a heads-up display in the dome that allowed her to track Ryan's falling body by his hand communication pad.

Kat ignited the jet pack and set it to full speed. She moved closer to Ryan and pushed the pack to its limits. Red alarms blared on the heads-up display. If he was going to die, she would not hesitate to die as well trying to save him. She closed in, wrapped her arms around him and pulled him in tight. The jet pack started to give out and Kat slowed down by coming out of the dive and letting the pack's AI system initiate an emergency vertical landing. The jet pack held on long enough to get them down into an open clearing with a large tree. As they landed, Kat fell to her knees, leaned Ryan against the tree, and gave a neural order to power down. The jet pack dome retracted and un-latched the harness. She let the pack fall to the ground as she fell next to Ryan.

Ryan's face and neck were bloody and burnt. Kat could see through his shredded shirt that his torso took the most damage. His chest was severely burnt, and blood oozed from multiple wounds.

Kat touched the side of his neck to check for a pulse and she couldn't find one. Tears ran down her face as she tried CPR. She even hit him with a small energy blast in an attempt to start his heart, but it failed to do so.

"Ryan, Ryan, can you hear me? Please…don't leave me, not now."

There was no response. Kat looked at him and caressed his face as tears fell rapidly down her cheeks.

She hit him the chest. "Why? Why now?" she screamed.

She fell into his shoulder and cried. She had failed him before and now she'd failed him again.

Kat kept crying, cursing herself and every god she could think of. Something hit her arm and she swatted it away. Other small soft things rained down on her head, body and arms. She looked up to see the leaves on the tree were shriveling up, crumbling into dust, and falling silently around them.

Without warning, she was pushed up as Ryan took a deep breath. The dust of the leaves fell faster, as did the closing of the wounds on Ryan's chest and face. Once all the visible wounds were healed, the leaves stopped falling.

"Ryan?"

Ryan slowly opened his eyes to see Kat smiling and crying.

"Thank the gods, you're alive. I thought I lost you," said Kat, smiling and caressing his face.

"I'm glad to be alive. There have been times in my life where I have woken up in bad situations only to feel comforted by the face looking back at me when my eyes opened. You're one of those faces. We just have to stop making a habit out of it."

Kat felt relief when he said that. She felt as if she was reborn again.

Ryan cringed as he sat up into a better position against the tree. "Why am I covered in crumbled leaves?"

"I'm not sure why, but somehow, as your wounds healed, the leaves on the tree died and fell."

Ryan put his head down and shook it. "You have to be kidding me. Out of all the damn powers I could get from the unknown Florarien DNA compound."

"What's wrong? If that's what did it, you're alive because of it."

"Yeah, well, I have a freaking Druid power. Not a mighty wizard or nimble thief, but a freaking tree hugging Druid. Just great."

Kat laughed at him as she wiped away the tears. "I have no idea what you're saying, but please don't ever stop being you."

Their eyes connected, and Kat leaned in to him as the roar of a ship's engine made her jump up and spin around. She reached for her holster, but it was empty.

She raised her hands up, ready to blast anything exiting the ship. "I'll blast them and then we run."

Ryan nodded as the ship landed about twenty feet away. The ramp extended as the transport's side door opened.

Kat felt relieved when she saw Tilli come rushing down the ramp.

"Ryan, you're alive! I saw you get blown up. How—"

Ryan held up his hand. "I'm fine. It's a long story but we—" He cut himself off when he saw Vicki, back in her human form, saunter down the ramp, covered in blood as if nothing just happened.

Kat quickly raised her hand and a blast of energy shot out, hitting Vicki and launching her off the ramp. Vicki sailed through the air and slammed into the side of the transport, slid down and crashed into the ground. She immediately changed into her vampire form as she jumped back up, but another blast hit her.

"Oh, don't be playing that vampire shit with me!" yelled Kat. She hit Vicki with yet another blast that sent her bouncing off the transport again. This time she was able to take a few steps forward before falling. Kat pounced on her and started pounding her fists into Vicki's face while cursing her out.

"Holy crap! Kat's gone all Van Helsing on Vicki," said Ryan. He cringed from some lingering pain as he got up, then ran over and lifted a screaming Kat off Vicki.

"Let me go! I haven't killed her yet!"

"Kat, calm down!" yelled Ryan, holding the flailing Kat.

"Don't tell me to calm down after what she did!"

Ryan put Kat down and pointed her in another direction. "Believe me, I understand your anger. Just let me handle it."

"Fine!" said Kat. She stormed away, rubbing her non-gloved hand, which was bleeding from the knuckles.

λ

Ryan squatted down to Vicki, who was back in her human form. One eye was closed shut and there were multiple contusions and bleeding cuts all over her face.

"How could you do that to us? I can't believe you sold us out like that."

Vicki leaned over, spit out some blood, and squinted at him through swollen eyes.

"I rescued you from near death. We had a conversation about good and evil. You were angry that I wouldn't give a vampire…I wouldn't give *you* the benefit of the doubt to be good. Then you prove me right by joining up with that freak to kill us."

Vicki laughed through the pain. "I've got nothing. I've run my course. Kill me and be done with it."

"If it means anything, Vicki did save me up on the ship from Fredrick's guard," said Tilli.

"You're just one big question mark to me," said Ryan. "You're right, I should kill you and spare anyone else from having to deal with your nonsense. I had every intention of doing so if I ever saw you again, but my gut tells me you have a bigger purpose, or I wouldn't keep ending up with you. So, here's what's going to happen. I own you now. We're going to fly back over to Kat's ship. Then I'm going to let you take this transport to whatever crypt you call home. If you don't make it, oh well. If you do—"

"You can't be serious! You're going to let her live?" said Kat, kicking the tree.

"Kat, I'll take responsibility for this, but let me finish," said Ryan, holding up his hand behind him. "Here is the key to this arrangement. When I call upon you, I expect you to drop everything and do exactly what I say. If not, I will help Kat test out every vampire killing technique I recall seeing in movies. Do we have an understanding?"

Vicki didn't make eye contact with Ryan and just nodded.

"Good answer. Tilli, please help Vicki up and get her on the transport."

Tilli knew enough not to say a word, but did exactly what he said.

Ryan walked over to Kat, who was leaning against the large tree with her arms crossed.

"You should've killed her. She has proved over and over again that she cannot be trusted," said Kat.

"You're probably right, but there is something else going on and I think she has some part yet to play."

"If she even blinks the wrong way, my next blast will take her head off," said Kat, storming off.

Ryan looked around and focused on the partially dead tree that saved him, gave it a nod and a pat, and headed to the transport.

CHAPTER 21

PORTALS

Tilli piloted the transport back to Kat's ship. Ryan sat between Kat and Vicki just in case either got any ideas of killing each other. Kat sat with arms crossed, staring into space, while Vicki held her head down and focused on the floor. Not one word was spoken; no one made eye contact. Once they landed, Ryan privately said goodbye to Vicki and reminded her of their agreement, before she flew off. The transport was a slow ship and it would take Vicki quite a while to get to wherever she was going. Ryan hoped it would give her time to think through what she did and to ponder her future.

Ryan, Kat, and Tilli spent the next two hours exploring the area a little and burying the bodies of LaRue's people. They even buried the three destroyed AIs from the *Tempus*. With the explosive on board the *Tempus*, the ship had to take off and leave the star system in record time, not allowing Commander Gordon to take them with him.

Tired and dirty, the three leaned against Kat's ship. It was quiet and there was a cool breeze coming off the lake. It was a peaceful and calming setting. The down time gave them all a chance to think.

"Well, this just sucks," said Ryan, breaking the silence.

Kat and Tilli both nodded in agreement.

"We got beaten and beaten bad. We lost the Orb and almost died," said Ryan.

"At least we all survived," said Tilli optimistically. "The clown doll being an AI was unexpected."

"Yeah, I guess I have to now worry about everything possibly being alive in one way or another," said Ryan.

"On another note, Nora did get away with the data crystal. Thanks to the passionate kiss you planted on her, lover-boy," said Kat.

"It was the only thing I could think of at the time. I'm sure she's going to sit me down and give me a lecture on it. Damn thing will probably consist of a full presentation with charts. Yay, me."

They all laughed. It had been a long time since they could all do that.

Kat reached into a hidden side pocket in her pants. "I still have this," she said, showing everyone a vial.

"The Gravel Goo. Well, at least we have a chance to possibly save the Gravel race. Anyone know of a young planet with some primordial ooze we can drop it into?" asked Ryan.

Tilli raised her hand. "I believe I may be able to assist."

"OK, I wasn't expecting someone to actually answer that," said Ryan.

"We're all ears," said Kat.

"When I was looking for additional data in the lab system, I found how the Orb works and coordinates for how to navigate to a young planet in another universe, so to speak."

Kat and Ryan perked up.

"That's awesome. We can get there in Kat's ship," said Ryan.

"Not that easy," said Tilli. "To do so we would need to hook up one of those Gravel Power Orbs to Kat's ship, and then we would need to fly it into the mini black hole at wormhole speed. Once we enter, we would need to emergency brake at specific coordinates to be sucked into the other universe."

"You're joking. No one survives going into a black hole, and we don't have an Orb," said Kat.

"The scientists who were once here traveled in and out of that black hole and documented their voyages. Plus, I found what I think is a prototype Orb. It's not fully stable, but it should work. I can try to hook it into your ship but there are some setup configurations I may have to guess at."

"Ryan, you have that look in your eye. You're not seriously considering this?" asked Kat.

"It's your ship. I'm willing to go if you are."

Kat turned around and put her head against the side of her ship. "I don't believe I'm going to do this. Ryan and I have seen an Orb setup on a ship up in the lab. I'll help you install the damn Orb and we'll go, but on one condition."

"That is?" asked Ryan.

"Tilli stays."

"Ah, come on," said Tilli. "This is an adventure of a lifetime. You know the technology I may find in another universe."

"Kat's right. Nora will eventually return, and we need someone who knows all the details here just in case things don't go well for us."

"Fine, but if this works, I get to go next time."

"Agreed," said Ryan.

⚓

It took Tilli and Kat about three hours to install the Orb from what they remembered, and another hour for Tilli to explain the proper way to exit the black hole and set up the AI to perform all the tasks. Ryan and Kat weren't too worried since Tilli could remember things in great detail like a mini-computer. Once they were ready, they said goodbye to Tilli and Kat piloted the *Retribution* into orbit, coming to a stop just outside the pull of the mini black hole.

"You sure about this?" asked Kat. "Once we get pulled in, there's no turning back."

"Not at all, but it's not like we're going to ruin a great day."

Kat had the ship's AI engage the energy Orb. A golden hue covered the ship and the energy readings for the engines went to max. The ship's AI was already configured with what needed to be done. "OK then. In three, two, one...."

The *Retribution* accelerated to wormhole speed and entered the mini black hole.

According to the research, the ship should've been torn apart, but the Orb somehow maintained the ship's shields and hull structure. As they went deeper, the feeling of being stretched increased and there was a god-awful screeching sound. Ryan and Kat covered their ears as they screamed from the pain. Ryan watched Kat pass out just before everything went black for him.

⅄

Kat grabbed her head as she regained consciousness. The emergency lights were blinking red, the view screen was down, and smoke emanated from the consoles. Ryan's head was slumped forward. The seat harness did its job of keeping him from sliding out of his seat or hitting the console.

"Ship status?" Kat thought, but there was no reply from the ship's AI. The neural link must have been down.

"*Retribution* AI, ship status," said Kat.

"Emergency landing initiated. Failure to AI sub-systems. Repairs have been started. Engines have overheated, and normal energy cells are depleted. New power source down to one percent and unstable. Use of power source in its current state will result in catastrophic explosion. Emergency solar cells have been deployed."

"Just great," said Kat.

Her thoughts were interrupted as Ryan started to wake up.

He grabbed his head and rubbed his face. "Wow, my head."

"You can say that again, but at least we're alive."

"Where are we?" asked Ryan.

"Not sure yet. Some of the systems are down. *Retribution* AI, what is our current location?"

"Current location is unknown. Planet and star system is not known to any system charts."

"Open front blast shields," said Kat.

The front of the command bridge opened to reveal the outside. They had landed on a barren rocky area near a small lake with a waterfall. In the distance, there were smoking volcanos, as well as a young forest.

"*Retribution* AI, what is the status of the planet we're on?" asked Ryan.

"Planet appears to be young, and currently at the end of a volcanic cooling phase. Atmosphere will sustain humanoid life. In addition, a ship of unknown configuration is just beyond the vegetation you are viewing. Due to system issues, scanning may not be fully accurate."

"*Retribution* AI, continue scanning planet and star system as systems allow. I want this all documented," said Kat.

"Request confirmed."

"I guess we should head out and take a look," said Ryan.

Kat smiled. "As a biologist, this is a dream to see."

Ryan and Kat eagerly headed out, but not before they each grabbed a las-pistol. Kat also took along a portable scanner.

They navigated the rocky plain and Kat took samples along the way. About an hour later, they had reached the forest. The trees were young, with wide canopies of hanging green branches with large white flowers on the ends. Ryan and Kat moved deeper into the forest, following animal trails as much as they could, and to their surprise, an old ship covered in vines of multi-colored flowers sat in a small clearing. A flock of red and green birds flew away as they approached.

"Take a look around the area while I scan the ship and go inside to investigate," said Kat.

"Sounds good to me."

Kat scanned the outside of the ship and it was remarkably similar to the one they had found back at the lab. Only this one was a smaller Gravel ship frame with add-ons from other alien races. Unfortunately, the ship's power sources were inactive. She realized she had not mentioned to Ryan that her ship was dead in the water, but figured it would be best not to scare him yet.

Kat entered the ship and looked around. Many of the parts had been scrapped over time. She noticed the interior had sound dampening devices installed. The explorers must have encountered the same sound effect that knocked her and Ryan out, and they did something to compensate for it; something she would need to remember should they ever be crazy enough to do something like this again.

Digging further into the ship, she located the main data system and pocketed all the data crystals for review later, should they ever get off this planet. Moving into the engine location, she found a pile of dust where a Power Orb must have been installed. The remains of another one was on the floor next to it.

"Kat, come out here," yelled Ryan.

Kat exited the ship to find Ryan waving at her from the rear of the ship. She walked over and followed Ryan around to the other side to see four graves. They must have been here a long time based on the weathering of the headstones, but the graves weren't overgrown with any vegetation.

"Guess we know what happened to the crew," said Kat.

"But who buried them and who is maintaining the graves?" asked Ryan. "They're not overgrown."

"I maintain them," said a voice from behind them.

Kat and Ryan drew their las-pistols and spun around. They looked at the creature and back at each other with confused expressions.

"Is there an issue?" asked the creature.

Ryan holstered his weapon. The creature was humanoid with giant butterfly wings on its back. The orange, black, and blue spotted colors of the wing continued into its chest with a touch of white here and there. Its head was humanoid with orange slicked-back hair and antennas that moved in different directions.

Kat holstered her weapon. "Fascinating. I have never encountered anyone of your race before. Black spots toward the back of the wings means you might be male?"

"That I am."

"How did you know that?" asked Ryan.

"Monarch butterflies have a similar pattern," said Kat.

"You are both humans. Mates?"

Ryan and Kat took a side step from each other and stumbled over their words.

"Nope, nope, just...you know...explorers. My name is Ryan Hunt. This is Dr. Katalina Winslow. And you are?"

"My designation is Shepard."

"Tilli had mentioned that name from one of the Old C-Tec's notes," said Ryan.

"The designation was given to me by the ones who came before you."

"Can you tell us about them?" asked Kat.

"The people came many times as explorers like yourselves. The ones in the ground have gone to be one with the universe. They were from races called the Gravel and Florariens. I liked the Florarien the best. Some of the vegetation is from her remains."

"How did they die?" asked Ryan.

"Their ship malfunctioned. The other explorers never came for them and they perished from time."

"So, what is your function here?" asked Kat, trying to change the subject.

Ryan gave her an odd look.

"I nurture the planet until the first beings of future higher intelligence crawl upon the shore, and then I move on to other ones."

"This planet has no life walking around yet?" asked Ryan.

"It has basic creatures, but the planet is young. In a few thousand of your centuries it will."

Ryan looked at Kat, she nodded and then pulled out the vial of Gravel Goo.

"I need you to look after this," said Ryan, pointing to the vial.

"It is Gravel," said the Shepard. "I can sense it, but why?"

"Back where we come from, the Gravel no longer exist. They were wiped out by another race. This is all that remains of them, and I think if this bacterium is put into the proper place, they may live again someday. Hopefully."

Shepard shook his head. "It is always the case. I help bring the planets to be and, in the end, there are always those who come along to hurt others. I must say, it is noble of you to travel so far to save a race when your only basis for its survival is hope. I will do as you ask."

Kat handed the vial to Shepard's outstretched arm using her gloved hand.

"You are part Gravel," said Shepard.

"Long story," said Kat.

Shepard turned to Ryan. "Are you part Gravel as well?"

"I'm probably a longer story."

Shepard approached Ryan and touched his arm.

"Oh, Florarien. You are part of that race…fascinating. Both of you are unique individuals. Please follow me."

Ryan and Kat followed Shepard to a barren area of small pools of steaming water.

"Here will be their new beginnings," said Shepard.

With a swift turn of his hand, Shepard broke the top off the vial and turned it upside down over one of the pools. The hardened matter slid out and fell into the pool. It floated for a few seconds and then began to melt until it was gone.

"Is that it?" asked Ryan.

"Yes, I can see they have taken to the pool nicely. Unfortunately, you will both be long gone before they can ever thank you."

"All we did was give them a chance. It's up to them now and I have faith they will survive," said Ryan.

"May the Gravel have a longer life in their new home," said Kat.

"Well said, Kat. Now on that note, we should be getting out of here. We left a friend behind, who is probably worried about us, and a situation we need to deal with," said Ryan.

"Yeah. About that…there is a slight issue," said Kat, rocking back and forth heel to toe.

"Slight issue?" asked Ryan.

"The energy Orb is damaged, and my ship is not doing well. We're marooned."

"Now you tell me. Don't you think you should've mentioned that earlier?"

"I was waiting to see if I thought of any solutions."

"Did you?"

"Nope."

"Well, this day just keeps getting better," said Ryan, throwing his hands in the air.

"Do you two always talk like this? Are you sure you are not mates?" asked Shepard.

"No!" screamed Ryan and Kat at the same time.

"You realize you can leave at any time," said Shepard.

"Say again?" asked Ryan.

"As I stated before, you are both unique. Whether it is by chance or fate you came to find each other, you both have powers far beyond what you know. She is energy, which can neither be created nor destroyed. You are one with the universe and I can guide you in the use of your abilities."

"Ohhhkayy, can we bring this down to a lower intelligence level. She might be there, but I'm not."

"In more simple terms, she can touch the Orb that brought you here and stabilize it. You can touch the lake and picture a place you want to go or have been to, and I can assist you with opening a portal to that location, so you may fly your ship there."

"Kat, is the giant butterfly serious?"

"I think he is and we have no other options. So let's just go with it."

Ryan looked up at the sky and then back at Shepard. "What the hell, let's go make a portal."

Shepard led Ryan and Kat to the beautiful lake near their ship. Its water was like azure glass.

"So, what do I need to do?" asked Ryan.

"Look into the water and let me know what you see."

"Simple enough." Ryan knelt next to the lake and looked in. "Let's see now. I see water, sand and rocks."

"Obviously, but look deeper and think about a place."

Ryan stared into the lake and thought. A few seconds later an image appeared. He was standing on the deck of his house after coming home from work. He was looking for his wife and he found her kneeling in her garden picking some vegetables and checking to make sure all the plants were OK. He called out to her and she looked up, smiled and waved to him.

Kat put her red-gloved hand on Ryan's shoulder. "She's very pretty."

"Yeah. Seems like yesterday. I miss her a lot."

"I am sorry to say portals cannot be opened into past time lines," said Shepard.

"I had a feeling you would say that," said Ryan. "But one can always dream."

Kat wiped a tear from her eye as she watched him.

Shepard touched the water with his hand.

As Ryan's thoughts changed, the image changed to the lake on the planet where they left Tilli. A face appeared in the water as he continued thinking about the planet in more detail, and then the face smiled. The lake swirled and became a mirror-like image of unmoving glass.

Ryan stood up and took a few steps back. "I was not aware water had faces. I'm guessing the swirling is the portal? Is that how you travel?"

"Yes, that is a portal. Water can be used as a source for traveling, but it is not how I move from world to world. All universes are connected and there are life forms that live in the connections. You have a rare gift that allows you to tap into the connections and summon portals, or what you would call 'wormholes'. Perhaps in time you will learn to create them yourself, but for now you need someone to assist you. The Orb will provide protection for your journey as it did on your trip here."

"Not sure what I just did, but I'll take your word for it if it gets us out of here."

"Now for you, Katalina. Your part is easy," said Shepard. "On your ship is an Orb that gave you the energy to bring you here. What I need you to do is place your hand on it and slowly add energy to it. The Orb will take in that energy. It should turn from a red to a yellow mist once it is stable. That should give you enough power to get your ship moving. You then need to fly it into the lake."

"Is this how the Gravel created the Orb in the first place?" asked Kat.

"No, but your minds are still too inferior to create such a sustainable energy source."

"At least he didn't call us stupid," said Ryan.

"You do not have much time. The portal will be collapsing soon. You should go. I will take care of the Gravel and nurture them as much as I can. Then it will be up to them to evolve."

"I will be the first person to admit I'm confused about what I just did and would love to learn more about you," said Ryan.

"The wonderful thing about life is discovering what you are capable of," said Shepard.

"Ryan, the portal is shimmering, and we should get going. I have no desire to be the next Eve to your Adam. Plus, I hate apples," said Kat.

Shepard watch them board the ship and listened to the continued bickering.

"How do you not like apples? Everyone likes apples."

"I don't like apples, they're icky," said Kat as the ship's side hatch closed behind them.

"They bicker like mates but yet deny it. The Earth humanoids were always the odd ones," mumbled Shepard, heading back toward the forest.

Ryan and Kat went to the engine area of the ship. The jury-rigged Orb was now partially filled with a red mist.

"*Retribution* AI, what is the ship's status?" asked Kat.

"Ship hull and shield repairs have been partially completed, but are still not safe for space travel. Combat systems and neural interfaces are still down, and we are running on converted solar energy, which is not enough for the ship to fly a long distance, break the planet's gravitational pull, or initiate a wormhole. AI interface to ship navigation is also damaged beyond repair."

"*Retribution* AI, monitor energy levels and alert me when the power source is stable and has sufficient energy for flight."

Kat hovered her gloved hand over the Orb, sent out a small beam of energy, and gradually increased it. The inside of the Orb started to swirl from red to a misty white as Kat's output increased. She started to sweat as she increased her power output to the most she had ever released in such a narrow burst. After a few seconds, the Orb started to swirl from the white mist to a bright yellow.

"Dr. Kat, energy reserves are now at a level for travel. Power source has also stabilized."

Kat stopped sending energy to the Orb and Ryan had to grab her as her legs buckled. She collapsed in Ryan's arms and passed out.

"Kat, Kat…Crap."

Ryan put Kat over his shoulder and hurried up the stairway to the top floor and to the cockpit area. He placed her in his usual chair and he jumped into the command seat. The portal in the lake was starting to waver.

"*Retribution* AI, keep me updated on the stability of the portal in the lake."

"Unknown command 'Portal'. Lake currently experiencing a wormhole anomaly that is destabilizing. Do you wish me to monitor the anomaly?"

"Yes! Yes! Monitor that!"

"Command confirmed, and for the record, Dr. Kat talks to me much nicer."

"Oh, bloody hell…A sensitive ship. Now, what did Nora teach me? Just relax and breathe."

Ryan started pressing areas on the console in front of him. The ship blast screen closed, and a virtual screen of the outside appeared, along with a virtual control panel in front of him. He hit the area for engines and could hear them come online as seat restraints shot around both him and Kat.

"Wormhole anomaly will collapse in eight seconds."

Ryan pushed a few more buttons and the ship's engines ignited. The ship crashed along the ground toward the lake as he used the virtual screen to navigate. Not having a control stick made things much harder, but he finally got the hang of it. The ship shot straight up in the air and then nose-dived into the lake as the portal collapsed.

The virtual screen went black as the ship kept moving forward. Red lights and alarms blared in the cabin and sparks flew from the systems around him. Ryan was jerked in his seat as the ship shot straight up out of the water. The virtual screen turned back on to reveal clear blue skies. Ryan brought the ship level to hover over the lake. He moved the ship in a circle to see a tropical jungle, the lab, and Tilli standing on the beach, looking up and waving.

They had done it. Now it was time to go home, of course after he figured out how to land the ship and assuming they could fix it. Just another wonderful day in his second life.

CHAPTER 22

POLITENESS

Fredrick LaRue stood in a command planning room on his ship with his hands crossed behind his back. His face was scruffy and his hair a little messy. He peered at the multi-colored lights of the wormhole through a viewing window. This time he was neither smiling nor listening to soothing music.

He looked over to the location where Mr. Jingles used to sit on his floating platform. The AI puppet he found in a scrap pile is what kept him sane all those years in an intergalactic prison camp until he was able to make an escape. Only he knew the puppet was a living AI and that they had a neural link to communicate. Unfortunately, the power source running Mr. Jingles was almost gone and could never be replaced without destroying the AI puppet, so he stayed in an extremely low power mode. They owed each other their lives, but it was Mr. Jingles who sacrificed his, and his sacrifice would not go unpunished. Fredrick now had a new goal and that was to make Ryan Hunt's life a living hell.

"Excuse me, sir. Am I interrupting?" said his Karyot assistant as she entered the room.

"You are, but what is it?" said Fredrick, continuing to stare out the viewing window.

"I have those updates you requested."

Fredrick squeezed his hands together. "Proceed, and be quick about it."

"Ship Eater systems are almost back to full. The team will need another few weeks to get everything fully operational."

"They have two."

"I will let them know."

"Next item?" asked Fredrick, still not turning around to acknowledge her.

"The rumors have finally been confirmed that Ryan Hunt did survive."

"That's unfortunate. Go on."

Beads of sweat started to form on the assistant's forehead. "The data crystal we received from Mr. Hunt was finally hacked and it was not what we expected. It's…a…um…"

"Finish your sentence."

"It's actually Mr. Hunt's daily journal, and rules to an odd game about dungeons with dice. He must have switched it somehow."

Fredrick gave an insane snicker, which made the assistant start to shake.

"He's a crafty one. I will give him that. Reminds me of *me* and there can only be one *me*," said Fredrick, bringing his hands to his side and sternly making fists and then releasing them. "Continue."

"Communication with our base has gone down. The last report was something related to an anomaly."

"Assume it has been destroyed since we have not turned over the Orb to our employer. We are no longer hired help but wanted criminals in this employer's eye."

"Yes, sir, I will inform the crew and operatives. Lastly, you asked me to remind you about our response to Victoria Van Buuren."

"Ah, yes, our little deal breaker. Send her sister back to her. I think one piece a day over the next six months will get our point across. Perhaps she can make a nice rock garden memorial out of her."

"I will have that taken care of, sir."

"You are starting to annoy me now. Anything else you wish to pester me about?"

"The package you wanted has regained consciousness and is waiting outside."

Fredrick spun around. "Excellent. Bring him in."

The assistant scrambled out the opened door and came back with two guards dragging a person with a sack over his head, followed by a black-cloaked C-Tec.

The guards lifted the man to his feet and removed the bag.

The old C-Tec hermit from the mining planet covered his eyes until they adjusted to the light and then he looked around the room.

"Wh-wh-what do you wa-wa-want wi-wi-with m-m-me?" stuttered the hermit.

Fredrick rolled his eyes. "Can someone please fix that before I shoot him?"

The black-cloaked C-Tec shuffled over and jabbed a wire, with a small box on it, directly into the exposed brain area, causing the hermit to convulse for a moment, and then his posture went straight.

"Now, old man, what did you say?" asked Fredrick.

"What do you want with me?" asked the hermit, looking around, surprised. "You fixed my speech. You know I used to know how to create things like that."

"Actually, we don't care. What we do care about is what you told the human man and Artesian lady who visited you a few weeks ago. We also want to know how to turn the Power Orb into a weapon."

The hermit looked at the ceiling and then the floor as he sorted through his memories.

"Oh, yes. The nice man and the cute young lady. I remember them. They were much kinder than you, but I'm afraid I cannot recall my conversation with them or how to use a Power Orb, as you call it."

"That's a shame, but we have ways to get the information from you. Kaimi, he is all yours."

"I will begin data extraction immediately," said Kaimi, the black-cloaked C-Tec.

The door slid open for the guards as they dragged the hermit from the room, followed by Kaimi.

The assistant waited until they could no longer hear the hermit's screams as he was forcefully escorted away.

"Is there anything else you require?" asked the assistant.

"No, be gone from my sight. I need to ponder in silence."

The assistant gave a slight bow and rushed out of the room.

Fredrick turned back around to stare out the viewing window. "Oh, Mr. Hunt, I will make you suffer. You will feel my pain."

⅄

Since the incident with Fredrick LaRue a few weeks ago, Ryan, Kat, and Nora attended daily briefings with CEO Klein and Jack. Of course, the meetings focused on what Ryan, Kat, and Tilli actually told everyone. On the return trip, they decided not to mention the second Orb they recovered, which they assumed was a prototype.

Tilli was now reviewing the crashed ship data crystals Kat recovered from the planet where they met the Shepard—something they also left out of their report—and she was retrofitting the second Orb to the *Tempus*. It took a while to convince Commander Gordon to bypass protocol to allow her to do so, and to keep it a secret from the chain of command. They all decided that the fewer people who knew what they had, the better.

Ryan and Kat kept a few other things a secret from everyone. They thought best not to mention how Ryan healed himself using a tree, helped to create a portal, had a blue glowing foot, and the fact Kat could charge up an Orb. They also hid the fact the Florariens went back to the hidden lab and destroyed the Dyson Bubble and the entire hill the lab was built on to keep old secrets safe. For now, it was best to just focus on finding Fredrick LaRue and stop him from whatever he planned to do with the Orb he stole.

Just like every morning, Ryan got up early, exercised, and grabbed some waffles before heading to the daily briefing. He entered CEO Klein's main conference room. CEO Klein and Kat were already sitting on the hovering chairs around the table. Jack was standing off to the side behind the CEO. Everyone turned to face Ryan when he entered.

"Sorry I'm late," said Ryan, taking a seat near Kat, who was sporting a yellow streak of color in her hair and matching glove.

"No, Mr. Hunt. Dr. Kat arrived early. We were just finishing up some details," said CEO Klein. "Would you like me to tell him, Dr. Kat, or would you?"

"Well, Mr. Hunt," said Kat with a smile. "I have been promoted to Director of the Scientific Division of OTKE Corporation."

"Congratulations!" said Ryan. "We should get some food later and celebrate."

"That we should."

"Yes. It is a celebratory occasion, but let us move onto other business first," said CEO Klein.

Ryan and Kat looked into each other's eyes for a second or two, and then turned their attention over to CEO Klein for the daily briefing. Ever since their return, OTKE Corporation had been on higher than normal alert levels.

"Jack, please start with the daily updates," said CEO Klein.

Jack moved forward to the table, his leg servos making a whirring sound as he moved. He gave everyone a disgusted look since he hated leading the updates, but CEO Klein thought he needed some practice at public speaking.

He looked around, cleared his throat, and brought up the data pad to read from. "There are accounts of a ship raiding small colonies for supplies. The reports indicate the ship appeared to be a friendly transport ship, but then changed shape once it finished the attack."

"It's LaRue with his Ship Eater. Has to be," said Kat.

"I would agree with your assessment," said CEO Klein. "Jack, please send word to all our bases to make sure proper protocol is followed for ships entering and leaving."

"Yes, sir," said Jack, making a note on his data pad before continuing. "The hostility between the Woland and the Florariens is increasing. There have been isolated reports of ground troop fighting at remote outposts and colonies. The Earth Consortium is doing its best to stay out of the fray and refuses to take any sides. Their main focus is the resettlement of the Earth home world."

"For now, let us do the same, but increase our network of ops in those areas," said CEO Klein. "As for Earth, Mr. Hunt, I did receive a formal invitation to pass on to you from the Earth Consortium. They stated you are free to return and live there if you like."

"Sounds very appealing. Nice large cabin on a lake in the mountains out west in what I called America." Ryan looked right at Kat and smiled. "But for now, I'm more interested in exploring new possibilities."

Kat blushed for a moment and then Ryan turned his attention back to the meeting.

"I can understand your intrigue on exploration and other endless possibilities away from Earth," said CEO Klein.

Jack shook his head. He hated watching Ryan and Kat act like little kids but continued, "There's something else I thought Mr. Hunt and Dr. Kat would like to know: Victoria Van Buuren has reopened the Little Lamb nightclub. It seems she now has a personal security force of Wolfkin at her disposal."

Ryan and Kat looked at each other.

"Oh, joy. She made it back alive. How wonderful for us," said Kat.

"I had a feeling she would make it," said Ryan. "An army of Wolfkin, you say. I wonder if she had something to do with those Wolfkin prisoners revolting on that mining planet."

"Anything is possible, Mr. Hunt, but I must first start off by apologizing for not telling you what Victoria truly was. I thought it better you did not know. I promise not to make that mistake again," said CEO Klein.

"No worries. I probably wouldn't have believed you anyway."

"With that said, it was compassionate of you to let Victoria live after what you reported she did. Most people would have killed her."

"Let's hope I didn't make a mistake."

Kat smirked at him. "Yes, let's hope not."

"Anything else, Jack?" asked CEO Klein.

"This was recently brought to my attention this morning. The man who arrived here impersonating the Earth Consortium delegate Glumet, was captured two weeks ago and today he is being transferred to an Earth Consortium holding facility. It was discovered he has links to Fredrick LaRue's organization."

"Good news for a change. What of the Earth Consortium fleet he commanded?" asked CEO Klein.

"Unknown. The Earth Consortium is still looking for it. Unfortunately, they found most of the fleet's crew dead. They were killed and then spaced in an isolated area in the Andromeda galaxy. From what my sources tell me, they still have no leads on the fleet's location."

"Great. An evil fleet of ships waiting to attack, and the thought of that lunatic having the Gravel energy Orb scares me," said Ryan.

"As it should. We need to be careful and make sure we are always vigilant. Especially you, Mr. Hunt—there is someone out there who wants you dead," said CEO Klein.

"Oh joy," said Ryan.

"Speaking of being vigilant. Where is Nora? She was here yesterday," asked Kat.

"I'm not really sure. It's the first time she ever skipped one of our early morning training sessions, but she did leave a note on my kitchen table."

"As in a handwritten note?" asked Kat.

"Yeah, she thinks my older mind will handle written notes over virtual holograms better. I try to explain I had email, text messaging and video phones back in my day."

"What did the note say, Mr. Hunt?" asked CEO Klein.

Ryan pulled the note out of his side leg pocket. "Mr. Hunt, I will be back soon. I went to finish a conversation. PS: Dr. Kat is OK but just to be safe, I have set up a DNA alert system in your apartment in the event she tries to sneak in and kill you. Signed, Nora."

"Well, at least I'm moving up in the world," said Kat.

"Smalls steps, Dr. Kat. Small steps," said Ryan.

"An odd note indeed," said CEO Klein.

"Yeah. I wish I knew what conversation she needed to finish," said Ryan.

The prisoner transport *Justice* exited the wormhole at the outskirts of the Earth Consortium Prisoner Star System. Its bearing was the one isolated planet orbiting a small sun.

The prisoner who impersonated the Earth Consortium delegate Glumet, sat on a hover bed wearing a red jumpsuit. A guard dressed in all black and a shaded helmet entered the prisoner area. The door shut behind him as he approached the cell, and an AI guarding the prisoner moved forward to intercept the guard.

"I was not informed of any guard changes, moving of or interaction with the prisoner. What is your authorization ID?" asked the AI guard.

The humanoid guard raised his hand and a pen-like device shot an energy burst at the AI. The AI twitched as its internal systems began to shut down causing it to fall backward.

The prisoner sprung from the bed and ran up to the energy barricade. "I knew Fredrick wouldn't leave me here to rot."

The guard walked up to the barricade and stared at the prisoner.

"What are you waiting for? Disable the barricade and let's get out of here."

The guard took off the helmet to reveal a pretty blonde woman with her hair pulled back in a ponytail.

The prisoner took a step back when he realized it was Nora.

"What...What are you doing here?"

"I had some time to ponder things and I realized I was rude to you the first time we met."

"I'm not sure what you mean by that."

"This." Nora reached into her jacket pocket and pulled out the Nora Barlow AI flower that had messed with her internal systems. "You gave me this beautiful gift and I never formally thanked you for the *unique* flower."

The prisoner put his hands up. "Listen. It was nothing personal. It was just business. You're just an AI. You should understand the difference."

Nora focused on the flower as she twirled it in her fingers. "Yes. I am just an AI, but there are still protocols I need to follow."

"What protocols? What are you talking about?"

Nora looked back at the prisoner, her eyes flared red and she smiled...

Book 3: Failover

The door groaned and sprang open.

Ryan jumped back, his scream echoing through the ship, causing Kat to dive to the side and fumble to draw her las-pistol. A mummified body fell forward, landing in front of him.

Kat moved to a sitting position and put her head on her knees while Ryan leaned against the wall and took a deep breath.

"Sorry," he said. "Wasn't expecting that."

"No worries. I like my heart beating outside my chest."

Ryan put his hand out and helped Kat up.

They moved onto the command deck. Most of the equipment was piled to the left side. How the body got to the door was unknown to them, but others were crushed in the mess of debris. They moved the lights around and found the command chair still anchored in place. The mummified remains of the commander were still belted in. A large piece of metal was stuck in his chest.

"I hope the guy didn't suffer," said Ryan.

Kat pursed her lips, nodded, holstered her las-pistol, and pulled out another power cube that had barely any power left in it. "I'm going to hook this up to the console in front of the command chair. If the cracked screen still works, it should be enough to bring up some data."

"How many of those things do you have?"

"Your next lesson in offworld archeology: always bring a bag full of power cubes."

"That is good to know. I will add that to the adventurer backpack item list for next time."

Kat rolled her eyes and shook her head, then attached the power cube to the console, and the screen flickered to life. She entered commands on the archaic keypad while Ryan focused his light at the open door and kept watch.

"There is a lot of data corruption. From what I can see, they engaged the Woland, and—"

The console flared, causing Kat to jump back and cover her face.

"Well, that sucks," said Ryan, waving his hand at the smoke pouring from the console.

"Yes, it does. We'll have to find the main part of the ship where those life forms are if we want to get any answers."

"Probably best we set up camp here for tonight," said Ryan, holstering his Glock.

"Makes sense. We—"

The loud bang and what sounded like a man screaming interrupted the conversation.

"That was a gunshot," said Ryan, rushing toward the opening with Kat behind him.

Past the sound of the pounding rain they could barely make out a man screaming again. Looking at each other, they nodded and rushed out into the swampy forest.

The rain was coming down harder, and their light source barely showed a way through the darkness, forcing them to navigate by the continued shouting.

The cries for help were now mixed with odd growling and clicking noises. They slowed down to better evaluate the situation when the ground under them gave away. Ryan and Kat slid down a muddy hillside and splashed face-first into knee-deep water.

Ryan sat up and wiped the muddy water from his face and eyes. As his vision cleared, he found himself in a muddy pool surrounded by fluorescent green glowing trees.

"Behind you! Watch out!" yelled someone in front of him.

He turned to his right, and his eyes shot wide open. A humanoid with two heads and red eyes was coming at him. Its mouth chattered quickly, causing its teeth to make a clicking sound. It brought a makeshift club up, ready to strike him. Ryan fired a three-round burst into the humanoid's chest. It spun backward and fell into the water. Ryan then moved to a kneeling position and swept the area.

Kat knelt behind him. "Over there, on the bank of the pool."

Ryan looked over to see a man leaning against a tree, holding a makeshift rifle across his lap. Two other bodies lay next to him, as well as more deformed humanoids.

Ryan and Kat spun around to the sound of cracking branches, and more creatures poured from the tree line. They were all deformed in some way, with multiple arms, heads, clawed hands, or body parts in odd areas.

Ryan opened fire, dropping three of the creatures and causing others to fumble back. Kat fired her las-pistol, which blew a large, cauterized hole in one of the creatures, but her next shot fizzled.

"Not now! Not now!" yelled Kat, shaking the las-pistol.

SECOND LIFE OF MR. HUNT SERIES

AUTHOR BIO

Gerrit S. Overeem is an IT professional whose passion for science fiction served as inspiration for *Second Life of Mr. Hunt*. In addition to enjoying Dungeons and Dragons and appearing at charity events as part of the 501st Legion Star Wars Costuming Group, he is also active in a local car club and has a black belt in Nihon Goshin Aikido. He lives with his wife, who has encouraged his interest in writing.

For additional details, short stories, pictures, and more,
or to contact Gerrit, go to: https://gerritovereem.com

Made in the USA
Middletown, DE
10 May 2022